I0587774

# Strait Over Tackle
a Flip-Flop Detective novel

# by Colin Conway

*"You are what you settle for."*

- Janis Joplin

# Strait Over Tackle
a Flip-Flop Detective Novel

# Chapter 1

As his eyes fluttered open, reality slowly returned to Sam Strait.

A light-skinned woman with sandy-colored hair hovered over him. Long hair framed her face as if she stood at the end of a short tunnel. She studied Sam with the stern concentration of an overbearing schoolteacher.

His eyes slowly closed again.

He'd been dreaming about a different woman—an alluring vision with skin the color of creamed coffee. They had recently been to a quiet cafe, sharing espressos and talking music. This other woman—her name was Lena—earnestly spoke about things as if everything should be more critical than they were.

At the quaint rendezvous from his dream, Lena had chosen to share the importance of protest songs from artists like Joan Baez and Credence Clearwater Revival and Public Enemy. She recently produced—assistant produced, she carefully clarified—a documentary on the subject, and the matter still greatly intrigued her. This, of course, intrigued Sam.

He listened intently to Lena's many commentaries on the subject. Some of the artists she referenced he knew, but that wasn't why he was so keenly focused. Instead, she fascinated him. He found that he enjoyed listening to Lena. Partly it was her accent—she'd grown up in the south—but of most significance was the intensity she brought to their conversations. Even if she didn't know much about a subject, she got passionate about it.

The other woman—the one now shaking his shoulder—didn't seem to care about the otherworldly visit from Lena. Sam blinked several times, then tugged the noise-canceling headphones from his ears.

"—prepare for landing," the flight attendant said.

Sam forced his eyes wider and stared at her.

The attendant's face relaxed, and she rested her hand on the edge of his seat. "Please bring your chair upright." The attendant moved forward to admonish another passenger in the first-class section about putting a tray into its stowed position.

He closed his eyes briefly, hoping to revisit the memory of Lena in the cafe. It wasn't difficult to picture her. She was beautiful.

And she smelled fantastic, he remembered. It was a scent he couldn't quite place, but it was one he couldn't get enough of.

She rarely laughed at his jokes. Instead, she frowned with curiosity at them, which he thought was strangely charming. He enjoyed that whenever it happened.

Lena's regular job was as a programming director for a national television conglomerate. She'd come to the islands to rediscover herself but found Sam instead. They spent three days together before he had to leave. She still had another week left on her vacation and asked Sam to stay with her. He considered it—seriously considered it—but doing so would have broken two of the rules he'd set for himself.

*No attachments.*
*Leave when it's time.*

He didn't have many rules to live by—he only had five that he'd bothered to write down—but those two were of paramount importance. In fact, they were the second and third listed on the small piece of paper he kept in his wallet.

So, abiding by his rules, Lena and he spent his final afternoon together before Sam caught the red-eye back to the mainland.

He brought his chair upright before running his hands over his face. His skin felt greasy, and a day's worth of stubble covered his cheeks. His tongue traveled across his teeth, and he wished he could brush them. The departure time and subsequent eight-hour flight left him feeling grimy.

As he stowed his headphones into their protective case, he rubbed his bare feet across the carpeted floor of the plane.

The woman next to him watched his feet swish back and forth. She was in her late thirties with short brown hair. He considered her attractive but in a severe and corporate way. Her gray business suit looked as uncomfortable as it was utilitarian.

After stowing her laptop in a bag, the woman tucked it underneath the seat in front of her. When she finished, she turned to Sam and said, "I should have done that."

"Done what?"

"Taken my shoes off." She pointed to his bare feet, still dragging lazily across the carpet.

For the entire duration of the flight, her feet had remained caged in pointy-toed medium heels.

With a nod toward her footwear, he said, "They look uncomfortable."

"I didn't think about them."

"How could you not?"

"I had work to do."

"On a red-eye?"

"The work won't do itself." She said it with what seemed to Sam a misplaced amount of pride.

For the entirety of the flight, he either read or slept, but mostly the latter. He wore the headphones for the whole trip, though. It was a defense mechanism he'd learned from his travels. When people thought he was listening to music, they left him alone.

Sam slipped his feet into a pair of flip-flops and crossed his legs at the ankles.

Even though he rarely started conversations with strangers on planes, he asked, "What do you do?" He was curious about the type of person who would choose to wear a suit and heels on an overnight flight.

"I'm an attorney."

When she announced her occupation, he almost ended the conversation at that moment. Instead, he forced a smile and politely asked, "On the islands?"

"Seattle. I flew to Honolulu for the disposition of a property portfolio." For additional clarification, she said, "A client's estate."

"Must have been fun," Sam said robotically.

Her brow corrugated. "Fun?"

"A free trip to Hawaii and all."

"It wasn't free. I worked, and one day was all it took. I didn't need more than that."

"You didn't take any time for yourself?"

Her face pinched. "I had work to do."

Sam's polite smile melted. This was a conversation he wanted to extract himself from. He pulled a book, *Ego is the Enemy* by Ryan Holiday, from the chair's back pocket in front of him. He opened it to the spot he had bookmarked.

"Self-help?" the woman asked.

"Uh-huh." He didn't bother to look at her. Continuing the conversation no longer interested him. His seatmate might be physically appealing, but her dedication to an occupation Sam found distasteful moved her into a category that he avoided as much as possible—people with repulsive careers. He'd actually created a rule concerning them.

Regardless of attractiveness, he didn't spend time with lawyers. He also didn't occupy his time with accountants, IRS agents, politicians, real estate brokers, or preschool teachers. The latter category was added after learning how irritatingly cheerful one woman was. He wasn't sure all preschool teachers would be this way, but why take the chance?

Life was short, and time was precious. It was best to adopt a few rules to live by. Therefore, he was careful to avoid preschool teachers at all costs. So far, it hadn't been a struggle.

Sam read a few lines in his book before the lawyer asked, "First time to Seattle?"

This, Sam thought, was the problem with removing the headphones too early. While they were in the air, the woman had ignored him as she focused on her laptop. She spent the trip perusing a variety of spreadsheets or crafting lengthy emails. Now, as they prepared to land, she was more than willing to engage him in conversation.

He didn't like chatty seatmates, of which he'd had a few over the recent years. The headphones or a book usually kept them at bay, but he'd made the mistake of talking to her in the first place to find out about her shoes. All bets were off now.

Not bothering to look up from his book, he muttered. "Seattle's a layover. Then home."

"And where's home?" She cocked her head to read some of Sam's book.

"Newman Lake."

The lawyer smiled. "You got me. Where's that?"

"Spokane County."

Her lip twitched as she fought the smirk he expected. Sam believed most Seattleites didn't appreciate the rest of the state beyond the Cascade Mountains. "What are you doing there?"

"Spending the summer."

This seemed to surprise her, and her lip returned to its natural form. She tilted her head to the opposite angle and studied him. They were roughly the same age, but while she looked business professional, he appeared beach-worn with his faded jeans and threadbare T-shirt.

"Do you live in Honolulu?"

"Just hung out there for the winter."

"Hung out?" she asked as if trying to comprehend the phrase. It shouldn't be a problem for her. She was too young to be confused by its usage.

"I stayed there for the winter," Sam clarified. "Well, for part of fall and spring, too."

"You… hung out?"

"Worked some, too, but mostly hung out. Yeah."

"What did you do?"

"Washed dishes."

The woman glanced around the first-class cabin. "You washed dishes?"

"Not always, but it's the work I found interesting this time."

"Dishes?"

"At Duke's."

"The restaurant on the beach?" She pointed at his pale blue T-shirt that bore the Dukes' logo.

"Uh-huh."

"And you did that for the winter?"

"Part of fall and spring, too."

The woman frowned. "Now, you're coming home for the summer?"

"That's right."

Her mouth dropped slightly open. "To do what?"

"Hang out." The conversation had now gone full circle.

"At Newman Lake," she slowly said. "Is your place actually on the lake?"

Sam nodded.

The woman studied him for a couple of seconds more before again glancing around at the other first-class passengers. When she faced forward in her seat, she bowed her head and thought.

Sam spent the rest of the flight in silence as he read his book.

\*\*\*

A green canvas bag appeared at the luggage carousel through a set of black rubber strips hanging from the wall. As it meandered slowly around, flowing in a river of bags, Sam was momentarily hypnotized by the duffel's movement.

His fascination with the baggage stream was broken by the travelers with whom he'd just shared a plane from

Seattle. Most jostled to get near the carousel. He watched with curiosity as they pushed by each other for a better position. Faces contorted with anxiety or anger when their bags did not appear quickly enough.

The last time he saw his lawyer seatmate was when he changed planes in Seattle. She had brought a small carry-on and left the aircraft without further word to Sam. He wasn't offended by her sudden aloofness. As she walked up the skybridge, her hips swayed in a hypnotic rhythm, and he developed a renewed appreciation for her.

Perhaps he should have spent more time chatting with her, but his stop in Seattle was only a layover, and she was returning home to do lawyerly things. The idea of spending time with her would have required him to violate one of his rules.

While lost in thought, his green duffel bag passed by, floating along the luggage stream until it disappeared through another black rubber curtain.

When he was jostled again, Sam decided to step out of the crowd. He wasn't in a hurry. There were others clearly desperate to get to the conveyor belt.

Nearby, a husband angrily barked at his wife, "I don't know where it's at!"

Sam assumed it was a missing bag the husband spoke about since the couple already had five around them, and the two intently watched the conveyor belt.

When the woman snapped, "Don't yell at me! I'm tired, too," the husband stormed off, muttering to himself.

A moment later, the wife's face lit up, and she turned to call for her partner. Realizing he was out of earshot, she shrugged, collected the bag from the stream, then sat on the edge of a rather large blue suitcase. Her elbow rested on a knee with her chin cradled in a hand. She looked like a woman waiting for the inevitable. Whatever that was, Sam didn't know.

When his duffel bag appeared a second time, he casually moved to the opposite end of the stream and waited. It would get to him in time.

The remaining folks in the luggage area continued to move to and from the conveyor belt hurriedly. The angry husband soon returned with a cart. He and his wife piled their bags onto it, and the man shoved it ahead of himself. The couple bickered as they moved out of earshot and eventually out of sight. Even when he could no longer hear them, Sam imagined they continued fighting all the way home.

Just before the green duffel disappeared through the black rubber curtain a second time, Sam grabbed it and slung it over his shoulder.

Then he opened the Uber app on his cell phone.

*** 

Outside at the ride-share stand, a Toyota Prius pulled to the curb. A guy in his late twenties hopped out and walked around to the trunk. "Sam?"

He nodded.

"I'm Kirby," the driver said with a nod. "Let me get that for you."

He grabbed Sam's duffel and carefully placed it into the rear of the car.

Once inside, Kirby checked his rearview mirror. "Good flight?"

"Ended where I wanted."

"First time to Spokane?"

"Hometown."

Kirby's eyes drifted down to his phone's mapping software. "Looks like we're headed to the Airport Mini-Storage."

"Uh-huh."

Sam wasn't sure why American Uber drivers, and taxi drivers, for that matter, insisted on chatting with their fares. It was an annoying tendency. He much preferred the drivers who had immigrated from other countries. Their silence was obviously from a lack of familiarity with the language, but Sam was nonetheless thankful. He wondered if immigrant drivers would be chatty if they drove in their home countries.

The Prius moved silently forward.

"I've never taken anyone to a mini-storage after a flight," Kirby said. "Airport parking for sure, but never mini-storage. Got a car stowed there?"

Sam watched the passing scenery. "Uh-huh."

"I had a friend who stored his car in a storage unit once."

"That so?"

"It wasn't a collector car or anything. Just his regular car."

Sam remained silent.

"He died," Kirby said.

That ended the driver's babble, which was okay with Sam. There was a time and place for small talk but chatting with an Uber driver was never it. Maybe he should add Uber drivers to his list of occupations to avoid. However, he relied on them for so much of his transportation that it would be hard for him to follow that rule. A necessary evil, he decided.

Five minutes later, the Prius stopped roadside in front of Airport Mini-Storage in Airway Heights, just east of

Spokane and they got out. Near Sam's foot was his duffel bag.

Kirby shoved his hands into his pockets. "Want me to wait until you get inside?"

"I'm good."

The driver nodded, then returned to his car. Before he climbed in, he said, "Sorry for being weird. The comment about my friend, I mean."

Sam shrugged.

As the Prius drove away, Sam removed a set of keys from his backpack and headed toward the front of the complex. When he held a fob to the entry box, the security gate buzzed and rolled inward.

At door H-11, he stopped and removed a padlock. With a jerk upward, the door clattered open. Inside sat a tarp-covered car. He carefully rolled the fabric back to reveal a pristine 1985 Ford Crown Victoria. Its burgundy interior was like new.

After a few attempts, the car started, and a low rumble emanated from under the hood. He pulled the vehicle out of the storage unit and let it idle. He tossed his duffel into the trunk along with the folded cover.

He returned to the storage unit, made sure nothing was left behind, and re-secured the padlock.

*** 

It was a beautiful mid-May afternoon as Sam pulled onto the freeway and headed east.

With the windows down, the Crown Victoria cruised at fifty-five miles per hour—five under the speed limit. A crisp breeze blew through the car, and the sun shone outside. There wasn't a cloud in the sky.

He pushed Sammy Hagar's *Standing Hampton* into the cassette player. The tape clicked into place, and "I'll Fall in Love Again" immediately pounded through the speakers.

The car had been his grandfather's, but the cassette tape once belonged to his father. Sammy Hagar had been his dad's favorite artist.

It's how Sam ended up with his name.

Samuel Roy Strait—named after the Red Rocker.

Traffic raced by him on the freeway, but Sam didn't care.

He was headed home.

*** 

It took thirty minutes to pass the sign welcoming visitors to the Newman Lake community. Along with the midmorning sun, a feeling of nostalgia warmed Sam.

It had been seven months since he'd been home, and he missed the area. He had a list of projects for the cabin that he needed to start on. He also had a couple of friends on the lake he hoped to see.

He turned on Northwest Newman Lake Road before dropping onto North Honeymoon Bay Road and heading toward the actual lake. Hagar now belted out "Sweet Hitchhiker" as he drove along the narrow road. At times, the roadway pinched so tight that it was tough for two cars to pass each other without one pulling to the side. Eventually, he turned the Ford into the driveway of his cabin.

When Sam switched off the car, it knocked and pinged for several moments. After stepping out, he arched his back and stretched. He smelled the pine trees, the lake, and the late spring air. His smile faded when he noticed beer cans scattered about the small lawn.

Sam glanced around to the neighboring properties. No one was outside. Instinctively, he crouched and moved slowly through his yard.

As he got closer to the front of the house, there were more beer cans. Then he saw food debris—a pizza box and hamburger wrappers—spread about.

The front door to his cabin was slightly ajar, and he peered inside. Not seeing anyone, he pushed it fully open.

The cabin was a small affair—two bedrooms, one bathroom, a living room, and a kitchen. It was the house where his father had been raised. It was the home where Sam grew up.

It didn't take much time for him to walk through and realize that his house had been ransacked. There were empty alcohol bottles and beer cans everywhere. A pizza box and dirty napkins were on the living room table. He walked out onto his deck to find more beer cans and liquor bottles. Several cigarettes had been snuffed out on the deck railing.

From where he stood, he could see his boat—a 1999 MasterCraft—tied to the dock below. A friend of his who lived on the lake had dropped it onto the water a couple of days ago. Someone—it appeared to be a woman with long dark hair—sat in the backseat.

"Hey!" Sam yelled.

When she didn't acknowledge him, he hollered again. "Hey!"

Again, she didn't respond.

Sam hurried down the deck stairs. He would find out who was responsible for this mess and make them pay for it one way or another.

This illegal party must have happened after his friend, Dominic, dropped the boat off. Had the party been going on when Dom arrived, he would have broken it up, then let Sam know about it. There's no way his friend would have allowed a party to happen.

His neighbors weren't the friendliest group, but even they wouldn't let a party of this magnitude continue for too long.

When Sam made it to the beach, he said, "Hey, lady, what in the hell are you—"

But he never finished the statement—there was no need.

The woman wore a black hooded sweatshirt and blue jeans. A Spokane Demons baseball cap was next to her on the bench seat. A plastic red cup lay on the floor along with a couple of empty beer cans.

Sam leaned into the boat to get a closer look at the woman. She stared unblinkingly back at him. The bruising around her neck was obvious.

He didn't know the woman. He knew that much immediately. Everything else about her was a mystery.

Sam took a step back and carefully studied the scene— the woman, the boat, the dock. He turned around and took in the debris scattered about the beach.

He pulled out his cell phone and dialed 911.

When the emergency dispatcher answered, Sam said, "I'd like to report a murder."

# Chapter 2

"And that's when you found her?" Spokane County Detective Shane McAfee asked.

Sam glanced around. This was the third time the detective had asked him to explain how he found the woman. He knew what McAfee was doing. The detective was making him repeat his story in hopes of finding inconsistencies.

"That's when I found her. Yeah."

"What did you do then?"

"I called nine-one-one like I said the previous two times you asked me that question."

He still hadn't told the detective that he recorded the entire crime scene with his cell phone. Sam had worked backward from the dead girl, the dock, the beach, his house, and then out to the front where he eventually met the first deputy to respond.

After what he'd been through, a recording of this moment might eventually come in handy. But telling a detective that he filmed a crime scene before the arrival of law enforcement might seem weird or even counterproductive. The guy might try to seize his phone as evidence.

"Then what did you do?" McAfee asked.

Sam's shoulders slumped. "I waited for a deputy. I didn't go back into the house. I didn't touch anything. For the third time."

Detective McAfee crossed his thick arms and frowned. He was a taller man, a few inches over six feet, perhaps. He wore a suit and tie, but he presented a trim figure—a man who spent time in the gym. His face was chiseled and lean. His short hair was combed to the side in a businessman's swoop.

McAfee also had appraising eyes—the type that judged without remorse. They probably did that even when he didn't know he was doing it. He silently watched Sam for more than a minute. It wasn't the quiet observation a casual stranger might do. Instead, it was the piercing study a scientist gave when a hypothesis wasn't turning out the way they hoped.

Finally, Sam had enough of the detective's glare. "What are you doing?"

"Thinking."

"About?"

"You."

"What about me?"

The detective flipped his notebook closed and tucked it into an inner jacket pocket. "You're not planning to travel anywhere now, are you?"

"I just got here."

McAfee smirked. "That doesn't answer my question."

Near the beginning of the interview, they had a conversation about Sam's seasonal relocation. He even showed McAfee the electronic ticket on his phone to prove that he'd just arrived earlier in Spokane. While he noted his travel times, the detective absently shook his head. At the time, Sam thought it was due to McAfee worrying about the woman's murder. Now, he believed it was something else.

"I'll stay through the summer," Sam said.

The detective's lip curled briefly, but he quickly forced it down. "Then where will you go?"

Sam shrugged. "I haven't decided."

"When will you leave?"

"Before it gets cold."

That seemed to frustrate McAfee, and the corner of his lip trembled again. He forced it down only to have the other side curl in response.

"Any further questions?" Sam asked. "I'd like to clean my house."

McAfee glanced toward the cabin. His tongue poked around his mouth while he thought. "We're going to be awhile."

"But my house—"

"Is a crime scene until I say it isn't," McAfee snapped. He leaned in, and his eyes hardened. "You remember how this works, don't you?"

The detective walked off without waiting for Sam's reply.

***

He sat in his car with the door opened and listened to Sammy Hagar belt out "Baby's on Fire." The cassette had finished the second side, and the tape player had automatically started over—eighties technology at its finest.

Four marked patrol units from the Spokane County Sheriff's Office blocked his car in the small driveway.

There were also two unmarked vehicles on the street. Sam knew one of them belonged to an on-scene supervisor, while the other belonged to Detective McAfee. A white van—the forensics unit—was parked at the edge of his lawn. There were no sidewalks in this part of Newman Lake.

Two lines of yellow SHERIFF—DO NOT CROSS tape were strung across his property. The first was along the edge of the property line to create the outer perimeter. The second line of tape had been near the boat to indicate an inner perimeter. Only Major Crimes and the forensic team were allowed in there. Anyone who stepped into either area would be recorded on a log sheet.

A news team showed up. Sam didn't know where they parked, but a female reporter and a male cameraman stood at the property's edge and surveyed the scene. The woman wore a teal blouse and tan slacks. The cameraman had on a T-shirt and khaki shorts.

The newswoman patted the man's shoulder and pointed toward Sam. The cameraman swung his lens in Sam's direction. After a moment, he dropped the camera to let it dangle around his neck.

It wasn't the first time a camera had been pointed at Sam, and he certainly didn't enjoy it. Unfortunately, there wasn't much he could do about it. He leaned back against the headrest and listened to the music.

From the east, Dominic Russo walked surreptitiously up the street. The only way he could have made it look more suspicious was if he pulled his hoodie over his head and darted from tree to tree.

As it was, Dom occasionally stopped behind a parked car to scope out what was happening at Sam's house. It was evident that he was searching for the presence of law enforcement officers.

Dom wore a black Hollywood Undead sweatshirt, faded jeans, and blue running shoes. On his head, a tattered baseball hat was turned backward. His spring clothing didn't reveal it, but Dom was top-heavy with bulging chest, shoulder, and arm muscles supported by underdeveloped legs. It was the result of an unorganized and undisciplined gym regimen. He spent too much time on the beauty muscles and not enough time on the rest of the body. Dom would be the first to admit he hated leg workouts.

Sam raised his hand through the open door, above the car's roof, and waved. Dom noticed the movement but didn't leave his place of relative concealment. Instead, he continued to search the area for the threat of law enforcement.

When Dom decided the coast was suitably clear, he hurried in a straight line for Sam's car. He yanked open the passenger-side door and dropped into the car.

Sam turned down the music until it was barely perceptible.

Dom asked, "The hell's going on? You throw a party and not tell me?"

"You left a dead woman in my boat."

"I *what*?" His face scrunched with disbelief.

"Relax. I know you wouldn't do that."

"That's not funny."

With the back of his hand, Sam tapped his friend's arm. "You're not the one with a bunch of deputies crawling through his house."

Dom's eyes narrowed and deepened the wrinkles at their edges. He was in his early fifties, which the off-season and his pale skin cruelly revealed. When the summer sun came and bronzed him to a dark hue, he'd pass for a man closer to Sam's age. The fruit of summer—waterskiing, parties, and younger women—was what Dominic Russo lived for.

"There's a dead woman in your boat?" he asked.

"Some homecoming, huh?"

Dom frowned. "Not really."

"When did you deliver the boat?"

"Couple days ago, like I texted. Prepped like normal. Then I turned on the cabin water and flipped the power switch."

Sam nodded, then shifted in his seat to watch the cameraman. His lens was directed at the house again. The reporter pointed to something Sam couldn't see.

"Looks like a helluva party," Dom muttered.

"They trashed the place. Garbage everywhere. Even down on the beach. You didn't see anything when you dropped it off?"

"I would have caused a stink if I had."

"That's what I figured." Sam pulled his phone from his pocket and started the video he'd taken.

"What are you doing?"

"I want to show you something."

Dominic Russo was the lake's version of the welcoming committee. He knew everyone. Sam paused the video and showed the phone to him.

"Ever see this girl?"

Dom's eyes widened.

"You know her." It wasn't a question.

"I've seen her around. Yeah, but Jesus. This. She's too young for that to happen." Dom turned away from the phone to look out the passenger window.

"How old do you think she is?"

Dom continued to look out the side window. "Twenty-one." He shrugged. "Maybe twenty-two."

"What's her name?"

"How would I know?" Dom glanced back to Sam. "Put that away, will you?"

Sam continued to hold the phone where his friend could see the woman's picture. "What was she doing when you saw her?"

"She was at the store." Dom eyed the paused video. The idea of a dead woman seemed to be less shocking now. "How'd she die?"

"Strangled from the looks of it. Who was she with?"

Dom shook his head. "No one. She was just hanging around."

Newman Lake had only a single convenience store on the water to service the locals and its visitors—Wagman's.

"Not a place for a stray," Sam said.

"Probably not," Dom muttered. He glanced at the phone again and grimaced.

"Can you ask around? See if she was visiting anyone?"

Dom lifted his head to study the various cars from the Sheriff's Office. "Shouldn't the cops do that?"

"She was dead in my boat at a party in my house. I'd like to know why she came here."

His friend frowned but nodded, nonetheless. "All right. I'll ask around." He sounded defeated.

Sam returned his phone to his pocket. "I'd appreciate it."

Dom twisted in his seat and surveyed the scene near the house. "I'm gonna get outta here before the cops decide they wanna talk with me."

"You didn't do anything wrong."

His friend raised an eyebrow. "When has that ever stopped the cops from railroading a man? You of all people should know that."

Dom lightly punched Sam on the shoulder before slipping out of the car. Without hesitation, he trotted down the way he'd come.

# Chapter 3

By five o'clock, the sheriff's office released the house to Sam. However, the beach remained off-limits. The forensics team was still processing it and the boat.

Detective McAfee instructed Sam if he discovered anything missing inside the house or found anything that might be useful to the investigation to let him know immediately.

A couple of deputies moved the yellow tape that marked the outer perimeter down to the beach's edge.

Sam carried his duffel bag inside and dropped it on the floor of his bedroom. His bed was messy—it had been slept in.

Or worse, he thought.

He stripped it bare and carried the bedding to the closet, which contained the washer and dryer.

Sam then systematically set about cleaning the house.

First, he went to the master bedroom, the room where his grandparents had slept. His grandfather had died more than fifteen years prior, and his grandmother kept the room nearly the same in his memory. She worshiped the man and spoke about him in revered tones. When she eventually passed, Sam did the same for her. He referred to her in the same honored way and had no intention of altering the room. It was a shrine to the last of his family.

Their bed had been used—he didn't want to think about what might have been done in it—so he stripped it as he had his own. He straightened up various items that had been knocked over—picture frames, mementos, knick-knacks. For a moment, he paused. When he first looked in this room, there were beer cans and bottles on the floor. They had been removed.

Likely the forensics team had collected them, but he wondered how useful the items would be. If there was condensation on either the glass or the aluminum cans, prints would be tough to pull. However, the forensics team wouldn't take the chance. They would still collect all the containers. He wondered how long it would take to fingerprint those items.

Sam left the room to grab a fresh set of sheets and remade his grandparents' bed. When he was done, he moved into his bedroom and did the same. If he accomplished nothing else, at least he'd be able to sleep for the night.

Considering the two bedrooms, it didn't appear anything had been stolen—simply that a party had been thrown. But he'd only been through the two rooms. He hadn't paid much attention to the rest of the house yet.

His room overlooked the lake. It had a small window as the house wasn't built for luxuries like the homes on fancier water bodies like Coeur d'Alene Lake or even some of the newer homes on Newman. He peered down to the beach.

Detective Shane McAfee stood cross-armed on the dock, but he faced the house. His expression was tight as he studied the scene. The woman's body was gone from the boat now. The coroner's team had responded to collect her, but Sam missed her removal. He wondered how that happened.

Was that what the reporter was pointing at that he couldn't see?

When Detective McAfee glanced up toward Sam, he moved away from the window.

The living room was the biggest mess in the house. The cans and bottles he had seen earlier were gone, but now fingerprint dust was everywhere—on the coffee table, end tables, and the old stereo system.

The record player's cover had been dusted, and it appeared several smudgy prints were taken. Sam opened it to find an album inside. It was Night Ranger's *Midnight Madness*—one of his father's. He liked the record but hadn't listened to it before leaving for Hawaii. Besides, he never left albums sitting on the turntable.

It was doubtful the intruders would have selected something his grandparents would have enjoyed. Records from Elvis Presley and the Beach Boys were in the collection. Even so, this choice of album surprised him.

If the dead girl's age was indicative of the partygoers, they likely would have been in their early twenties.

How many of them would have known Night Ranger?

More than likely, they would have streamed something from their phones, but this stereo wouldn't work with modern technology. The whole house was old school, and Sam liked it that way. There wasn't even a computer in the cabin, much less wi-fi.

Above the stereo, along the wall, were a series of family pictures. There were a couple of Sam's parents. Some were of Sam's father, but the rest were of Sam through his school years. He stared at his graduation picture. In it, he proudly wore the cap and gown of East Valley High School.

The glass within the frame was cracked, and it appeared someone had thrown a beer at it, which sprayed some of its contents across the wall.

Was the party random, Sam wondered, or had they come to the cabin as some sort of vendetta against him? He doubted it was the latter, or the house would have been ransacked far worse.

Sam picked up the remaining litter in the living room before turning his attention to the wall. As he applied a damp rag to the dried beer, the alcohol's staleness irritated his nose.

Anger rose in him now. It hadn't shown when he first discovered the break-in, and the discovery of the dead woman had tamped it down. But someone had been in his house, his grandparents' home, the home where his father grew up. He stood in front of the picture wall for a moment and struggled to contain his fury.

Why did they choose this house to break in? And how—

He paused.

*How did they get in?*

He hurried through each room—checking the doors, checking the windows—until he found it. The small window in the bathroom was open slightly. He pulled it fully opened to discover the screen missing. He stuck his head out to find the screen leaning against the side of the cabin.

On the windowsill was the little wooden dowel that he kept in the track. He studied the window closely now. There were no pry marks anywhere.

Did he forget to secure this window before leaving for Hawaii?

The Beatles song "She Came in Through the Bathroom Window" sprang to mind. It was on one of his grandfather's albums—the one where the band was walking in a crosswalk.

He nudged the memories aside and left the bathroom, returning to the living room. He considered the sliding glass doors. It would have been more convenient to enter through there, but if he forgot to secure the bathroom window—the Beatles song again ran through his mind—that way inside would be cleaner and faster. The intruder—or intruders—would not have had to break anything. However, it would require someone to take the time to check all the windows. That would demand some measure of patience, however small.

Standing in the corner of the living room was the large wooden dowel he'd dropped into the track of the sliding glass doors before leaving. Even if someone were to pry open the lock on the large windows, the door wouldn't move because of the stick in the way.

He finally decided he must have forgotten to secure the bathroom window. Maybe he should make a checklist, so this wouldn't happen next time. Although, he'd never forgotten before. Perhaps he had, and no one had found his mistake. He could twist himself up playing the game of, "What if?"

Sam went to the kitchen sink and rinsed out the cloth he'd been carrying. He wiped down the living room's picture wall once more. Unfortunately, the smell of stale beer still lingered. Sam rinsed the rag another time and wiped the wall again. When he was finally convinced the wall couldn't get any cleaner, he looked through the sliding glass doors to the beach.

Detective McAfee was no longer in sight. No deputies were either, but the inner perimeter's yellow tape remained. It rippled gently, almost hypnotically, in the wind.

He walked into his grandparents' room to look out toward the front. Several patrol cars remained parked along Honeymoon Bay Road. Deputies had to be milling about somewhere. If they didn't bother him, Sam was okay with them being on the property.

Back in the living room, it took longer than he liked to remove the fingerprint dust from the various surfaces. The black stuff was horrible. He wondered if the forensics team ever considered the mess they left behind for the victims of a crime.

The kitchen was the final area, and Sam found it surprisingly clean. Most of the mess had been outside this small room. He carefully wiped down the counters and sinks. Then Sam opened the drawers to check for missing items.

The break-in seemed to be for a party, not to steal things. This led to more questions for Sam.

*Why would a twenty-something need to break into a house to party?*

*Was she homeless?*

*Couldn't she go to a friend's house?*

He opened the refrigerator and found a nearly empty half rack of Rainer beer along with another full twelve-pack on a shelf underneath. Beyond the alcohol, there wasn't much else except a slew of condiments. Sam hadn't left much in the fridge when he left for the winter.

"Find anything?"

Sam jumped.

Detective McAfee pushed the refrigerator door closed. "Have you found anything missing?"

Sam took a deep breath to settle himself before answering. "Not that I've noticed."

"Huh."

"Did you see the bathroom window?" Sam asked.

"The point of entry? Looks like you forgot to secure it."

"I must have." Sam's brow furrowed. "But I thought I did."

"The dowel needs to go into the track. Not sit on the windowsill."

Sam rolled his eyes.

"We're not taking the boat." The detective pointed toward the dock. "It's not necessary. They fingerprinted the hell out of it, so don't be upset when you see its condition."

"Is it any worse than what they did in here?"

Ignoring Sam's frustration, McAfee asked, "Anybody use the boat beside you? We want to identify as many prints as possible for elimination before they start showing up."

Sam nodded. "Dominic Russo. He delivered the boat. Not sure if anyone was in it at the storage yard, but I doubt it."

McAfee nodded as he wrote Dom's name in his notebook. When he was done, he handed Sam a little folded card. On top of it was a handwritten number. "That's your incident report."

"I know."

The detective sniffed dismissively. "Of course, you do. Any questions?"

"Who's the dead girl?"

McAfee's lips twisted. "You sure you don't know her?"

"Never seen her."

The detective rubbed his chin as he thought. "Isabella Taylor."

Bella, he thought and had a brief memory of a movie series with sparkling vampires. He'd met a woman in Corpus Christi who insisted he watch them with her during a winter romance. Those were hours of his life he'd never get back.

"We found her driver's license in her pocket," the detective said.

"She have a record?"

"Not really. Couple of shoplifting charges when she was a teenager. Nothing as an adult."

"Which means we have no idea why this happened."

"*We?* We who?"

Sam frowned. "It was a figure of speech."

"It better be. You aren't getting involved in this investigation."

"I didn't think I was."

"You said we like you were part of the team. You're not."

"I know that. I said we like I was careless with my words."

McAfee's eyes narrowed.

"Seriously. I could have easily said, you have no idea why this happened and left it at that."

The detective smirked. "I have an idea."

"You do?"

"It always boils down to one of two things—love or money."

"What about drugs?"

"That's a version of money." The detective was about to say something, but Sam interrupted him.

"What about a serial killer?"

"You think a serial killer did this to her? In your boat?"

"No. You said everything boils down to love or money, and I wanted—" Sam stopped talking then. He realized what McAfee would say. Serial killers loved to kill. He didn't need to get in a discussion about killing motivation with a detective. Sam said, "Sorry," then remained quiet.

McAfee appraised him again with those judging eyes. He must have decided something for himself because the detective nodded a couple of times before asking, "Any idea how they found your place?"

Sam considered mentioning Dom had seen Isabella Taylor around the lake but doing so would give McAfee another reason to look at his friend beyond delivering the boat. Dom had a checkered past, and he didn't need any more attention paid to him.

If Shane McAfee were any kind of detective—and Sam figured he was—he would contact Wagman's convenience store soon enough and discover the girl hung out there. Sam wouldn't need to mention Dominic. Besides, he'd already said his friend's name once in response to possible fingerprints on the boat.

"I've been gone for months, Detective. A lot of these cabins are empty for the off-season. You'd think this would happen more often."

McAfee grunted. He gave a final glance around the house. "If you remember something or find anything missing," he tapped the incident report card in Sam's hand, "you call and leave a message. Got it?"

"Uh-huh."

The detective hesitated as if he wanted to say something further, but he left it unspoken. He turned and left. The door clicked behind him.

Sam walked into his grandparents' bedroom and watched through their window as the last of the patrol cars left.

With them gone, it was as if a dead girl had never been in his boat.

# Chapter 4

The Mariners and Rangers were stumbling their way through a game, and Sam was on his second beer when she slipped onto the stool next to him. On the bar before him sat a plate of picked-clean bones which thirty minutes prior had arrived as jumbo-sized hot wings. Next to the plate sat his book, *Ego is the Enemy.*

At first, he didn't pay much attention to the woman. The Super Fan is in State Line, Idaho, and the dancers from a neighboring strip club often wandered over after their shifts. Lots of attractive women came in, but it was best to look and not touch. Getting involved with an exotic dancer led to unintended consequences. Sam knew this from experience, and he liked to think himself a man not to repeat the same mistake twice.

"How are they doing?"

He glanced over to see her considering his book, then turned his attention back to the TV. "Up by one. Bottom of the sixth. Two outs. Runner on third."

When the bartender approached to collect his plate, Sam nodded his thanks. The woman said, "Bud Light," before the bartender could ask for her order. As he walked off, the woman faced Sam and studied him.

He frowned until she turned away and examined herself in the reflection of the mirror behind the bar. Maybe she was still studying him. Sam didn't know.

She was in her early thirties and wore a Lulu Lemon baseball cap with an expertly curled brim. Her light blue T-shirt hugged her appropriately, and her white shorts rode high on her toned thighs. Her skin color was store-bought—it was too early in the season for a deep tan. Bright white sandals covered her feet, and straps wrapped around her ankles.

Sam gave her a final glance before staring at the TV. His thoughts didn't leave the woman, though. She looked familiar, but he couldn't place her.

Until he recalled *how* he knew her, he didn't want to start a conversation. He would have remembered if they had been together intimately. That wasn't the type of thing Sam forgot. Even though he wasn't in a long-term relationship, hadn't been in one for many years, he never forgot anyone he spent time with.

Sam was sure they had never met before, but the fact she seemed familiar bothered him. He struggled to place her while he absently watched the ballgame.

The bartender returned and placed a beer in front of the woman.

On the screen, a Mariner's batter drove a deep shot into left. Sam leaned forward slightly. With a leap, the right-fielder caught the ball above the outfield wall. Sam settled back on his stool and wrapped his hand around his beer.

In the mirror behind the bar, he noticed the woman analyzing him. Frustrated that he couldn't place her, Sam asked her reflection, "I know you?"

"Not yet."

The way she held eye contact perplexed him. Via the mirror, she studied him in the way a woman reads a man she's about to make a move on, but she just sat.

The lady was moving way too fast, Sam thought.

"Are you working?" he said, which is the polite way a law enforcement officer asks, "Are you a prostitute?" He didn't think it was an unusual question due to the proximity of the strip club.

She must not have understood his question, though. Instead, the woman said, "I want your story."

He rolled his eyes, put his hand on his book, and turned his attention back to the game. Now, he knew her. She was the reporter who had earlier stood at the property line of his cabin. Only she'd changed out of her professional work clothes.

Her stool squeaked as she faced him directly. From the corner of his eye, he caught the motion in the mirror.

"This has the makings of a great story," she said.

"For who?" Sam asked over his shoulder.

"For everyone."

"Not for me," he said to the TV. Hopefully, the woman would take the hint and leave.

"Then tell your side."

"I already have."

The pitcher threw a called strike before the reporter asked, "Who did you tell?"

He shook his head but didn't bother to look at her.

They sat quietly for several moments. The Rangers cleared the side after a pop-up to shallow right field. The television switched to a commercial. Sam grabbed his book and pulled it to him. He opened it and prepared to read.

The woman leaned forward until she was in his right ear. Sam could smell her perfume. It was a sweet smell and reminiscent of the woman he'd recently met in Hawaii. "I know about you."

He closed the book and turned slightly to see her.

"The paper has your history. I had a researcher pull it up when we found out it was you. I don't need a comment from you. My story can run with what I've got."

"And what is that?"

"Exonerated deputy finds a dead woman in his home."

He fully faced her now. Sam was about to say something but stopped. She had a small notepad on the bar, and her pen hovered above it. In a moment of self-preservation, he pushed his beer further away from himself. Saying something—*anything*—would end up in the paper. He knew how it worked.

Her eyes searched his as she waited for him to reveal a useful nugget.

"How'd you find me here?"

"I followed you."

He frowned.

"It wasn't hard. I saw you driving away on Newman Lake Road." With a single finger, she made a circle in the air. "I flipped a U-ey and followed you here."

He looked at the half-empty beer—his second—and thought about the empty plate of hot wings that were now gone. "I've been here long enough for you to come in."

"I gave you time to eat. I thought it would be easier for you to talk on a full stomach."

"You mean a stomach full of beer."

She shrugged. "I was being polite."

Sam squinted and fought back the expletive he wanted to utter.

The reporter leaned in slightly. "The county paid three-quarters of a million for wrongful termination. I think the public would like to know what happened to you and that money."

"Lady—" he began but stopped his thought. "I don't even know your name."

"Jordan Withers."

Sam inhaled deeply and tried to calm himself. "Jordan, I'd like to say you seem like a nice woman—"

"I am nice."

"—but you're going to make trouble for me."

"I'm here for a story."

Anger built within him. "You want a story?"

"That's all I'm asking."

He wanted to tell this woman about his grandmother and her failing health. That as she aged, she refused to move into the city where it would be easier for her to get assistance from social services. Sam moved back into the cabin with her for selfish reasons because he didn't want to lose his last close family member. He had maternal grandparents who lived in Florida now and a couple of other shirttail relatives scattered about the country, but his grandmother was the last of his family.

She'd been on the lake for more than fifty years. It was her home. It was where she had lived with her husband—Sam's grandfather. She raised Sam's father there. After his parents died, his grandparents took Sam in and raised him as their own.

Jordan stared expectantly at Sam and absently turned her beer on the bar.

When his problems with the department started, it deeply hurt his grandmother. She told the friends who would listen that the department was coming after her little boy. Then the media piled it on. Seeing what they said on television didn't change his grandmother's mind, but when the accusations were put into print—a woman her age—

she believed some of it was the truth. It was the newspaper, after all.

Sam wanted to tell the reporter all of this, but he held it back. Instead, Samuel Roy Strait said, "Good things don't happen when you put my name in print."

"But I have a story to write."

Sam slipped off his barstool. "Write what you want, but you need to think about something."

Jordan raised her eyebrows. "What's that?"

"Sticks and stones."

"The nursery rhyme?"

"Whoever said words could never hurt lied."

"It's called the news."

He tossed several bills onto the counter. "After you get your byline, those of us you write about have to deal with the fall-out your words create."

Sam left her sitting alone at the bar. He didn't bother to look back.

# Chapter 5

At least, Sam thought, the trespassers had the decency to leave some beers in the fridge. The deputies thankfully hadn't seized them for evidence. Would there have been any evidentiary value to the beer?

He reached into the nearly empty box of Rainer and pulled a can out. Only a single beer remained after this one.

Sam snapped open the can then gulped down a deep swallow. He hadn't been home an entire day yet, and he already knew this summer would be full of drama.

He didn't like drama, and he wanted to avoid it, so he made it one of his rules. The fourth was plain and simple.

*No drama.*

Maybe he should move it to the top of the list, he thought ruefully. No, the first rule was still the most important. That should always remain where it was.

Sam left the kitchen. At the stereo, he realized he hadn't put the *Midnight Madness* record away. He lifted it from the turntable but soon returned it to where it had been. The cover wasn't sitting out. He searched through the mix of albums—a collection of both his father's and grandparents—until he was confident the Night Ranger record cover was missing. He stood and looked behind the stereo to make sure it hadn't slipped behind. No luck.

He hadn't seen the album sleeve while cleaning. If he had, he wouldn't have filed it away without the actual record.

Did that mean the deputies took it as evidence? Or had one of the partygoers taken it? If so, why would they do that *without* the record? What good was an empty record sleeve unless someone had a coverless album at home that needed protecting? The thought didn't make sense.

He turned on the stereo and dropped the needle at the edge of the record. After a few moments of light crackle, "(You Can Still) Rock in America" boomed from the stereo.

Sam stood at his window and stared at the blackness of the lake. There were a few twinkling lights in the distance.

For a moment, Sam wondered if the tune could be considered a protest song. The title and chorus initially might sound like a stand against censorship, but as he listened closely to the lyrics, he realized it was really about partying. Slightly disappointed, it wasn't a song of dissent, he sighed. By the second chorus, though, he shrugged and no longer cared. It was still a damn good rock and roll song.

Sam listened only to his father's music while he was home. His father had been into rock and roll. Listening to those records and cassettes was a way for Sam to connect with his past. He didn't have any memories of his dad, but the music allowed him to imagine what his father was like.

While he sipped his beer, his thoughts turned to his mother. He felt terrible he didn't have many ways to connect with her. He should, he thought, but most of what he knew about her came from what he saw in old photographs.

Maybe he knew his father better because his fraternal grandparents raised him. Therefore, he heard stories about Peter Strait most of his life. Adoring son, loving father, and dead at eighteen.

It was a habit of the Strait family, Sam knew, to idolize their dead. His grandparents did it to their son. They spoke of him in revered tones and only of his highest qualities. His grandmother would often say he was the brightest boy and achieved some of the highest school marks. He played on several sports teams and often earned starting positions.

Peter had such a way with the girls, his grandmother told Sam, there would be so many coming through the house she couldn't keep them straight. His grandfather would chuckle at those memories, no doubt enjoying the roguish behavior of his only child.

Of course, that behavior led Peter Strait to be the only boy in his high school class to be married and a father during his senior year.

His grandmother often said Sam was the spitting image of his father. Sam played various sports in school, earned high marks in his classes, and also had a certain charm with the girls.

Sam tilted back his beer and finished the last of it. He wondered what about his father, if anything, *wasn't* ideal? Did he have the same shortcomings that Sam did? The few times he asked his grandmother, she could never point to a single failing. He smiled at the thought and returned to the kitchen.

How lucky was it to be so loved by someone that they couldn't find fault in you? Was that a mother's love? Did his mother, Cynthia Strait—Cindy to her family and friends—love Sam in that way? He was only a baby, so maybe she couldn't have found fault with him then. Or was he so troublesome at times that she couldn't stand him? That would be human nature, wouldn't it?

Never having children of his own, Sam didn't know.

Sam opened the fridge, reached into the Rainer box, and grabbed the last can. As he pulled his hand out, the box came with it. He tugged the empty cardboard container from his hand and tossed it on the counter. Before closing the fridge, he spied the remaining half-rack in the fridge. It appeared to have been taped. Someone had likely dropped it at the grocery store, and it tore. He'd purchased cases of beer like that before. If the cans inside were okay, no one would care what the cardboard box looked like.

He closed the fridge and went to the couch. With a sigh, he dropped into it and lifted his bare feet to the edge of the coffee table.

For several minutes, he drank his beer and listened to the music. Nostalgia was always a part of returning home. It had been for the past six years, but a more profound melancholy was creeping in with each return.

He didn't feel these regrets while he was gone for the winters. Never once. Perhaps he should sell the lake place and move permanently. Go somewhere new—someplace where no one knew him—and just enjoy his life.

If he did that, he could leave everything behind.

Such as the Strait legacy, which often felt constraining. How could he ever live up to the memory of Peter Strait?

Back home included his history with the sheriff's department. This was something he loathed and would happily have abandoned. However, every time he returned, he ran into people or situations that reminded Sam of that tumultuous period. Forever leaving the lake looked good when weighed against this consideration.

However, doing so would mean leaving behind the few friends and acquaintances he did have. Unfortunately, the older he got, the fewer they became. Would he—could he—change his life for a handful of people that may not be there the next day?

It didn't take a psychologist to tell Sam that his fear of abandonment came from an upbringing without his biological parents. He'd developed a life perfectly suited around this underlying angst. Leave before attachments became too deep and could hurt too much. Return to make sure he still had a touchstone to his past.

Doctor Sam, he thought sardonically, heal thyself.

Is that why he read books like *Ego is the Enemy*? Was he searching for ways to deal with the loss in his past? If that were true, why didn't any of them stick? He'd finish a book, feel good for a few weeks, then slip back into the Sam of old. His head dropped to the back of the couch.

Why did he only feel sad when he returned to Newman Lake? While away for the winter, he felt alive. Then he came home and was greeted with melancholy, nostalgia, and despair.

That was a new one—*despair*. He'd never thought about that word before.

Perhaps it was the beer talking. He held up the can. This was his fourth of the night, but he wasn't a lightweight. He knew how to hold his liquor.

If it wasn't the beer, then what allowed these feelings to sneak in and overwhelm him? His chin dropped to his chest, and he noticed the Duke's logo on his T-shirt. For several moments, he considered it.

"Idle hands," he mumbled.

When he returned to the lake, he mostly laid about for the summer. He didn't do that when he snowbirded for the winter. He always found a seasonal job to offset his expenses.

Perhaps he needed something to occupy his mind while home—a way to keep his thoughts off the emptiness of his life.

Maybe I should start a family, he thought. He barked a single, sharp laugh then shook his head. He wasn't the wife-and-kids type of guy. He didn't even have a pet because he didn't want to be tied down.

Sam sipped his beer and allowed his thoughts to drift away on the music. After a while, the album finished playing, and the needle lifted to reset on the record player. Suddenly, the room was silent.

He sighed, then slowly leaned forward as if to stand. He paused in mid-motion and stared at the record player. His thoughts whirred with other, more immediate considerations.

Night Ranger's *Midnight Madness—what happened to its album cover?*

The party—*why did they pick my house?*

The dead woman—*why was she murdered in my boat?*

Sam struggled to remember her name. He leaned back on the couch and rested his head. Detective McAfee had told him what it was. He should have written it down. For several moments, he concentrated. He lifted his beer to his lips, paused, and pulled it away without drinking.

Sam was reminded of something when the detective said the woman's name. What was it? he wondered. A movie? That's right—a film about vampires.

Bella, he thought. *Isabella!*

"Isabella Taylor," he muttered and leaned forward again. He pulled his cell phone from his back pocket and called up the Internet browser. As much as he pretended to prefer the ways of the past—his grandfather's car, the turntable, the small cabin—there were moments where technology did come in handy.

Sam entered the dead woman's name into the browser's search field, pressed enter, and waited for the results. Most of them came back either related to Facebook or Instagram. There was more than a dozen Isabella Taylors, and he suspected one of them lived in Spokane County. However, he didn't have an account on either social media platform so he couldn't find her without joining. Sam figured someone on the lake with an account would help him.

"Isabella Taylor," he repeated.

She would be his mission, he decided. She would give his mind something to focus on rather than despair. He would find out who she was and why she was at his house. The melancholy about returning home faded.

He leaned back into the couch and finished his beer.

"No more idle hands," he said to himself.

# Chapter 6

"You're not going to like this."

Dominic Russo tossed the newspaper onto the counter. Sam pulled it toward himself. Below the fold was an article by Jordan Withers titled *Exonerated Deputy Finds Dead Woman.*

The article identified Isabella Taylor as the victim because the department had already notified her next of kin. It was a matter-of-fact piece devoid of speculation. There was some back story on Sam that was worked in—wrongfully terminated, cleared of wrongdoing, and later awarded a settlement—but none of it was salacious. It seemed his conversation with the reporter might have scored a few points.

Sam laid the paper down. "It's not bad."

"Not bad?" Dom repeated, taking a seat at the table. Just as the day before, his baseball hat was turned backward, and he wore the same Hollywood Undead sweatshirt. "I wouldn't want my name in the paper."

"She did a fair job."

"She?"

"The writer." Sam folded the paper and tapped the byline. "The reporter. Her."

Dom lifted his eyebrows and stared at him, indicating he was done talking about the article unless Sam wanted to continue down this path.

He tapped the newspaper again. "You find anything about the girl?"

His friend nodded. "Izzy was with—"

"Izzy?"

"Her nickname."

"How'd you know that?"

Dom shrugged. "The cashier at Wagman's told me. Ernie hired her friends, and she hung out at Wagman's while they worked."

"What did they do for Ernie?"

"Yardwork, I guess."

It was the guessing that caused Sam to pause. Dom was tuned into happenings around the lake. He would know about a couple of guys over at Ernie Holstrom's place since it sat almost directly across the water from Dom's.

"Wagman's cashier knew about the guys working at Ernie's, but you didn't?"

Dom shrugged again. "Maybe I knew something about that."

"Why would you lie?"

"I didn't lie," Dom said as he crossed his arms. "I just didn't know if Ernie got himself into something."

"You think the old man could be responsible for the woman's death? He motored across the lake to a party and strangled her? Does that make any sense?"

Dom shook his head. "When you put it that way."

His friend seemed slightly off. It wasn't like Dom to be coy, but maybe it was the dead woman. Most people had never been near a recently murdered person. It affected everyone differently. "But you talked with him."

"Yeah."

"What did he say?"

"Nothing." Another shrug. "Just that he hired a couple guys for yard work. You know, to get the cabin prepped for the season. The girl tagged along."

Sam gnawed on his lip while he thought.

"Why's it matter if I talked to him before the cops?"

"It doesn't."

"Your face says different. I didn't tell him about the girl being killed."

"Why not?"

Dominic shrugged for the fourth time. Sam never noticed Dom affecting that gesture so many times. "I don't know. I wasn't sure I should tell him or not. I wasn't trying to hide anything, but I didn't want to get into trouble either."

"Who would you get in trouble?"

Yet another shrug.

Sam cocked his head. "Dom, is something going on?"

"Besides a girl getting murdered?"

That must be what was causing his friend to act so strangely. "The big question remains," Sam said. "How did Izzy and her friends—I'm supposing it was her friends—make it to my house? Ernie's place is around the way."

"Don't look at me like it was my fault."

"I'm not."

Dom's face reddened. "Yeah." More nodding. "You kind of are."

"Why are you getting so mad?"

"I had nothing to do with any of it."

"Dom—"

His friend stood from the table.

"Where are you going?"

Dominic stalked out of the cabin, leaving the sliding glass door open as he went.

Sam walked to the big window and watched his friend trot down to the dock. He hopped into his boat and revved it to life.

What the hell just happened? Sam wondered and slid the door closed.

***

Located in Cherokee Bay, Wagman's convenience store served as a one-stop catch-all. Customers could get snacks, sodas, beer, fishing supplies, and ice. They could even order a custom-made pizza. Visitors to the lake could request—if they got lucky—one of the few RV spots along the bay, but they had to hurry as they always filled early in the spring.

Sam carefully pulled his boat alongside the dock and hopped out. He tied it to a cleat before walking toward Wagman's.

It would likely remain quiet on the lake for another week or two. The average temperature for May wouldn't top seventy degrees. At night, it could fall below forty. That meant the weekend warriors—those who came to party and water ski—wouldn't arrive until next month. Due to its depth, the lake warmed considerably by July. In that month, the water would become unruly. By August, it would be a choppy mess with the number of visitors.

Regardless, it was still a wonderful place to call home.

He opened the door to Wagman's and was greeted with the smell of coffee and the sound of oldies rock & roll—stuff that his grandfather listened to. The song "Be True to Your School" was a Beach Boys classic.

Behind the cash register stood a teenager with hair the color of cotton candy. Long bangs peeked out from beneath a black Carhart beanie. Begrudgingly, the girl lifted her eyes from her smartphone. She didn't bother acknowledging Sam before returning her attention to the small device.

Standing in front of the counter, he waited for her to finish whatever she was doing. Her fingers jumped across the keyboard. When she slowly looked up again, her eyebrows lifted in a bored, questioning manner.

"Ready?" he playfully asked.

"What?" she snapped.

That wasn't the response he was expecting. "Can I order?"

"Yeah, fine." She jerked her head as if she were talking back to an inquisitive parent.

"Black coffee and an egg sandwich."

She rolled her eyes before stepping to the prep counter.

He sat at one of the two small tables and watched her work. The teenager moved with efficiency, but anger masked her face. While his egg cooked, she paused at the counter to notice him watching. She sighed, shook her head, and turned toward the coffee pot.

In a moment, she stopped by his table and placed a Styrofoam cup in front of him.

"Sorry," she muttered.

"About?"

"My attitude."

"No worries." He was surprised the teenager had apologized.

She returned to the grill and worked a few minutes further. When she came back, she handed him a paper plate with an egg sandwich wrapped in tin foil. A ticket for his order was slipped under the sandwich.

He stood and pulled a couple of bills from his pocket.

She tucked the money into the till. "You hear about the girl they found?"

"The dead one?"

The cashier handed him his change. "Uh-huh. Izzy was my friend."

Sam's eyebrows rose, and he leaned in. "Really?"

The teenager nodded.

"How long have you known her?"

"Long enough."

"What's your name?"

"Nicki."

"Hi, Nicki. I'm Sam."

She stared at his extended hand like he was handing her a dead salmon. Nicki was new to Wagman's, which wasn't necessarily a surprise. The work was seasonal, so the cashiers tended to change often, sometimes yearly.

Sam pulled his hand back. "She was found in my boat."

Nicki's eyes narrowed. "No way."

"While I was away, someone threw a party at my house."

"I didn't have anything to do with that."

"I didn't say you did."

"Good because I didn't."

"Were you there?"

"No. We weren't those kinds of friends."

"What kind of friend were you?"

Nicki frowned. "Are you some kind of cop?"

"I'm the guy whose boat Izzy died in."

Her frown deepened. "Oh, yeah. Sorry."

"So, what kind of friends—"

"The work kind."

"Meaning?"

"She came in and hung out."

"What was she doing?"

"Drinking coffee. Using the Wi-Fi. Charging her phone."

"For how long?"

"Not very long. Just a couple days."

He had expected her answer would come in the form of hours, but the response she gave was better than he hoped. "So, you never drank with her? Never went to a party together?"

The girl's face pinched. "I'm only nineteen."

Sam smirked. "You mean I found the only nineteen-year-old at the lake who doesn't drink?"

Nicki glanced around as if she were checking to see if anyone else could hear their conversation. They were the only two in the store. "Okay, I drink. It's no secret."

"But you didn't drink with Izzy?"

"I told you we weren't those kinds of friends. She came into the store and leeched the Wi-Fi. That's how I knew her."

"You ever see her with anybody?"

"Just the guys she was waiting for."

"The ones doing yard work for Ernie Holstrom?"

"That's right," she said with a nod. "They came in here to pick her up."

"What'd they look like?"

"Big."

"Like tall?"

"And sort of fat."

"You see her talking with anyone else?"

"Not really, no."

"What about Dominic?"

Nicki shrugged. "Well, sure, she talked to him, but he talks to everybody. That doesn't mean anything. He's like that. I mean, he's in here every day. He's friendly, is what I'm trying to say—to everybody."

Sam pointed to her cell phone. "Are you on Facebook?"

"Only because I have to be."

"You *have* to be?"

"My mom is on it with her friends. I joined so she would quit asking me what I'm doing with my life. I post a picture now and then so she'll—"

Sam interrupted. "Were you Facebook friends with Izzy?"

"No."

"What about the other ones?"

"Her friends?"

"No, the other social media sites. Are you on those?"

"Instagram and Snapchat?"

"Sure. Did you connect with Izzy on either of those?"

"Why would she ever Snap me? She just hung here when her friends were working. I'm sorry I made such a big deal of us being friends. It's not every day someone I know dies. It's sort of bothering me, you know?"

"Can you look her up?" Sam asked. "I want to see what her profile looks like."

Nicki's face pinched. "Stalk much?"

"She was inside my house. She was found in my boat."

The teenager stood on her toes and looked out the window toward the docks.

"I figure that allows me to know something about her."

Nicki dropped to her usual height and picked up her phone. She paused for a moment and frowned. "What's her real name?"

"You were friends, but she never told you?"

The teenager tossed her phone back onto the counter and crossed her arms. "Look it up yourself, grandpa."

"Listen," he said. "I'm sorry." He'd forgotten what it was like to be young and accept someone based only on a first name or a nickname. "Her name is—"

Nicki held up her hand. "Whatever, Boomer."

"I'm not a Boomer. I'm still in my thirties."

"You're old enough to be my dad. That makes you a Boomer." She moved her hand, palm first, in front of his face. With a jerk of her head, she said, "Buh-bye."

Nicki spun and walked into the back room.

Sam smacked his hands in frustration, collected his sandwich, and left the store.

# Chapter 7

Sam ate his breakfast as he motored slowly across the lake. The sun was still low in the east, and it seemed cooler out on the water. In moments like these, he was reminded of why he loved being home. It was the freedom that even a small lake embodied. He could zip to and fro, or he could putter along. If he wanted, he could come to a complete stop in the middle of the water and just bob along for a time. It didn't matter—it was his choice.

After growing up at the lake, he knew almost everyone who lived along the shoreline. Of course, some homes were rented out, but most folks chose to participate in the community, either as full-time residents or summer attendees.

By the time he arrived at Ernie Holstrom's dock, he had devoured his egg sandwich and finished his coffee. He stuffed the garbage into an inner pocket of the boat so it wouldn't blow away.

As he secured the MasterCraft to the dock, the screen door on the rear of the Holstrom cabin opened, and an older man stepped out. He wore black pants and a yellowing shirt that Sam was sure had once been white. A camouflage baseball cap sat cockeyed on the man's head. He hooked his thumbs in his red suspenders as he ambled toward the dock.

Sam said, "Morning, Ernie."

"Must be summertime when that fool friend of yours puts that boat in the lake."

"Dominic isn't so bad."

"Aw, hell. The boy's an idiot. So are his parents, but it's generational, which means it ain't his fault. But you bein' his friend and all… Well, now, that's another story. Your parents raised you to be smarter than that."

Ernie referred to Sam's grandparents as his parents— almost everyone on the lake did. Sam never bothered to correct them.

"If you only got to know Dom—"

"I got to know the clap during the war." Ernie pointed an accusatory finger. "It didn't make me like it any better."

Sam shoved his hands into his pockets. "I heard you hired help for some yard projects."

"Russo must have told you that. He was over here asking about them."

"That's right."

"Why do you care? You looking to hire somebody or something?"

"Not really. From what I heard, it was a couple guys and a girl."

"Just a couple fellas. The girl, she just came the one time and sat on her butt until they took her over to Wagman's."

"She didn't pitch in?"

He chuckled. "She was worthless. I didn't mind too much since I wasn't paying them by the hour, but she distracted them both. They worked a helluva lot harder when she wasn't around."

"Did you get her name?"

"Hell no. She looked like trouble."

"Trouble?"

"Pretty enough, but with tattoos. Them type of girls is nothing but trouble." Ernie winked. "I can tell."

"You hear about the dead girl over at my place?"

Ernie's eyes narrowed. "She the same one?"

"That's what I'm thinking."

The older man tapped his toe as he thought. "Ain't that something? You think she found your place while they was working over here?"

Sam shrugged with his hands still in his jeans. "We're not exactly neighbors."

"Opposite side of the lake when you think of it that way."

He glanced toward his cabin. Sam couldn't see it due to the bend in the shoreline. "It would take some doing for them to find my house."

"That it would," Ernie agreed.

"But you hired them?"

"Uh-huh."

"How'd you find them?"

"They came recommended."

"By who?"

"A deacon at church. He used the fellas to clean up his yard. Big strappin' kids. Moved some heavy stuff for him. The deacon gave me the number to one of them, and I called him up. He came out, looked at the job, and set a price. Didn't seem unreasonable, so I agreed to it. It was only a couple days' worth of work."

"They do a good job?"

Ernie made a sweeping gesture toward his cabin. "I'm happy with it. The girl, she seems to be the one you're interested in, she didn't do too much with them. Mostly stayed over at Wagman's while they worked 'cept the one time she came over and distracted them like I said."

"Two days is a lot of time for a young woman to waste."

Ernie pulled on his suspenders. "Who knows what's a waste of time to the young? She seemed to flirt with them both. I couldn't figure out which was her boyfriend. These young people. They're too easy with themselves. Too easy with their affections."

"You said you had a number?"

"Up in the house."

"Did you get a name, too?"

"Of course." Ernie turned then and trundled towards his cabin. Sam fell in step behind him.

Inside, it was a tribute to a bachelor's life. Fishing gear was spread across the kitchen table. Photographs of Ernie with a variety of fish were on the kitchen wall. Paintings of jumping salmon proudly hung in the living room above a threadbare couch. A small box TV stood in the corner. Several wildlife magazines were haphazardly spread across an oval coffee table. On top of one magazine sat a spiral notebook. Ernie grabbed it and flipped to a back page.

He pointed to a name and number that had been crossed through.

"Tom?" Sam asked.

"That's him. Big dark fella."

"Dark?"

"As in negro. Although he was more of a caramel color. Like he was a mulatto maybe. Although, I don't think I'm supposed to say that anymore. The ladies at church are on me about my words, but I ain't saying nothing bad about the kid. He was a hard worker which is the best compliment I can give any man. He didn't say much, though. The strong silent type if you will."

Sam pulled his cell phone from his back pocket. "Mind if I photograph the page?"

Ernie smirked. "I didn't pull this out for my health."

"What did the other one look like?"

"Like Mr. Potato Head. Big ol' ears sticking out from the side of his melon." Ernie waggled his hands near his ears. "And white as the inside of a spud, too. Never got his name and didn't care. I don't think he was the brains of the outfit. Even though he talked a lot, the kid never said nothing."

Sam positioned his cell phone over the notebook and snapped a picture.

On the way back to his boat, he said, "Thanks for the info, Ernie. I appreciate it."

"You going to tell the cops about this?"

"You want to talk with them?"

"Why'n the hell would I want that?"

"I just figured."

"Well, you figured wrong. Since you were asking about the fellas who worked for me, I thought maybe you was going to share that info with the cops. I wanted to prepare myself for a visit from them if'n you was."

"What have you got to be worried about?"

He snorted. "It's the cops. What more do we need to know?"

Sam untied his boat from the dock. As he did so, he considered responding to Ernie, but he didn't see the point, especially since the man had just spoken the truth.

Instead, he jumped into the MasterCraft, waved a silent goodbye, and motored away.

\*\*\*

He knocked on the door and waited for either Ginny or Bert Vaughn to come to the door. Not hearing anything, he knocked again.

There wasn't a car out front of their home. Their boat wasn't tied to the dock when he motored past on the way to his house. Like him, they were snowbirds, escaping the region's harsh winters by fleeing for the warmth of the south. More than likely, they were still gone for the season.

When he gave up on the Vaughns, he walked past his house to Mary Jo Brakke's. She lived alone, having survived the divorce of her first husband and the death of her second. After a single knock, she answered the door. She wore a white blouse, faded blue capri pants, and white leather flats.

Her silver hair was short but recently cut and styled. Light make-up was expertly applied around her eyes and lips. In her youth, Mary Jo Brakke was likely to have broken many hearts. In her golden years, it was clear what she was after.

Her eyes took in Sam from head to toe and then back again. "Look who it is."

"Mrs. Brakke."

She waved off his formality, then reached for Sam but stopped just shy of touching him. "I've been telling you for years there's no need to be so formal. I haven't been committed to Mister Brakke since his passing. Why don't you call me Mary Jo?"

"I don't know, Mrs. Brakke. My grandmother would disapprove."

She raised her eyebrows. "I won't tell if you won't."

Even though she was in her early seventies, Mary Jo smiled at him with a lasciviousness reserved for dirty old men.

"Did you hear a party a couple nights ago?"

She nodded. "I read the paper. Just terrible. I should have called the police."

"Why didn't you?"

"On you, Samuel?"

"But I wasn't home, Mrs. Brakke."

She glanced towards his cabin. "I thought you were."

"No."

"But your boat—"

"Dom dropped it for me. I got home yesterday."

She lifted her hand to her mouth. "It's an honest mistake then. Plus, there were several young women at your house. Real pretty things. The type I've seen you with before."

"Have I ever thrown a party like that, Mrs. Brakke?"

Mary Jo reached for his arm but again stopped just before touching him. "Now, Samuel, I've seen you with women before." The way she said it was full of suggestion.

"All at once?"

Her finger touched her chin as if pretending to be in thought. "I don't know about that. I thought perhaps you were experimenting."

Sam raised his eyebrows.

After a moment, Mary Jo frowned. "It wasn't too loud. Mostly talking."

"Did you hear what they were saying?"

"Not really. Near the end, I heard some yelling, but that was it."

"Could you tell if it was a man and a woman?"

"There was some of both. You know how parties go. The arguments didn't last long, and the party ended early enough for me to get some sleep."

"And nothing seemed suspicious?"

"Not really, no. I thought you were home, so I ignored it."

"You couldn't see the woman sitting in the back of my boat?"

Mary Jo put her hands on her hips. "Why do I get the feeling, Samuel Roy Strait?" This was the tone she took with him when he was a young boy and caused trouble in the neighborhood. "That you think I'm partly responsible for what happened over at your place? I've already told the policemen everything that I saw and heard."

He apologetically lifted a hand. "Mrs. Brakke, we both know you had nothing to do with what happened over there. I'm not looking to make trouble."

"You better not be." She put her hands on her hips and slightly arched her back. This action thrust her breasts toward him.

"Mrs. Brakke—"

"Mary Jo."

"—I'm trying to figure out why those folks picked *my* cabin to break into and why someone decided to murder a young woman there."

She didn't blanch at the mention of the murder. "I can't help you with that. I try to keep my nose out of other people's affairs." Her eyes traveled his length again, and she blinked slowly. "Still. It's nice to have you back in the neighborhood."

"Thank you, Mrs. Brakke."

"How many times do I have to tell you?"

"My grandmother wouldn't approve."

As he walked away, Mary Jo muttered, "I wish I had that swing in my backyard."

Sam glanced back. "You don't have a backyard, Mrs. Brakke."

She winked at him. "That doesn't mean I don't want a swing."

He shook his head and continued on his way.

# Chapter 8

Sonja Boyd walked into the cabin without knocking. It was lake etiquette among friends to enter unannounced, and Sam Strait wasn't annoyed or bothered at her behavior.

"Why didn't you call?" she asked. In her left hand was a coffee mug from the Liberty Lake Coffee Company.

"It's nice to see you, too."

He was seated at the small dining table, making a list of what he needed to accomplish. The search for Isabella 'Izzy' Taylor's killer couldn't stop him from putting his life in order. When returning from a winter away, he still had lots to do, like buying groceries and checking the cabin for repairs. Spring cleaning around the grounds was always a good idea.

She set the coffee cup on the dining table and raised her eyebrows. Sonja then pushed her hip to the side and rested a manicured hand on it. Her short red hair was tucked behind her ears. The body he knew well was hidden under an oversized sweatshirt and a pair of coveralls. All its lovely curves and bends were now muted and flattened by denim and cotton.

On anyone else, those clothes would have been dowdy, perhaps even dumpy, but Sonja was neither of those things. Sam suspected if anyone checked the well-worn sweatshirt or the faded denim coveralls, a designer label would be revealed on both.

His eyes flicked to her feet. She wore slip-on tennis shoes with no socks.

When his gaze returned to meet her eyes, she still hadn't responded, so Sam offered, "I just got home."

"You've been home since yesterday."

Sam leaned back in his chair and crossed his arms.

Sonja was once Lilac City Queen, the honorary leader of the county's annual parade. It was the highest honor for a high school girl interested in titles such as head cheerleader and prom queen.

As recently as four years ago, she was named Miss Spokane. Now, Sonja made her living acting as a spokeswoman for a variety of local businesses. She'd also had bit parts in several films made in the region.

"You could have called before you arrived," she said. "You said you'd do exactly that before you left."

"Sonja—"

"Don't start." She unbuttoned the strap over her right shoulder, and the flap of denim flipped forward.

In this part of the world, she was a minor celebrity—often stopped and admired, especially by young girls and overly fit men. Sam still couldn't place his finger on why she insisted on pursuing him.

"This isn't a good idea," he said.

"I said, *don't* start."

After she unbuttoned the second strap, the bib of the coveralls fell forward.

"I'm still leaving at the end of the summer."

She tugged her sweatshirt over her head, exposing her pale skin.

"You won't convince me to stay. We've been over this."

With a little shimmy, the coveralls fell to the ground, leaving her completely naked. She stared at him now, defiant.

"*Sonja*," he said.

"Let's go." She stepped from the coveralls that had puddled around her ankles.

"I'm serious. I'm gone at the end of the summer."

Her defiance turned to challenge. "Then there's no time to waste." And with that, she headed toward his bedroom.

Sam Strait glanced at his list of chores.

They could wait.

***

Afterward, they lay in bed with her head on his chest. They'd fallen asleep for some time. When he awoke, she asked, "Seriously, why didn't you call?"

"I thought you had a boyfriend."

"Not anymore. You knew that."

He did but decided to ignore it by simply saying, "Huh."

"I thought after last year…"

"Sonja, this is how I live my life. We've talked about this repeatedly."

She pushed herself onto an elbow. "Why don't you love me?"

"We're doing this *now*?"

"Sam, there are plenty of men out there—"

"No doubt."

"Hundreds, probably."

"Maybe thousands," he agreed.

"Who would kill to be with me."

"Killing might be an exaggeration."

She pouted. "You don't know that."

"Are you saying you want them to kill me?"

"No." Sonja sucked her lip in before saying, "I want you to want me."

He thought about telling her there was a song by that same name in his father's record collection, but he figured pointing that fact out now might be seen as inappropriate. Instead, he said, "I do want you."

"I want you to want me beyond this moment."

"Sonja—"

"Why couldn't I go with you at the end of the summer?"

"I've told you why."

Her eyes hardened. *"Hundreds* of guys," she threatened.

"Maybe thousands."

For a moment, they stared at each other. Then Sonja angrily flipped the covers back on the bed and stood. She collected her clothes into a ball and stomped into the bathroom. The door slammed behind her.

Sam climbed slowly out of bed and dressed.

\*\*\*

When she walked out of the bathroom, she was put together, but the fury had not left her eyes. "I'm leaving."

"You don't have to."

"Yes, I do."

"Want to get a drink later?"

"No." Her tone was laced with things unsaid.

Sam shrugged. When Sonja got this way, there was no changing her mind. She'd have to work things out for herself.

Sonja stared at him for a few seconds longer then stalked to the front door. She whipped it open and left. The door remained wide, and daylight poured in.

Sam settled into his chair. He lifted his pencil and stared down at his list of tasks.

A minute later, Sonja returned. Her face was red, and her eyes filled with rage. She set her jaw, and her head shook slightly. "Where?"

"Where what?"

"For that drink."

# Chapter 9

Sam first noticed the pick-up after he turned onto Starr Road. It was a reconditioned mid-eighties Chevy 4X4. It was hard to miss with a bright red and white paint job, but trucks in Spokane County are as ubiquitous as mosquitoes in the summer.

However, noticing something and paying attention to it were two different skills. Sam failed to do the latter.

Turning eastbound onto Trent Avenue, the truck pulled in behind him. There were only two ways to go at that point—east or west. He hadn't expected anyone to follow him. Besides, Trent was the old state highway, having served the purpose of shuttling commuters back and forth before the eight-lane freeway took over sometime in the sixties. Nowadays, Trent Avenue was a smattering of worn-down retail and industrial concepts on the north side of the street, while to the south, the Burlington-Northern rail line ran parallel with the roadway.

This occurred until Argonne Road, where Sam turned south, drove under the elevated tracks, and looped into a shopping center anchored by a grocery store. He pulled into the parking lot, paused long enough to hear Sammy Hagar hit the final notes of "Heavy Metal," and got out.

That's when he finally paid attention to the red and white pick-up. It pulled up directly behind his car.

Two rather bulky men—one white, the other a dark Samoan—climbed out. The truck groaned in appreciation at the release of weight.

With a deferential nod, Sam said, "Fellas."

The pale man had a fat face and wore a purple beanie cap with a Spokane Demons logo on it. The hat was pulled down over his ears.

Mr. Potato Head, Sam thought.

"We want our stuff," Potato Head said.

"Stuff?"

The Samoan stepped forward and shoved Sam back into the trunk of his car. He pointed at Sam but remained silent.

Sam leaned forward as if waiting for the man to say something. When nothing came, Sam finally said, "The strong, silent type."

The Samoan slapped him, which buckled his knees.

Sam blinked repeatedly while rubbing away the stinging on the side of his face. "That's not helping my first impression."

"Toma is a man of few words," Potato Head said.

"And here I didn't think you were the brains of the outfit."

Toma slapped Sam again, which further buckled his knees. Sam hollered, "Quit doing that!"

"We want our stuff," the pale man said.

Sam was completely confused now. He glanced at Toma, who watched him intently.

"Our stuff," Potato Head demanded.

"I don't know what you're talking about."

Preparing for another slap, Toma opened his raised hand.

"Wait!" Sam yelled and lifted his arms in surrender. "Just wait."

"Remember now?" the pale man asked.

"Tell me what I'm supposed to have, and I'll find it for you."

The two hulking men glanced inquisitively at each other.

"That's convenient," Potato Head said. "We tell you, and you leave to get it. Then what? Call the cops? Keep it for yourself?"

"I don't know what you're talking about."

"Why don't we go together?"

"I don't like that idea."

"Why are you making this so difficult?" the pale man asked.

"Me?" Sam glanced between the two men. "I'm the one getting smacked around."

Toma chuckled.

Potato Head said, "Answer our question, or there's another smack coming."

An older woman, stooped over from age, strolled out of the grocery store. Alongside her, a clerk pushed a cart full of bags. The two seemed to be chatting amiably. When Sam saw them, he hollered, "A little help!"

The pale man's attention turned to the oncoming citizens, but Toma didn't have the same worries. Instead, the big Samoan punched Sam in the stomach, which doubled him over.

It felt like the man's fist touched the back of Sam's spine. He wanted to squeal, but he couldn't breathe. He wanted to vomit, but nothing came up. Instead, he silently gagged.

"You two!" the woman yelled. Her frail voice was filled with the tone of righteous indignation. "Leave him alone."

"Get in the truck," Potato Head said.

Toma bent over. "I'll remember this."

Sam glanced sideways at the Samoan and wanted to say something witty about him finally speaking, but he couldn't catch his breath to talk.

Toma must have sensed he intended something snarky because he punched Sam in the kidney. The strike straightened him, and Sam bellowed like a lone wolf howling at the moon.

The sound of his voice surprised him.

The two men climbed into their truck. It squeaked in discomfort when they added their weight. The Chevy backfired as it sped away.

"Are you okay, my dear?" The woman gently held Sam's hand.

He nodded and struggled for breath. "Fine," he croaked.

"What was that about?" the grocery clerk asked.

"Misunderstanding," Sam whispered. He couldn't say much more.

"A misunderstanding?" the woman said. "It seemed much more than a misunderstanding. That man assaulted you."

The grocery clerk watched the truck speed from the parking lot. "What was the argument about?"

Sam straightened fully to stretch his back. "My parking spot."

The woman and clerk both glanced around at the several empty slots that surrounded Sam's car.

"What's so special about this one?" the clerk asked.

"I was in it."

"Want me to call the cops?" the pimply-faced kid asked.

Sam shook his head and walked around to the driver's door. He climbed into his car. He sat for several minutes with his head rested against the steering wheel.

*\*\**

Before leaving his car, Sam scanned the neighborhood, looking for the red and white truck. He then carried several grocery bags just inside the cabin. Once he had the last load in, he locked the front door.

Lake etiquette be damned. Visitors could knock for a while—at least until he figured out what was going on.

In the kitchen, he set the bags on the counter and removed the various items. As he did so, his mind worked through the problem of the two men and their missing stuff.

He didn't have anything that belonged to them. He already cleaned the house and was sure the interlopers left nothing behind. Maybe someone at the party had taken what they were looking for. That would explain why he hadn't seen it and why they thought it was missing.

With a yank, he opened the refrigerator and placed a variety of vegetables into the appropriate drawer.

For him, restocking a refrigerator was always a slow process. He didn't run out and buy everything at once. He wasn't a great cook, so he tended to purchase things as he needed them. When the appliance again resembled an appropriately stocked refrigerator, it would be time for him to leave.

He pushed the half-rack of Rainer to the side to make room for a package of chicken.

His body hurt from Toma's punches. The guy only hit him twice—once in the stomach and once in the kidney—

but it felt like he'd been in a collision with a freight train. He'd been slapped a couple of times, and his jaw hurt, but nothing like the shots to the midsection.

Slowly, he finished putting the remaining items away. When he was done, he gently touched his side. Could anything be busted in there? Could he have a lacerated kidney? What about an ulcerated stomach? Did those injuries come from getting punched hard? Sam didn't know, and maybe he was worried about nothing.

He thought about taking some ibuprofen but worried it might be hard on his aching stomach and his tender kidney. A beer, though, might do the trick.

He reached for the taped-up half-rack of Rainer and pulled it toward him. When he did so, the rear flap of the box flipped up. Maybe someone had already taken a beer out. He spun the cardboard container around and saw several clear baggies of white powder inside.

Sam quickly stepped back as if just being in the vicinity of the powder could somehow link him to its existence. He wasn't concerned about it being a substance like anthrax. No, he instinctively knew by its packaging and casual hiding place it wasn't something as harmful as that. It was still an illegal substance, though. Otherwise, there would be no need to hide it in this manner. No one hid specialty baking powder—was there such a thing?—in baggies tucked inside an empty Rainer box.

Sam relaxed then and pulled a baggie out to examine it. He couldn't be sure what was inside. Perhaps it was cocaine. Maybe it was heroin. Whatever it was, there was no way to know from just eyeballing it. He certainly wasn't going to taste it.

He knew for sure this was what the goons were after.

Someone had hidden it inside his fridge. Presumably, the dead girl, and that's why someone killed her. They wanted their drugs, and she had refused to give them back.

*Presumably.* Don't get ahead of yourself, he thought.

Sam considered the baggie itself. It was reusable and resealable with a plastic zipper. The type everyone referred to as the brand Ziploc. He'd never seen drugs packaged this way before. Probably because the resealable bags were an unnecessary expense. Why package the drugs this way?

Crumpled up, the Ziploc baggie was about the size of a baseball, but that didn't mean anything to him. He was terrible at guessing the weight of drugs. It had been that way while on the department. Some guys had a talent for it, but not Sam. He tossed the baggie and caught it to test its weight. That didn't tell him anything, so he did it again.

Was it a kilo? An eight-ball? He knew the terms but not what they applied to. Maybe if he'd studied a little harder in math during high school. Or would it have been science?

As he continued to toss the little baggie, his thoughts migrated to the Samoan and his pale friend. He considered Toma's slaps and punches. Based on that fact alone, they were men not to be messed with. If they wanted these drugs—

A pounding at the door ripped Sam from his thoughts. He jumped in surprise and immediately looked toward the knocking. Doing so caused him to misjudge the arc of the descending baggie. It clipped the side of his palm, and his hand clamped shut around nothing but air.

In what felt like agonizingly slow motion, Sam watched with horror as the Ziploc fell to the ground.

When it hit, the plastic baggie popped open, and white powder cascaded across his bare feet and flip-flops. A fine white mist descended over the kitchen floor.

The knocking continued.

Even though he suddenly felt frozen in place, Sam's heart raced.

Could it be the two men wanting their drugs? The white powder scattered across his kitchen floor and over his toes mocked him. If they saw this, how bad of a beating would Toma give him?

It was at this moment he wished he still had a gun.

The pounding continued.

Reluctantly, Sam left the kitchen and looked through the peephole of the front door. He reared back and inhaled sharply. Sam glanced down the hallway at a trail of white footprints that marked his path.

Sam made a quick decision and yanked open the door. Detective Shane McAfee stood there with his arm raised mid-knock.

"What took you so long?"

"Baking accident," Sam said and stepped outside. He didn't know why he lied but having done so he pulled the door behind him. "I dropped a bag of flour."

The detective considered the white powder that covered Sam's ankles, feet, and footwear.

Sam had a small window to tell the truth. He could stop right now and admit he'd found a container of drugs in his refrigerator.

McAfee sniffed dismissively. "Flour? For what?"

"Cookies." Oh God, Sam thought. *A second lie. Why am I lying?*

The detective's eyes slanted. "You bake?"

"Can't a man bake?"

The detective cocked his head. "Doesn't seem like something you'd do."

"That's a sexist attitude."

That gave McAfee pause.

Blood pounded in Sam's head as his heart raced. He'd lied to the detective twice now, and his bare feet were covered with some type of illegal drug. The further he got away from this moment, the more trouble he brought himself.

Tell the truth, Sam thought. *Tell the truth!*

Detective McAfee shrugged. "Whatever."

"I'll give you some when I'm done."

The detective smirked. "I'll pass."

And right then, Sam no longer felt bad. It wasn't even that big of a slight, but it was enough for Sam not to feel guilty about lying to the detective anymore. "Was there a reason for your visit, or did you stop by just to insult me?"

"Dominic Russo."

"What about him?"

"He hasn't returned my calls, and I've left a card at his house. Is he around?"

Sam stared at the detective. He didn't like the sound of his questions. They seemed accusatory. "Dom didn't have anything to do with the woman's death."

"I'll be the judge of that."

"You're a judge now?"

The detective's lip twitched. "You know what I mean."

"Yeah, I do. Remember, I was judged before the truth came out."

"I didn't do that to you."

"Still. It cost me my reputation and my career."

McAfee smirked. "Okay, then. What *was* the truth?"

"The brass believed one of their own over one of their deputies."

"You took a pay-out and left. Nobody's heard boo from you in how long? That doesn't seem the behavior of an honest man."

There was no use in arguing with a true believer like Shane McAfee. He would bleed the green and gold of the Spokane County Sheriff's Office. The man was a Major Crimes detective. A person doesn't get to that level by not believing in the system.

"You want to talk with Dom," Sam said. "That's why you're here?"

"That's why I'm here."

"Next time I see him, I'll tell him to get in touch with you."

"Why don't you call him now?"

"I'll do that."

"How about *right* now? While I'm here."

Sam glanced at his powder-covered feet. He realized his pulse had slowed. "I'm baking," he said. "When I'm done."

"Yeah. Whatever." McAfee muttered. "Have fun with your cookies."

Sam watched the detective walk across the small lawn to his unmarked car. He remained outside until McAfee left the neighborhood. Then he stepped inside, locked the door, and returned to the kitchen.

Seeing the busted Ziploc bag and the white powder on the floor, he needed a plan. It wasn't a good one, but it would have to do. He reached for the Dustbuster hanging on the wall but stopped.

First, he needed to call Dominic. When his friend didn't answer, it went to voice mail.

"Dom," Sam said, "call me. A detective is trying to reach you. Why are you avoiding him?"

# Chapter 10

"I didn't think you would call so soon."

"I missed you," Sam said.

"Missed me, *missed* me?" Sonja asked. "Or did you miss me in the way that means you want to get back in bed?"

"Why do you have to make everything so complicated?"

"I don't try to make it complicated with you. That's just how it is."

They were seated on the patio at The MAX. The sun was almost below the horizon, so most of the tables were now in darkness. The shade umbrellas were down for the night. The other tables were filled with quietly chatting patrons. Nearby, tall propane burners provided extra heat. It was still early in the season for eating on a patio without the sun.

"You look nice," Sonja said.

Sam glanced down to his zippered sweatshirt, jeans, and flip-flops. "I look like I always look."

"I know," she sarcastically said. "Are you still adhering to your rule?"

Sonja was one of the few people who knew about his list. Since she was talking about his wardrobe, he was fairly sure she meant the first one.

*Only be where flip-flops can be worn.*

"The one about my shoes?"

Sonja rolled her eyes. "Flip-flops are not shoes."

"They're in the shoe department."

"Shoes cover your feet. Those aren't shoes. They're barely footwear."

"Why do you hate my flip-flops?"

"Because it's a childish impulse to base a life philosophy on them."

"Tell me how you really feel."

"As someone who…" she paused to make sure she had proper eye contact, "cares for you, I've learned to resent your footwear. Whenever you scamper out of town—"

"I don't scamper."

"The first thought that comes to mind are those stupid sandals."

"They're not sandals."

"Whatever. I hate them. No matter how attractive your feet are, I will always hate your stupid flip-flops."

Sam sipped from his drink before calmly saying, "The flip-flops are a symbol."

"Of what?"

"Of how I choose to live my life."

"Like a surfer."

"Like a free man."

"I've seen you wear shoes."

Sam's smile was soft. "Contrary to your earlier statement, I'm not a child. I wear shoes when it's appropriate. I'll wear them when I'm in the gym, if I'm on a run, when I go to work—"

"Speaking of."

"I washed dishes."

Sonja frowned.

"It paid."

"*Barely.*"

"I only need to cover my expenses."

The settlement he received from the county wasn't enough to live comfortably forever. His grandmother had left him an eight-unit apartment rental that sent him some monthly spending money after a property manager pulled out the operating expenses. Even with that, he needed to make sure he covered his costs, or his nest egg could be gone someday.

"I'll eventually run out of money," Sam said, "unless I take the occasional odd job."

"But washing dishes—"

"Is honest work. Besides, it's not only about making money. It's about finding something to do."

Her brow furrowed so he continued.

"If I keep myself busy for part of the day, then I'm not spending money. Eight hours a day, five days a week, not spending money is a fairly good way to save. Plus, it gets me into a routine as well as allows me to meet some locals."

Her eyes slanted. "Were there any locals I need to be worried about?"

"What does that mean?"

"You know exactly what that means."

"We're not exclusive, Sonja."

Her face pinched. "You made that abundantly clear last year."

They sat in silence for several minutes while Sonja stewed over the state of their relationship. Finally, Sam asked, "Do you have Facebook on your phone?"

Her lower jaw moved to the left and right several times before she said, "You know I do."

"What about Instagram?"

"Why the sudden interest in social media? Are you going to join?"

"I want you to look up a woman."

Sonja's eyes widened. "Oh, my God. What is wrong with you?"

"Excuse me?"

"You say we aren't exclusive, and then you ask me to look up a woman. How dense are you?"

Sam lifted a hand to stop her. "It's not what you think."

She stood. "I don't know why I put up with you. You are the most irritating and cruel man I know."

Her voice rose on the quiet patio, and the other customers turned their way. Sam reached for her, but Sonja whacked his hand.

"No," she said. "I won't let you smooth talk me."

"It's about—"

"I don't care what it's about," she loudly said. Her face reddened, and her shoulders hitched up. "You always do this to me!"

"—the dead woman."

"You take me for a—" She blinked several times before swallowing. Sonja glanced around to the other customers watching them. Even a couple of servers stood by with open expressions. She smiled, batted her eyelashes, and gave them an "everything's fine" wave. It was the type of performance she usually saved for the camera. Several patrons grinned back, and one of them—an elderly man— even returned her wave.

Sonja turned to Sam and whispered, "The dead woman?"

"I want to know more about her."

She slowly sat and grabbed her water glass.

"Her name is Isabella Taylor."

"That's the woman? In your boat?"

He nodded.

"She's not some girl you want to meet?"

"Sonja, if you want to be with me while I'm home, then we're exclusive. If you don't want to be with me—"

"Stop talking," she interrupted and reached into her purse. After pulling out her phone, her fingers bounced over its screen. "Isabella what-was-it-again?"

"Taylor."

More finger bouncing.

"Huh. There are several Isabella Taylors on Facebook, but none of them are from this area."

"Try Izzy Taylor, instead."

"Izzy," she muttered as if she found the name distasteful. Her fingers tapped again. "There it is."

Sam stood and moved behind Sonja so he could peer over her shoulder. They scrolled through a variety of photographs showing mostly tame pictures. A couple showed her posing with a dark-haired woman as they held coffees in the air. Both wore black T-shirts, and racks of flavors were in the background.

"You think she's a barista?" Sam asked.

"Looks like she's inside a coffee stand. Maybe she's visiting a friend?"

"But they have the same T-shirt on. Can you see the logo?"

"Not really."

They flipped through a few more pictures, but nothing revealed much about Isabella Taylor.

"Doesn't look too exciting," Sam said.

"Let's see what she's got on Instagram."

"Think it will be different?"

"Probably, if she runs it like I do. Facebook is for my family. My mom and grandmothers are on there. I don't post anything I wouldn't want them to see and tell their friends. Instagram is where my friends are."

It didn't take her long to find Izzy's Instagram account. Those photographs were more provocative. They featured bikinis, parties, alcohol, and marijuana.

They found more pictures of her with coffee, but she was scantily clad in a bright yellow bikini in these. A background logo showed a cup of coffee planted in the sand with the ocean behind it.

"Must be one of those bikini joints," Sam said.

"Beach Bikini Brew. Skanky." Sonja glanced at him. "Ever been to one?"

He hadn't and said as much.

They continued to search the Instagram account and found a promotional shot with Izzy in a cheerleader uniform. She stood in a formation with a multitude of other similarly dressed women. In the corner of the picture was a logo for a football team. It was the same logo he'd seen on one of the men who attacked him in the grocery store parking lot. The same symbol on the baseball hat found in his boat.

"What are the Spokane Demons?" he asked.

Sonja cocked her head. "A semi-pro football team. How do you not know this?"

They continued to search through the photographic evidence of Isabella Taylor's life until they found some with football players.

He told her to stop as she came to one. In it, Izzy stood laughing between two bulky men—one white and one dark Samoan—both wore the Demons' uniform. The white guy's ears stuck prominently out from his head. Izzy's arms were around their necks, and each man held her by a wrist. Her feet dangled off the ground.

"Does it say their names?" Sam asked.

"No."

"Can you send me the picture?"

"I'll have to take a screenshot to get it, but—" Sonja's fingers hopped around her phone, then Sam's phone buzzed. The photograph was now on his device.

"Thank you," he said.

"I'm glad I could be good for something."

He considered making a joke in poor taste but knew it would go over badly. Instead, he said, "Can you go to the Demons website and see if you can find out who the two men are?"

"Anything else? Maybe see if she's got a Tinder account?"

"What? No."

"Just checking."

She worked her phone and hunted for the information he wanted. He could have done this himself but having Sonja involved felt important. For several minutes, she moved about the website. "It doesn't look like they have a roster on here. There are players mentioned in some related articles, but nothing that gives pictures and names."

"Thanks for checking."

She put her phone back in her purse and then studied him for a moment. "Remember what you said."

Sam tilted his head. "What did I say?"

"As long as you're home, we're exclusive."

"Is that what you want?"

Sonja smirked. "That's all you're giving, so what choice do I have? You and your stupid rules."

Sam lifted a foot and dangled a flip-flop. "But you said my feet were attractive."

She rolled her eyes.

# Chapter 11

Sam awoke as the light began to shine through the windows. Carefully, he pulled his arm from underneath Sonja's sleeping form. Her soft purring stopped briefly but soon resumed.

He started a pot of coffee then pulled from underneath the sink the Rainer box with the plastic baggies.

After dropping the Ziploc the previous day, he picked up the exploded clear bag. He then carefully folded it around what remained inside it and tucked it back into the box with the other baggies. Then he vacuumed the floor with the handheld Dustbuster and wiped down any surfaces the stuff managed to get on.

Through the clear plastic, he now studied the white powder. He wished he had a drug test kit, the type he had while he was a deputy. It would help him narrow the powder down to whether it was cocaine or heroin.

*Could it be meth*? Maybe, Sam decided. He had no way of knowing without a kit.

But a test kit wasn't conclusive proof. The proper identification of such a substance wouldn't occur until it was sent to a lab for processing.

And the baggies themselves bothered him. Why package it in Ziploc bags? Maybe criminals were doing that now. He'd been away from the streets for six years. Things change.

As he considered the plastic baggies and their contents, Izzy Taylor entered his thoughts. Was she the one who brought the drugs into his house? Had she taken them from the men, and they wanted them back?

If so and they killed her for it, why would they have left the drugs in the house? There seemed to be a disconnect in his reasoning.

Maybe she got the drugs from them legitimately and, now that she was dead, they wanted them back. That *could* work as an explanation.

No, he thought, it was more likely she took the drugs, and they wanted them back. How did they know Sam had them?

The men must have been at the party. Did one of them have sex in his bed? In his grandmother's bed? His stomach turned.

Sam should call Detective McAfee right now and alert him to the drugs. That would be the smart move—the *right* move.

Those two men had been inside his house. At least, he assumed they had since they claimed this was their stuff. There was no assumption necessary in the fact that they assaulted him. His sore body was conclusive proof of that.

Therefore, he didn't want to hand the drugs over to the sheriff's department just yet. Doing so would mean he would have to step back from looking into Isabella Taylor's death.

Would they care about her murder like he would? Not likely.

It was in his boat that she was found.

It was his house they broke into to throw their party.

To the deputies who responded, it was merely a call. To Sam, this was personal.

Where was the harm if he decided to dig a little further? Maybe he could provide a few more answers for Detective McAfee.

If he was honest with himself, the idea of doing some police work again gave him a charge. He hadn't done anything like this since he was removed from the department, and he had loved being a deputy. He'd felt the most alive when doing the job. Even the fight with the two men felt oddly good—not the losing part, but the actual confrontation.

Sam knew he should alert McAfee to all he had discovered, but there would be time for that.

He heard her moving before he saw her. Sam casually tucked the drugs back into the beer box and placed it under the sink. Sonja shuffled into the kitchen. She was completely naked and unashamed of such. She mumbled, "Good morning."

"Morning."

She wrapped her arms around his neck and nuzzled her head under his chin.

After a moment, he gently pushed her back and said, "Let me get you a cup."

Her lower lip pushed out in a pout while he poured her some coffee. When he handed her the cup, he said, "There's milk in the fridge."

"I guess the affection is over."

"That's not it. I've got some stuff to do—"

"The night is over, and you've had your way. Time for me to go. Is that it?"

"Now, Sonja—"

"Don't *Sonja* me. I know how you operate."

He snorted. "How I operate?"

"You laugh as you kick me to the curb."

"I'm not doing that."

"But you don't want me to stay."

"You can stay."

"I can take a hint."

"I just said you could stay."

She spun on her heel and marched down the hallway. Sam watched her butt rhythmically sway until she disappeared into his bedroom. He sipped his coffee and waited patiently for her return.

In a couple of minutes, Sonja reappeared. She was a disheveled version of the previous night's vision. "I'm leaving," she announced with a stamp of her foot.

"You don't have to."

"I most certainly do. If you don't want me here, then I'm not staying."

"Why are you doing this?"

"Me?" Sonja asked with a second stomp of her foot. "You! You're the one doing this."

"I don't know what I'm doing."

"That's the problem! You never know what you're doing."

Sonja spun again, but this time she included a dramatic whip of her head. She hurried toward the front door. It slammed closed behind her.

He walked down the hall and locked the door.

It was still too dangerous to allow lake etiquette to remain in effect.

\*\*\*

Sam took his time showering and let his thoughts drift to Sonja.

He hadn't intended to get involved with her again this summer. They'd only had a brief relationship last year before he left. She'd pursued him on and off since high school, but Sam usually kept her at bay. Not because he didn't find her attractive, she was off the charts in that category. He also didn't keep her at a distance because of her slightly crazy behavior. He sort of liked that, although it conflicted with the *No drama* rule.

No, the reason Sam and Sonja never got involved over the past years was that one of them always seemed to be in a relationship. Sam never was interested in dating two women at once or being involved with an already committed woman. Even before his rules, he liked his life as drama-free as possible.

Maybe it would take care of itself, and Sonja wouldn't be back. If that were the case, there was no point in worrying about it.

Sam's thoughts shifted to the dead woman. When they did, he kept coming back to one question—should he continue to involve himself in trying to find Isabella Taylor's killer?

It started as a way to avoid idle hands, but there needed to be a higher reason for staying involved now that he'd been assaulted.

Why am I doing this? he wondered. *Do I really care who killed her?*

Of course, he wanted to know how and why they selected his house for their party. There must have been other empty lake houses they could have chosen for an illegal get-together.

Besides, why couldn't they have thrown a party at one of their own houses? It wasn't like they were teenagers and needed a place to drink. That would at least make some sense.

And the pictures he'd seen on her Instagram account led him to believe she at least was employed as a barista. He didn't know if she got paid for being a cheerleader—probably not much, if any—but partying in a vacant lake house seemed like a risky proposition for someone who had something to lose.

So back to his question—did he care who killed her?

Sam felt bad about the young woman's death, but he didn't know her. Should he run off and risk life and limb for a woman who meant nothing to him? Especially if that young woman had taken part in defiling his home?

He loved the mystery novels from the sixties and seventies that once belonged to his grandfather, but he wasn't a knight errant in need of fixing some hole inside himself by saving a damsel in distress.

Besides, this damsel was beyond distress—she was dead.

So, he didn't care about her, he decided. *Does that make me a bad person?*

Lots of people didn't care that the woman died in his boat. From his neighbors, to Sonja, to Dom, to the people attending the illegal party since none of them seemed to have come forward to report what they may have witnessed.

Even the deputies didn't care that the woman died in his boat. They would only pretend to care because it was their job. They were paid to respond to that crime scene. Detective Shane McAfee wanted to solve the riddle of her death, of course, but that was to help his clearance rate.

It was a cynical way to look at law enforcement, Sam knew, but his days of believing cops and deputies to be beyond reproach were in the rearview mirror.

Why would Sam's lack of remorse make him a terrible person? It didn't. Regardless, he still felt bad about not caring. Izzy had been in his boat, moored to his dock, and at the edge of his property. He found her.

Was she, therefore, his responsibility? Was she tied to him in some metaphysical way? Save a life, and you're responsible for it, he'd heard. Did it apply when you found someone dead, too? Only a moron would think that, Sam thought ruefully.

Was this about retribution then? Because some unknown people violated his house—his grandparents' home. Did Sam want to find them and get even? Was it about payback because the two men attacked him in the grocery parking lot?

If it was about wanting payback, then he should stop immediately and call Detective McAfee. That'd be the best way to achieve any measure of revenge. There was no way him going it alone would end well. He should stop and turn it over to the Sheriff's Office. Let them deal with it.

If it wasn't about retribution, responsibility, or duty, why did he want to get involved?

He lifted his face to the hot water.

The truth was he had plenty of free time—that was the reason. He had returned to the idea of idle hands. He could help Izzy Taylor, and no one would stop him. Wasn't that a good enough reason?

Besides, she was dead and couldn't help herself.

Why couldn't he just help her and not worry about the justification behind it?

He turned off the shower and got out.

# Chapter 12

"What can I get you, baby?"

The barista was in her mid-twenties, which meant she was too young to call him 'baby.' Even though there was a slight chill outside, she stood unabashedly before him in a red bikini that barely contained her. There must have been a space heater inside the little sea-blue shack.

As she leaned over the counter to make sure Sam got a good, long look at her, the bikini top struggled against the heft of the woman's breasts.

She wore too much blush, fake eyelashes, and a pretend smile. Her blond hair curled away from her face.

"Medium black coffee," he said.

It was the first time Sam had ever visited a coffee stand like Beach Bikini Brew. He instinctively knew why he never went to one before. Now, he could safely say for sure.

The whole bikini barista experience made him feel like a dirty, old man—the type who might wear sweatpants to a strip club. At least strip clubs, which he didn't make a habit of visiting, were usually dark and located in out-of-the-way places.

This coffee stand was out in the open on East Sprague Avenue and in the heart of Spokane Valley. There weren't many people he was concerned with seeing him sitting here, but the idea of publicly idling in front of a half-naked woman still embarrassed him. It was an odd feeling because he saw bikini-clad women all the time on the lake.

The barista pouted and squeezed her breasts by slightly pinching her elbows together. It wasn't supposed to be obvious, but it was, nonetheless. "You don't want something more exotic?"

He *was* hungry, so he said, "Plain bagel with cream cheese."

Her fake smile widened to show bright white teeth. "That's hardly more exotic. Maybe a latte or a mocha?"

"Americano then."

The woman chuckled and shook her head. "That's a fancy way of saying black coffee."

Sam figured she would continue this banter unless he hardened his stance on the coffee—which he didn't care about—or he changed his order. "Latte then. No flavor."

The barista relaxed her elbows and purred. "I don't want to force you into anything."

"I'm not so sure about that."

As she turned away, her chuckle turned into a full-throated laugh.

Many others did not share Sam's discomfort at being there. Even with the possibility of being seen by a family member, a friend, or a co-worker, Beach Bikini Brew was hopping at that time of the morning.

Both sides of the drive-thru coffee stand were busy. Long lines of waiting customers—work trucks, rusted pick-ups, and dented cars—moved slowly by the order windows. Right now, a shiny Dodge Ram waited patiently behind Sam's classic Ford.

He'd driven through plenty of coffee stands before, and time was always of the essence. However, efficiency was not essential at this stand, as evidenced by his exchange with the flirty barista.

As she attended to his order, he noticed another woman working in the opposite window. She wore a black bikini and appeared to be incredibly toned, as if much of her life was dedicated to a fitness regimen. Tattoos covered both her arms, and a tribal graphic was on her lower back. When the dark-haired barista turned toward the coffee machine, Sam saw it was the woman in the picture with Izzy Taylor.

The blond barista reappeared in the window to announce Sam's total. As he counted out some cash, he asked, "Did you know Izzy Taylor?"

A sadness crossed the woman's face. "You've heard?"

"Yeah."

The other woman glanced in Sam's direction. He was about to say something when his barista spoke again.

"I can't believe she OD'd."

"Who said that?"

"That's the rumor. Crazy, huh?"

"Crazy," Sam agreed.

The barista took his cash and finished processing his order. When she returned, she handed him his change. "How'd you know her?"

"It was my house."

"Huh?"

He spoke loudly and clearly, so the tattooed woman in the small shack would hear. "Izzy died at my house while I was away on vacation."

"Oh, my God." The barista covered her mouth with a hand.

The tattooed woman stiffened. She didn't turn to face him, though.

"I'm looking for information on her. Maybe learn why she was there."

"Deidre was friends with Izzy. Maybe she might know." The barista turned to the tattooed woman. "Dee?" the barista said as if she expected the other woman to have heard their conversation.

"What?" the tattooed woman snapped, still refusing to turn in Sam's direction.

"Izzy died at this guy's house."

Deidre spun and glowered at the barista. "How do you know?"

"Huh?"

The tattooed woman pointed at Sam. "He's never been here before and now he shows up? He might be some creeper looking for— Who knows what he might be looking for? I don't have time for this." Deidre glared at Sam. "Move on."

"But my order," he said.

Deidre turned to the other barista. "Get this jackass his coffee, then move him on."

***

Sam waited across the street in the post office parking lot. He slowly ate his bagel and sipped his unflavored latte. The roll was under-toasted, and the coffee was lukewarm. Customers didn't go to Beach Bikini Brew for the quality of their products.

After a time, the line of cars thinned, and the back door to the tiny blue building opened. Deidre slipped out and hurried across the small lot. She now wore a faux fur jacket, black shorts, and Ugg boots.

She climbed into a red car—an older Toyota Camry—and raced from the parking lot. It dropped into westbound traffic on Sprague Avenue.

Sam left his parking spot and followed her from a distance.

When she turned northbound on Argonne Road, he struggled to keep her in view. At Montgomery, he blatantly ran a red light so as not to lose her.

Whipping in and out of traffic, Deidre drove like a maniac. This required Sam to drive aggressively just to keep her in sight. He didn't think she was trying to lose him, though. She was just a terrible driver.

Near the top of Argonne Hill, she turned abruptly into an apartment complex, and the little Toyota bounced into the parking lot. Sam slowed and followed her through the community. Finally, she parked and exited her car. She strolled across the lot and climbed three flights of stairs. Without pausing to knock or unlock a door, Deidre let herself into an apartment.

He took his time parking.

*\*\**

After he knocked, a tall, broad-shouldered woman with short dark hair opened the door. She didn't have the toned body of Deidre. Instead, she looked like she could bench press a horse—a female version of Arnold Schwarzenegger. She wore a tight T-shirt, volleyball shorts, and white running shoes.

"Yeah?"

"Sorry," Sam said. He leaned so he could look past the woman blocking the apartment's entrance. The inside appeared well-maintained, but he didn't see Deidre. "I might have the wrong apartment."

"Probably."

Sam decided to ask, anyway. "Is Deidre here?"

"Excuse me?"

The tattooed barista suddenly appeared around the corner, and her eyes widened.

"Nope." Sam smirked. "Right apartment."

"That's him!" Deidre shouted.

The tall, broad-shouldered woman punched Sam in the face.

\*\*\*

When consciousness returned, Sam slowly pushed himself upright and leaned against the wall of the small landing. The door to Deidre's apartment was now shut.

Above a ringing in his ears, he heard footsteps ascending the stairs. Fear clutched him, but his body was slow to respond.

Get up! he thought.

The soles of his flip-flops slid helplessly across the concrete landing.

Perhaps it was the bodybuilder from the apartment returning to punch him again. It was bad enough to get bested once by her. But he couldn't stand the humiliation of a woman trouncing him for a second time.

Move! Sam thought.

He tried to roll to the side, but that seemed to be a monumental task. His head pounded an angry warning.

Maybe it was the two bulky men from the grocery store coming to help. It was a jump in logic caused by fear. He didn't know if there was a connection between them and Deidre, but he didn't want to be hit again.

Do something! he mentally yelled. Anything!

Sam squeaked something unintelligible as he tried to push himself to his feet.

"Stay down."

A slightly chubby officer with the Spokane Valley Police came into view. Sam gratefully dropped to his seated position.

"Keep your hands where I can see them."

Sam pulled his feet in toward him and placed his hands on his knees. His wrists felt like he had weights around them.

The officer knocked on the nearby door but kept his eyes on Sam. When Deidre appeared in the doorway, she scowled at Sam.

He swallowed and blinked. He wanted to say something, but the only thing he managed to get out was a weird grunt. There was a disconnect between his brain and his tongue. Maybe he had a concussion.

"You the one who called?" the officer asked.

"I am." Deidre pointed at Sam. "That's the guy."

"All right. Close the door. I'll be back."

When the door shut, the officer motioned toward Sam. "Stand up."

"Listen—" The word sounded thick, and he thought he lisped it. He wasn't sure.

The cop snapped his fingers. "Up."

With the officer's help, Sam struggled to his feet. When he was upright, he read the silver name tag on the officer's breast pocket—*Posluszny*.

Sam almost fell when the cop grabbed his arm and spun him around. "Hands on the wall."

If he could have grabbed a handful of the building, Sam would have done so. Instead, he leaned on it and sighed in contentment. Then Posluszny wrenched his left arm behind his back, and a handcuff slipped over the wrist.

"Let me explain," Sam mumbled.

"Inna minute."

The officer grabbed Sam's other arm, twisted it behind his back, and snapped a second cuff into place. Sam's face was now pressed against the building. He could taste the accumulated grime on the gray siding.

"You're not under arrest," Posluszny said. "You're only being detained."

"Yeah," Sam mumbled into the building. "I got it."

"Been through this before?"

"Sort of."

Posluszny patted Sam down and removed his cell phone and car keys from his pockets.

When the officer finished, he roughly turned Sam around and pushed him in the chest. Sam's shoulders thudded against the building.

"Lean against the wall."

It was an uncomfortable position but tactically sound. The only way Sam could run was first to push himself upright or roll off the wall. Either way would waste time. It didn't matter, though. Sam wasn't going to run. He only wanted to sit and reconsider his earlier desire to investigate the death of Izzy Taylor.

"What's your name?"

"Sam. Samuel. Strait."

The officer wrote it in his notebook. "Middle name?"

"Roy."

"Birthdate?"

After Sam gave it to him, the officer tucked his notebook away. He then grabbed Sam by the elbow and led him toward the stairs. As they descended, Posluszny said, "I'm putting you in my car for safekeeping."

"Call Detective McAfee." His head felt better, and his words sounded clearer. Maybe it wasn't a concussion.

"McAfee?"

"He's a homicide detective."

"I know who he is." The officer eyed Sam with disdain. "You're not going to tell me he's a high school friend, are you? That won't carry any weight."

"He's investigating a dead girl found in a boat."

"The one in Newman Lake?"

"The woman upstairs knows her."

"You a private investigator?"

"No."

The deputy jerked Sam by the arm. "Then why are you messing around in McAfee's case?"

"It was my boat."

There was no further conversation until they were at the officer's patrol car. Posluszny opened the rear passenger door and turned Sam's back toward the plastic-covered seat. "The best way is to sit, then swing your legs in."

Sam dropped onto the seat but looked pleadingly up. "Please call him."

"Swing your legs in."

"Detective McAfee," Sam said.

"Move your legs." The officer's voice dropped an octave. "Or I'll move them for you."

Sam lifted his legs inside the car. "Please call—"

Posluszny slammed the car door and headed back toward the apartment building.

# Chapter 13

Time passed slowly. At least, it felt that way. Sam had no way to tell the passing minutes. There was no clock in the dashboard of the silent patrol car. There probably was a digital one while the engine ran.

Sam twisted sideways in the backseat to take the pressure off his handcuffed hands. He lay the side of his head on the plastic-covered headrest and watched vehicles come and go from the apartment community's parking lot.

Several people walked by the patrol car. As they did, they gawked at him with mouths agape. One mother abruptly turned her daughter's inquisitive gaze away from Sam after he smiled sadly at the girl.

He sighed.

An unmarked patrol car pulled into the lot and drove slowly toward where he was. When it was close enough, Sam could see the man behind the steering wheel. He straightened as he felt a surge of hope.

Detective Shane McAfee parked and glanced at Sam. Then he lifted his cell phone to his ear. McAfee spoke with someone for a few moments, then hung up. After the detective exited his car, his eyes drifted toward the apartment building.

Sam struggled to turn in the backseat so he could see out the rear window. Officer Posluszny sauntered down the stairs, lifted his chin as a familiar greeting toward McAfee, then extended his arm as he neared. The two men shook hands. They chatted for a couple of minutes before Posluszny thumbed toward Sam.

The two lawmen approached the car, and the officer opened the rear door. "Get out," Posluszny said with a wave of his hand.

Sam wriggled himself across the backseat—the plastic cover squeaked as he did so—until he could get his feet back on the ground.

When Sam stood, the detective asked, "The hell were you thinking, Strait?"

With his hands cuffed behind his back, Sam shrugged. "I wanted to ask the woman some questions."

Posluszny said, "The same woman who said you stalked her?"

"I never stalked her."

The officer's eyes narrowed. "That's not what she said. You've been coming to her stand for weeks."

"Weeks?" Sam glanced at the detective.

Posluszny continued. "Uh-huh. That's right. You've made lewd and inappropriate comments during that time."

Sam's gaze whipped back to the officer. "C'mon, that's bull—"

"Until today when you follow her home from work and attacked—"

"No!"

"That's why her friend hit you. Self-defense. Both confirmed it."

"I wouldn't do that. I wouldn't attack anyone, especially a woman."

Posluszny chuckled. "A woman knocked you out."

Sam smirked at the officer. "She was strong."

"They said you went out like that." The cop snapped his fingers.

"Whatever." Sam faced McAfee. "You know I wouldn't do that."

"And I know that how?" the detective asked. "Your reputation isn't that great, my friend, and that's the only way I know you."

"Reputation?" Posluszny asked with raised eyebrows.

"That's right," McAfee said, "you weren't around when this guy was on the department."

The officer's eyes slanted. "You were a deputy?"

Sam didn't want to rehash his life right then and there. He needed to deal with the current problem. "I got home two days ago," he said. "That's when I found the woman in my boat. So, I haven't been around long enough to stalk anybody."

"Can you prove that?" Posluszny asked.

"My phone—my itinerary and ticket are on it."

Detective McAfee crossed his arms. "Uncuff him."

"Seriously?" Posluszny muttered.

"He wasn't in town," McAfee said. The man sounded almost disappointed.

With a single finger, Posluszny motioned for Sam to turn around. In a moment, the cuffs slipped from his wrists, and the officer handed Sam his phone. His fingers tapped the screen and called up his flight itinerary. Sam lifted the phone to show both men. "See?"

"You showed me that at your house," the detective said. "I already believed you."

"He didn't." Sam jerked his head toward Posluszny.

He lowered his phone and his fingers danced across the screen again. When he lifted the cell phone a second time, he said, "And here's my ticket from Seattle to Spokane, matching up to the itinerary."

McAfee eyed the officer before nodding at Sam. "You made your point, Strait. Now, we all know the woman's story is bogus, but that still doesn't tell me what you're doing here."

It had been a long time since Sam had done any investigative work. He'd clearly bungled this attempt to find Izzy's killer, so it was time to come clean. "I think Isabella Taylor was murdered because of drugs."

"Drugs?" McAfee and Posluszny said simultaneously.

"I found some hidden inside my refrigerator."

McAfee leaned toward Sam. "And you didn't call me?"

Sam lowered his head, looked away, then returned to meet the detective's accusatory glare. He weakly said, "I wanted to know what happened to her."

The detective stepped forward. "You're interfering in a homicide investigation."

Sam didn't acknowledge or deny that statement. Instead, he stared at the ground. The detective stepped back, crossed his arms again, and seemed to be considering a course of action.

When neither McAfee nor Posluszny said anything further, Sam asked, "So, do you want the drugs?"

"Yes," McAfee yelled. "I want the drugs!"

\*\*\*

They traveled as a two-car caravan back to Newman Lake—Sam led, and McAfee followed. The detective allowed Sam to drive his own car. However, McAfee warned, if Sam diverted course at all, the courtesy would end. The detective would immediately pull him over and handcuff him. Sam would finish the rest of the journey in the back of a patrol car.

Officer Posluszny remained behind to interview Deidre and the broad-shouldered woman who punched him. Sam didn't hold out hope the cop would get anything from the dark-haired barista. He imagined Deidre to be the type who would stack lie on top of lie, even when they were tumbling in on themselves. She avoided talking to Sam at the coffee stand, and she lied to the cops about him. He knew he didn't have much to build his impression on, but Sam didn't care—he didn't like the woman.

When Sam pulled in front of his house, he noticed the front door was open. He hurriedly got out of his car. He thought about rushing into the cabin, but at this moment, prudence was the better course of action. He waited for McAfee to pull up behind him.

After slipping from his car, the detective asked, "What's wrong?"

"It's open." Sam pointed toward the door. "I didn't leave it that way."

"I thought you lake people did that sort of thing."

"What sort of thing?"

"Left your homes unlocked."

From the front steps of her house, Mary Jo Brakke called to Sam. "You missed your friends."

"Who?" Sam asked.

"Two big fellas," Mary Jo said loudly. She spread her arms wide at shoulder height. "They just left. You probably passed them on the way in."

Sam didn't wait any longer and hurried toward the house.

"Wait," McAfee said. When Sam didn't slow, the detective hollered, "Strait!"

As he passed the front door, Sam could see it had been kicked in. The wood near the lock was splintered. Had he followed lake etiquette, they could have just walked in and saved him a costly repair.

Sam turned toward the kitchen but immediately stopped. Even from there, he could see the open cabinet door under the sink. His shoulders slumped.

McAfee noisily entered the house, angrily grabbed Sam's shoulder, and ordered, "Wait."

The detective went by him then with his gun drawn. Sam knew that was protocol—to clear the house—but he was sure there was no one there. Especially now that he could see the lower cabinet was open.

It only took a minute for McAfee to announce, "Clear."

Sam headed into the kitchen. "It's gone," he said glumly.

"What is?" McAfee holstered his gun.

Sam pointed to the space under the sink. "The drugs. That's where they were."

There was a noise at the front of the cabin, and both men turned to see Officer Posluszny standing at the doorway. He paused to examine the damage to the door frame.

"Bruno," McAfee called.

Posluszny stepped further into the hallway but remained near the entrance to the cabin.

"What are you doing here?" the detective asked.

"The complainant wouldn't come to the door. Either that or she and her friend took off, but I didn't see them leave while we were talking. Did you?"

McAfee ignored his question. "We can deal with her later. The drugs are gone."

Posluszny eyed the damaged door frame again then glanced at Sam. "They probably took them while we were dealing with him."

The way the officer said *with him* made Sam think Posluszny blamed him for the drugs being stolen. Sam was about to point out that his house was broken into when McAfee spoke up.

"Go next door." The detective motioned toward Mary Jo Brakke's house. "Get the neighbor woman's statement. She saw a couple guys here. See if she can give you descriptions."

The officer nodded reluctantly and said, "Yeah, all right," before leaving.

After Posluszny was gone, Sam said, "I can tell you who they were. At least, I have a pretty good idea."

McAfee raised his eyebrows. "How's that?"

"I got jumped outside a grocery store."

The detective leaned his hip against the kitchen counter. "You report it?"

"No, but an employee witnessed it."

McAfee clicked his teeth a few times. "What about it?"

"Couple guys. Big guys." Sam spread his hands apart at shoulder height, the same way Mary Jo had. "They wanted their stuff."

"Stuff?"

"That's what they called it. I didn't know what they wanted when they attacked me, but when I found the drugs later that night, I figured that had to be it."

"Yet, you didn't call me."

Sam ignored McAfee's accusation and continued. "I found out who they were, though—a couple football players for the Demons."

"The local football team?"

"Uh-huh. Izzy Taylor was a cheerleader for them."

McAfee rubbed his chin. "What are their names?"

Sam looked at the ceiling.

"You didn't get their names?"

"Well, no."

"So, you don't know who they are."

"I know what they look like, and I know they play football for the team. Here's their picture." He held up his phone to show McAfee the photograph of Izzy and the two men. "That's more than you had when you showed up here."

"I would have had it *if* you shared that information when you discovered it." The detective's face flattened. "And I would have had the drugs now, too, *if* you shared that information when you discovered it."

Sam looked away.

"Email me that photo."

"Can't I just text it to you?"

The detective's eyes narrowed. "Do I look like a teenaged girl? I said, email it to me, so I have an official record of its arrival."

"Fine."

McAfee provided his email address, and Sam sent him the picture. After the detective verified the arrival of the photo, he put his phone back in his pocket. "These two never told you what this stuff was?" McAfee air-quoted the word 'stuff.'

"No."

"They just called it stuff?"

"I assumed they assumed I knew what it was."

"That's a lot of assuming." McAfee bent to study the area under the sink. "So, why didn't you call me?"

Sam shrugged, even though the detective wasn't paying attention to him. Suddenly, his reasons for inserting himself into the investigation seemed selfish and stupid.

"Were you planning to keep the drugs?"

"I wouldn't do that. I didn't even know what kind of drug it was."

"What did it look like?"

"A white powdery substance."

McAfee frowned as he straightened. "That's right out of Report Writing one-oh-one. Was it consistent with cocaine?"

"It could have been baby powder, for all I knew. I didn't have a test kit around to tell you one way or another."

McAfee glanced at Sam's flip-flops. Then he looked around the kitchen. "Where are those cookies you baked?"

Sam opened his hands and exposed his palms.

"You didn't taste the drugs, did you? That's only stupid Hollywood stuff."

"I'm not an idiot, Detective."

McAfee snorted. "No, Strait, you most definitely are an idiot. The jury is still out on whether you're a *complete* idiot."

Sam's shoulders slumped. "Was that necessary?"

"How'd you get the powder on your feet?"

"I dropped a baggie, and it popped open."

"You were playing with the drugs?"

"I wasn't playing with the drugs," he said but immediately thought about tossing the bag into the air to test its weight. If that wasn't playing with the drugs, it was pretty damn close.

McAfee's gaze swept over the kitchen then went to the floor. "How did you clean it up?"

"I washed my feet and flip-flops. I vacuumed the rest."

The detective's eyebrows raised. "You vacuumed— with what?"

Sam grabbed the graying Dustbuster attached to the wall.

McAfee took the small, handheld vacuum and examined it. "Some of the drugs are in here?"

Sam now understood McAfee's line of questioning. "That's right."

"Let's get a drug kit." Without waiting for Sam's agreement, the detective headed for the door.

As they crossed the front lawn, Officer Posluszny stepped onto the front steps of Mary Jo Brakke's house. He noticed the detective's urgency and hurried toward the parked patrol cars.

"She give you a good description?" McAfee asked.

"If black, white, and big is a good description of a couple guys, then yeah, I'd call it good."

"That's all she gave?"

Posluszny smiled. "No. That's not all. The old bird gave me her number. She suggested I call her when I was off-duty."

McAfee glanced at Sam, who said, "She likes the company of men."

The detective shook his head. "Lake people." To Posluszny, he said, "Grab your test kits."

For the next several minutes, the two officers worked together. McAfee carefully pulled apart the Dustbuster. Posluszny dipped a test strip into a sample of its contents— a grayish dusty mess—then plugged it into a small plastic reader.

It only took a moment for Posluszny to make a pronouncement. "Nothing."

McAfee squinted as he registered the results. "Which one is this for?"

"Cocaine."

Posluszny pulled out a second strip and another plastic reader. "Heroin," he said. Repeating the process, he dipped the strip into the dusty mess. In a moment, he announced, "Negative."

The officer repeated the process twice more. The first was for fentanyl, and the second was for meth. The results were the same.

Posluszny tossed the last reader on the trunk of his car. "A big zero all the way around."

McAfee pointed at the kits. "Could the dust and other stuff in there be throwing off the results?"

"Maybe," Posluszny said. "I dunno, but there should be enough to give some sort of reading. At least, I would think."

McAfee glanced at Sam. "How was it packaged?"

"Ziploc bags, which I thought was weird."

"Why?" both officers said in unison.

"I've never seen that before."

"Drugs get transported in all sorts of things," Posluszny said. "I've found it in washed-out cottage cheese containers before."

"Seriously?"

The officer nodded. "The guy I arrested said it was the only thing he had available. People use what they have. It wasn't packaged for sale—I mean individual sale—right?"

"I don't think so."

"There you go," Posluszny said. "They were just transporting it. The Ziploc baggies were probably available, and they grabbed them. Don't over-think it."

"But the tests," Sam said and motioned toward failed kits, "say the powder isn't drugs."

"No," McAfee said. "The readers failed to test positive. That's a big difference."

Sam rolled his eyes. "Right. I get it. It's not a real test until it's done in a lab, but let's assume it confirms these tests. What does it mean?"

The detective exchanged a knowing look with the officer.

"What?" Sam asked.

"Maybe it was a scam," McAfee said.

"Scam?"

"Maybe they wrapped up a bunch of baking soda to fake out some buyers."

"But the two goons attacked me at the grocery store. And they broke into my house to get it back."

"Then it's probably not baking soda," Posluszny said.

The detective frowned. "Or maybe those guys bought it and still haven't figured out that it's baking soda. Regardless, it's worth considering due to the negative result."

Sam lifted his chin toward the Dustbuster. "Are you taking it back to the lab?"

McAfee nodded.

"Can't you just take the contents? So, I can still have the—"

"Evidence," the detective said. "I want the Dustbuster in evidence so we can show how we came into its possession." McAfee tapped the trunk of the patrol car near the failed drug kits.

Sam fought back a sigh. The hits kept coming following the break-in. "How long will it take for the lab results?"

McAfee shrugged a single shoulder. "Who knows? Even as part of a homicide investigation, it'll be weeks at best. More than likely, a couple months."

"Has anyone from the party come forward yet?"

"I don't need to tell you that, but no one has."

Sam glanced at Posluszny, then returned his gaze to the detective. "Doesn't that seem strange?"

"What? That people don't come forward after a dead girl was found in a burglarized house? Come on. Anyone coming forward would openly admit to participating in a felony—burglary. Now, we found out that there are possible narcotics on scene. It's even less likely people will want to raise their hand and say 'I was there.'"

"I was just asking."

"And I answered."

Sam's gaze went to the open front door of his house. "What about the break-in?"

McAfee jerked his head and said to Posluszny, "Bruno, grab your camera and take some photos. I'll file the burglary report." Then the detective smirked at Sam. "Seeing as how Mr. Strait has been so helpful and forthcoming with my investigation."

# Chapter 14

The training facility for the Spokane Demons was in the Sullivan Industrial Park. The team's website provided the address with an invitation for fans to come out and watch. It wasn't hard to find with the help of his smartphone's GPS.

Sam probably should have left investigating the football players to Detective McAfee. The man would get to it sooner or later, but Sam had plenty of time to check on them. Also, the fact that the two men not only assaulted him but broke into his house angered him. Sam wanted to be involved in their apprehension. The least he could do was figure out who the two men were. Once he did that, he would turn over their names to McAfee and step back from the whole situation.

No idle hands, he thought.

The Spokane Demons were part of the upstart International Minor League Football Foundation. The acronym's international aspect came from the fact that two Canadian teams—Calgary and Vancouver—were part of the league. This was only the second year of the IMLFF and the Demons.

The website did a decent job of promoting the foundation and the individual teams, but it did a horrible job of highlighting its players. Sam mused this could be due to a couple of reasons.

The league was a start-up, so they couldn't spend a lot of money on constant website maintenance. Or perhaps the lack of player highlights was due to turnover in positions. Since the players weren't paid, there wasn't much reason to stick around if something better came along—even if it was in the form of a regular, hourly-wage job.

Sam searched online for a team roster but only found references to the most popular positions—quarterback, receivers, and tight-ends. It seemed the minor league was a mirror of the professional world.

There was a small lobby just inside the training facility. It was done up in the team's colors—black and purple. Painted on one wall was a grinning face reminiscent of a cartoon Satan. Behind a waist-high counter sat a cute mid-twenties woman who flipped through spreadsheets. As she did so, she highlighted things with a yellow marker.

When she looked up, the woman asked in a pleasant yet slightly high-pitched voice, "Here to watch practice?"

"That would be great," Sam said.

She grabbed a clipboard from her desk. "May I have your driver's license?"

He removed his identification from his wallet and handed it to her. The receptionist then slipped the card under the clipboard's clapper.

"Is this your current address?"

"It is."

Sam didn't like her writing his address on the form, especially since he suspected a couple of Demons had just burglarized his house. But what would it hurt? If his home had been violated by two of their players, then they already knew where he lived.

She looked up. "What's your phone number?"

He gave it to her, then asked, "Why do they practice in a warehouse?"

"We play our games at Joe Albi." It was the football stadium where the city's high school teams played. "We got permission from the school district to do so, but we can't practice there. Instead, we were using the city's parks, which means we were competing against families and church events and other whatnot. You understand."

He did.

"Anyway," she continued, still not looking up from the clipboard, "there are a couple of benefactors for the club. Former NFL players who live in town. They leased this space to help give back to the community."

"Huh."

She glanced up now. "I know, right? So cool. We've got one of the better clubs in the league because of it. We're expecting big things this year."

The receptionist finished completing the form and handed Sam his driver's license. Then she gave him a lanyard with a rectangular purple pass. "Put this on and go through that door. Feel free to sit in the bleachers, but the locker room and team offices are off-limits."

"Got it." He slipped the guest pass around his neck. "Do you have a team roster?"

She pulled open a drawer and removed a single sheet of light-purple paper. "Here you go. Have fun."

Sam smiled and felt foolish when he waved the paper at her.

\*\*\*

The Demons practiced in modified uniforms. The players wore their helmets, T-shirts, and shorts. The body types of the men involved were varied.

On the offensive line, the men tended to be figures of undefined mass. Sam wouldn't call them fat as they moved quickly and shoved oncoming players around. But they weren't ripped like the running back and receivers. Those men—Sam thought of them as being in the highlight positions—wore shirts cut above their stomachs and had the sleeves removed. It was clear they were proud of their bodies. They probably had close to zero body fat.

The quarterback was surprisingly soft around the middle, though. One word came to Sam's mind as he watched the field general move about the pocket—*doughy*. He wasn't fast, but he did seem quick. The man knew how to make the most of his movements—a simple step up into the pocket to avoid an oncoming rusher or a sidestep to create more distance. The quarterback's greatest asset, however, was that he had a cannon for an arm. He accurately threw it the length of the warehouse practice field, which was fifty yards.

Sam was a decent baseball player when he was younger and could throw a ball from the outfield to the catcher. However, accurately spiraling a football fifty yards downfield was a completely different skill. The quarterback's arm impressed him.

The defense seemed to be a mirror of the offense. There was a mass of men on the line while athletic linebackers stacked the middle. The defensive backs and safeties were all ripped like they spent their free time in a gym.

Sam had never seen a minor league football game before. He'd heard about some minor leagues around the nation but never bothered to attend a game. He did not play football in high school but had grown up watching it with his grandfather. Now, he only caught a game if it was on at a restaurant or a friend's house. He didn't own a TV, so he rarely went out of his way to watch sports.

Witnessing this practice, he was surprised at the speed of the men on the field. Even though they were minor leaguers—part-timers doing it for the love of the game— the men flew around. For a moment, he appreciated the joy of the sport that allowed grown men to continue to pursue an activity like this.

The two sides lined up, and the quarterback called a series of signals. After the center hiked the ball, the field general faked a pass to a streaking wide receiver. All eyes went downfield. Then the doughy quarterback ran to the right and followed one of the offensive linemen. It was a favorite play of Sam's grandfather, who often simply called it straight over tackle.

After the whistle blew, the separate sides—offense and defense—huddled around their respective coaches.

Sam studied the light-purple sheet of paper he'd been given. Every player was listed along with their hometown and college. The offense was on the left side of the page while the defense was on the right. A small black and white photo was next to each player's name.

It took only a moment for Sam to find two faces he recognized.

Toma Papani—Left Tackle. Hometown—Yakima, Washington. College—San Diego State.

Hoyt Jefferson—Right Tackle. Hometown—Walla Walla, Washington. College—Montana State University.

Sam tapped the paper. He'd found the men who had assaulted him in the grocery store parking lot.

He noticed the quarterback's name as well. Tucker Jacobson. Hometown—Post Falls, Idaho. College—North Dakota State. His face didn't look doughy in the picture. Maybe he'd put on some weight since he'd graduated.

When Sam looked up, both sides of the team still huddled around their respective coaches. A couple of offensive linemen looked toward him, though. He couldn't see the faces behind their helmets, but one was caramel-skinned, and the other was pale white. He had a good idea who they were. A coach barked something to the two bulky players, and they turned back to the huddle.

Sam's attention returned to the paper—Toma Papani and Hoyt Jefferson.

His phone buzzed once—a signal for a text message. He checked it and saw that it was from a former co-worker. SAW YOUR NAME IN THE PAPER. WANT TO MEET FOR COFFEE?

Sam thought about watching the practice further, but what was the point? He'd gotten enough by finding the men who assaulted him and likely broken into his home to steal their stuff.

NAME THE PLACE, he typed.

# Chapter 15

Cozy Coffee is a little cafe on Barker Road. It doubles as a drive-thru with a lane on each side of the building. Behind the stand is a storage facility for recreational vehicles. People who leave their RVs there during the off-season make their payments to the baristas.

It's a set-up that Starbucks would never find itself in, but a neighborhood coffee joint does what it must to survive. Based upon the fullness of the cafe, the locals seemed to like it just fine.

Aaron Keller sipped his coffee and eyed Sam. "You've let your hair grow long."

"I take it that you don't like it."

Keller frowned. "Makes you look like a surfer."

"That's bad?"

"No. It's... I don't know." Keller waggled his hand. "It looks undisciplined."

Sam laughed. "You wish you could do what I'm doing."

"And what did you do this time?"

"Washed dishes."

Keller clucked. "You gave up being a deputy to wash dishes."

"In Hawaii. Over the winter, I remind you. And I didn't give up being a deputy to do that."

"Still."

"There was more to that decision, and you know it."

Keller dismissively waved his hand. "I didn't have anything to do with that."

"Yeah. I know."

"And you could have come back."

"If the department treated you that way, would you have come back?"

Keller fell silent.

"Here's something I've learned since leaving."

"What's that?"

"Being a deputy is a job," Sam said. "Nothing more, nothing less. It's like washing dishes or being a janitor."

Keller's face flattened. "You're not going to use the trash collector metaphor, are you?"

"Metaphor. Someone's been reading."

"Because I've heard it before, and I don't buy it. We do more than collect the county's garbage."

Sam held up an apologetic hand. "What I'm trying to say is that it's only a job. It's not a higher calling."

Keller appeared offended. "I think it's a higher calling."

Sam smiled softly at his friend. "Then, I apologize."

"Most of the guys in the department probably think so, too."

"And someone may think washing dishes is a higher calling."

"No one would think that," Keller said.

"But you get my point."

"Of course, I get your point, but you could have come back."

Sam sipped his coffee. "Not after what happened. There was no way I could ever come back."

A car zipped by on Barker Road. Its loud exhaust gave both men a moment of pause. When it was quiet enough to talk again, Keller leaned forward.

"What's with the woman they found in your boat?"

"How do you mean?"

"What do you mean, *how* do I mean? A body was found in your boat. How did it get there?"

Sam shrugged. "I returned home, and she was there. I don't know any more than that."

"That sucks."

"For both of us."

"Us?"

"Her and me."

"Yeah." Keller nodded. "Her and you. And McAfee is investigating." The way his friend said the detective's name led Sam to believe he disapproved.

"You don't like him?"

"He's a tool."

"Why? What'd he do?"

His friend crossed his arms and twisted his lips.

"You can't throw out chum like that and not expect me to go after it."

Keller glanced around. "McAfee's got himself a girl."

"So? You've got a girl."

"I mean a real girl. She's like eighteen or something."

"Eighteen? For real?"

Keller's face relaxed. "No, she's not eighteen, but she can't be much older. Maybe she's twenty-one."

"So, he's dating young, and she's got daddy issues. It's not illegal."

"I don't care that she's young. Good for him."

"I'm confused. Then what do you care about?"

"She's the mayor's daughter."

"Which mayor?"

"The Spokane Valley mayor. The city we have a policing contract with. Remember? Do you know how big of a deal that is for the department?"

"And somehow McAfee's love life is screwing that up?"

"Literally," Keller said with a disbelieving chuckle. "The mayor is pushing to create their own independent department now. If that happens, a lot of our brothers and sisters won't have jobs anymore."

"*Our* brothers?"

Keller frowned. "Don't be that way."

"A lot of your brothers and sisters let me twist in the wind."

"And a lot of us didn't."

Sam shrugged. "A new police department won't happen. It'll be too expensive. They'll keep the contract with the Sheriff's Office."

Keller shook his head. "You don't get it, man. The seeds are planted. The council only works with the sheriff because they *have* to, not because they *want* to. First chance they get, they'll dump that contract."

"That was going on long before Shane McAfee's love life got in the way."

"Yeah, whatever. I'll tell you this. McAfee's not helping the situation."

"Because he's seeing a woman he likes."

"He's selfish. It should be all hands on deck, but his choices are affecting the rest of us. As far as the union is concerned, Shane McAfee is a man without a country."

"Like I was."

Keller thought about it for a bit. "But you walked away."

"And McAfee isn't willing to do that with this woman?"

"Shane McAfee is a hard head," Keller said. "If there's one thing I know about the man, he'll stick around even when it's bad for his health."

# Chapter 16

She was seated on his doorstep when he returned home. Her long, tanned legs were pressed tightly together at the knees. Her LuLu Lemon ball cap was pulled down around her eyes. She wore a red sweater and jean shorts. On her feet were white Converse.

"Your door isn't secured," Jordan Withers said.

Sam shrugged. "Lake rules."

She stood as he approached. "I didn't go in."

"That's nice of you."

As he went by her, he caught the scent of a different perfume than she had previously.

Jordan hurried to her feet and asked, "Who kicked it in?"

Sam knew better than to give the reporter any leads, so he said, "I don't know."

"Did you call the police?"

He turned to her now. She was inside his home—in the living room, to be precise—waiting for him to answer.

"Are you here to follow up on your story?"

Her eyes slowly drifted about the cabin. She moved to the pictures on the wall. "Did you buy this place with the settlement money?"

"It belonged to my grandparents."

"They left it to you?"

He nodded.

"Did you grow up around here?"

"I grew up here."

Jordan straightened. "In this cabin?"

"That's right."

Her face brightened. "On a lake. How awesome would that be?"

"Are you writing a story?"

She shook her head. "Not right now."

He considered what he should tell her. After a pause, Sam pointed to a picture on the wall of a young couple holding a baby. "That's my mom and dad."

Jordan leaned in to study the young family. "Cute."

He could smell her perfume again, and he lingered on the scent. He never smelled it before, and words began to flood his mind describing it—fresh, airy, spring—

"Where do they live?"

The descriptors of her perfume stopped immediately. "They're dead."

Jordan's smile faded.

"A car crash." He studied the faces of the parents he never knew. "I was still a baby. My parents had gone out to see a David Lee Roth concert. Know who he is?"

Her brow furrowed. "It sounds familiar."

"He was the lead singer for Van Halen."

"Oh, my dad listens to them."

He was still focused on the picture. "Cinderella opened for him. Must have been a great show." Sam had listened to David Lee Roth's *Eat 'Em and Smile* and Cinderella's *Night Songs* so many times growing up, he lost count. "On the way home, they were hit by a drunk driver. Killed instantly."

Sadness washed over her face. "And you grew up here with your grandparents."

"On the lake."

"So, that wouldn't be awesome at all."

He shrugged. "My grandparents were great. They treated me like their own."

Jordan's eyes swept over the wall of photos. A series of conflicting emotions washed over her face. "I should tell my dad I love him."

"He would probably appreciate it."

She continued to stare at the picture of the young family.

"Why are you here?" he asked.

"I came to apologize. About yesterday. About catching you at dinner."

"It's your job."

She turned to Sam. "Do you…"

"Do I what?"

"Are you seeing anyone?"

Sam typically avoided committed relationships. It was one of his rules that he tried to live by.

*No attachments.*

However, he never saw two women at the same time. Doing so created drama, which violated another rule. Since Sonja came back into his life, there was no need to meet anyone new.

When he didn't answer immediately, Jordan said, "I better go."

"Did you want to ask some more questions?"

Her eyes drifted back to the picture of his parents. "They're not important."

"Another day."

Jordan's eyes lowered. "Yeah," she whispered and left the house.

\*\*\*

"How long are we going to do this?" Sonja Boyd asked.

She'd already finished her first vodka tonic. With another drink on the way, her questions were about to get more pointed. Sam knew this from experience.

They were seated at Barlow's in Liberty Lake.

"Doing what?"

Sonja moved a finger back and forth between them. "This. Us."

"As long as you want, I guess."

"I want forever."

He winced. He had walked into that one. "Sonja—" he said, but she cut him off.

"I love you, Sam Strait." Her earnestness surprised him. "Since high school, I've loved you. I said you were going to marry me one day."

"We never even dated in school. And we were kids when you said that."

"So, what? I meant it. It didn't matter if I had to wait. I figured, big deal. But you've always kept me at arm's length, even when we're together. I'm not going to wait around forever—you know?"

"I'm not asking you to."

Her face reddened.

"Haven't I been clear with how I want to live?"

Her jaw flexed.

"Haven't I?"

"Yes," she said, biting off the answer.

"Am I leading you on?"

"No. You're *definitely* not doing that."

"Then what's the problem?"

"The problem is you don't love me."

"Sonja—"

"I would travel with you."

"*Sonja*—"

"You won't let anyone get close to you."

"I've let you get closer than anyone."

She laughed loudly, and several patrons in the restaurant turned to watch them. "You think we're close? I don't even know you, Sam. I want to, but you keep things bottled up. You won't talk, and you don't share."

He stared at her.

"This is what I'm talking about."

The server delivered her vodka tonic. "Is there anything else I can get you?"

Sonja curtly shook her head, and the young woman walked away.

"You won't even tell me you'll do better."

Sam shrugged. "I'm not doing anything wrong."

Sonja rolled her eyes. "Either you like being with me, or you don't."

"I like being with you, but I like the way I am. I should be able to live my life the way I want."

"Can't I want you to change?"

"This is who I am."

Sonja studied him. "You haven't even told me about Hawaii."

"You don't want to hear about it."

Her eyes narrowed. "There was another woman, wasn't there?"

Sam sipped his beer to avoid answering.

Sonja's face reddened. "I should leave."

"Please, don't take this wrong, but I didn't call you when I got home." He looked at her pointedly. "You showed up at my house. You already know my rules. I'm here for the summer, and then I'm leaving."

"I hate those stupid rules."

"I know you do."

"And I hate your stupid flip-flops."

Sam smirked. "Now, that's mean."

She turned away, and he watched her sulk for a minute. When she worked through whatever she needed to, she turned back to him. "What's going on with the woman they found at your cabin?"

"Do you really want to talk about that?"

She thought about it for a second, then shook her head. "Not really. No."

They sat quietly and finished their drinks. When hers was empty, Sam asked, "Want another?"

"No, I have to drive."

He sighed. Sam wanted it to go well tonight. He enjoyed spending time with Sonja, but he wasn't going to get into a long-term relationship. He'd been straightforward with her about that. They had a late summer relationship last year. They occasionally dated during their twenties, but she always wanted more out of it than he wanted. When he failed to respond the way she expected, she would dump him and move on.

After a while, the cycle repeated itself, so Sam refused to get involved with her for a couple of years. He couldn't help it if she wanted something else out of her life.

Sonja might be demanding and slightly crazy, but he liked her—a lot. He was honest when he said that of anyone in his life, she was the person he'd let get closest to him.

She put her empty glass on the table and stood.

"Want to meet again?" Sam asked.

"Are you kidding?" Sonja seemed genuinely confused at his question.

"For another drink or something?"

Sonja's face pinched. "We're leaving," she said flatly. "I'm following you to your house. Some of us have to work in the morning."

"Oh," Sam said and waved for the check.

# Chapter 17

Sam awoke after Sonja slipped out of bed. She wasn't quiet about getting ready. Instead, she clunked, bumped, and thunked her way through his cabin. The woman created more noise than was necessary. She didn't even say goodbye before leaving.

He knew she had left when the front door banged shut and the engine of her car revved. He slowly climbed out of bed as her car raced out of the neighborhood.

Sam feared their relationship would continue this way throughout the season. This violated his fourth rule for living—*No drama*, but he made a concession when it came to Sonja. He didn't necessarily want to, but he seemed to push the fourth rule aside whenever she showed up. Now that he thought about it, when it came to Sonja, he pushed aside his second rule as well—*No attachments*.

He either needed to reconsider his rules or reconsider Sonja.

\*\*\*

Sam motored across the lake. He could have made breakfast for himself, but he wanted an egg sandwich from Wagman's.

In the distance, he saw Dominic's boat leaving the dock of the convenience store. He accelerated to catch up with his friend.

Now, the two of them chatted in the middle of the lake. They tied the two boats together loosely and drifted in the morning sun.

"How come you're avoiding the detective who's calling you?"

"I'm not avoiding him," Dom said through a mouthful of food. He was eating a ham and egg sandwich and sipping coffee from a Styrofoam cup.

Watching Dom eat, Sam's stomach rumbled. He wished he'd gone straight to Wagman's instead. He could have talked with Dominic afterward. "He said you weren't calling him back."

"A number kept coming up as restricted. I wasn't going to answer that. When he finally left a message, I called him."

"You did?"

"I did. Yesterday. We're meeting later this morning, in fact."

"Oh."

"Yeah," Dom said through another bite of the egg sandwich. "Put that in your pipe."

"Yesterday, a couple guys kicked in my front door."

"The hell for?"

"They wanted their drugs."

Dom stopped eating.

"You knew there were drugs, didn't you?"

"I did not."

"But you knew the girl."

"I know a lot of people."

"Come on, Dom. I've asked around."

His friend wrapped the aluminum foil around the remaining portion of his sandwich. For several moments, he struggled to find the right words. "Yeah, all right. I knew her."

"How'd you meet?"

"Wagman's."

"She was hanging around?"

Dom nodded.

"And you what? Started chatting? Is that it?"

"Something like that."

Sam was about to follow up with another question, but Dom glanced away. When he looked back, there was something in his eyes that Sam hadn't seen from his friend but once before. It was the same look he'd noticed at his house the day after Sam found Izzy. He wasn't sure what it was at that time, but Sam knew it now—guilt. But why? He was sure his friend hadn't killed Isabella Taylor. Dom wasn't that type of man. If that wasn't it, what did he have to feel guilty about?

Then Sam realized what it was. "You showed her my house."

Dom's eyes slowly lowered.

A jet ski zoomed by on its way toward Wagman's. The rider—an older woman—waved to Dom and Sam. Neither man waved back.

When quiet returned to the center of the lake, Sam said, "It happened when you dropped the boat."

"It's not what you think."

Sam knew he was on the right track. "She was at Wagman's when the boat was delivered."

Dom remained silent.

"Did she want to know what you were doing? Did she offer to go along for a ride?"

His friend shrugged.

"No," Sam said and turned to watch the jet ski rider who had just passed them. The woman was nearing the convenience store now and slowed. "You asked her to follow along on your jet ski. That's what happened. Isn't it? When you delivered the boat, she saw where my cabin was, and then you two went back to the store. That's how she knew where I lived and how she knew it was vacant."

"I towed it," Dom muttered. "I towed the ski like I always do."

"She rode in the boat?"

"I was big talking around her, so she went along with me. I didn't see the harm in it. I told her we were friends and that I dropped your boat to help you out. You know how it is." He cocked his head and sighed. "Listen, man, I'm sorry. I told her you were gone. I didn't know she would do what she did."

"Why were you talking big around her?"

Dom wouldn't make eye contact then.

"She was young and pretty."

His friend shrugged.

"Did you let her into my cabin?"

Dom nodded. "To use the bathroom. I figured, what could it hurt?"

And that's how the bathroom window got unlocked, Sam thought. "Why not tell me this?"

His friend looked away.

Sam couldn't understand Dom's level of guilt. Okay, the man had made a poor choice by taking the young woman to his cabin and letting her in so she could use the bathroom. It wasn't like he gave her an engraved invitation to burglarize his house. Dom had simply shown her a simple kindness.

He leaned over the edge of his boat to study his friend's face. Dom turned further away from him. That's when he realized his friend's guilt wasn't just from showing Izzy the location of his house or letting her in to use the bathroom.

"You *didn't*."

Dom glanced sheepishly at Sam.

"In my house?"

His friend shrugged.

"Not in my bed. Tell me you didn't."

"I wouldn't do that."

"Not in my grandparents' bed!"

"I wouldn't do that, either." He tapped his chest. "I've got more class than that."

"Then where?"

"The living room."

"On the couch?"

Dom shrugged. "And the floor."

"Damn it, Dom." Sam rubbed his face. Dom had a notorious reputation around the lake, but this took it to a new level. "What were you thinking?"

"Like you said, she was young and pretty and, well, you know." Dom hesitated, then shrugged again sheepishly. "If you had seen her when she was alive, you would have understood, Sam. The girl was—"

"Why didn't you tell me?"

"Seriously?"

"It wouldn't be the first time you hooked up with someone in my cabin."

Dom smirked. "I've never done it while you were away." He lifted his hand as if he were appearing before a judge. "I swear."

Sam sighed.

"Then the girl threw a party at your house. And was murdered. Let's not forget that."

"How can I?"

"Her ending up dead, well— admitting to hooking up didn't seem like something I should do."

A thought ran through Sam's mind, a consideration from his days as a deputy. "The sex," he said.

"What about it?"

"It was consensual, right?"

Dom's face pinched. "Of course, it was consensual. I'm not a monster. Why would you even ask me a thing like that?"

"Evidence." Sam tapped his temple. "Think, Dom, think. Did she have any evidence of you on her body? Did she scratch you during—"

His friend's face flattened and suddenly paled. Dom seemed to have trouble swallowing. He then slowly turned and lifted his shirt, exposing his skin. Faint scratches crossed his back.

"That's not good," Sam said. "Did this happen the day she was killed?"

The T-shirt fell back into place, and Dom faced him again. His skin tone had shifted from pale to ghostly white. "The day before."

"They'll check under her fingernails," Sam said. "Maybe the remnants of your skin are gone. I don't know how long it would stay behind. I was never a detective."

Dom swallowed with great difficulty and blinked repeatedly.

"Dom, did you use protection?"

"She said she was on the pill."

In frustration, Sam threw his hands in the air.

"That's what she said," Dom whined.

"Come on, man! I'm not worried if she got pregnant. Did you leave DNA on her?"

Dom's eyes widened with realization. His body involuntarily spasmed then, and he quickly covered his mouth. "I think I'm going to be sick." He turned and rushed to the other side of his boat. Dom bent over the side, but nothing came out.

As Sam watched his friend prepare to vomit, he knew the answer to his question.

# Chapter 18

When Sam walked into Wagman's, Nicki looked up from her phone. The teenager eyed him with a mixture of suspicion and respect. "I asked around about you."

"Yeah? Well, good morning to you."

"You used to be a cop." She slipped her phone into her back pocket.

Sam stopped in front of the counter. "That a problem?"

Nicki scrunched her nose, pretended to be in thought, then relaxed her face. "Not really."

"Why are you asking around about me?"

"That's what lake people do."

"Gossip, you mean."

"None of the boomers out here have social media, so they get in everyone's business. Ask someone about their neighbor, and you'll get an earful."

"Something you want to ask me?"

Nicki nodded. "Oh, yeah."

"Fire away."

"What do you want for breakfast?"

Sam shrugged. "Same as before, I guess."

The teenager rolled her eyes. "A challenge," she muttered and turned to the grill.

Sam sat at a table just as the door to the store opened. Ernie Holstrom walked in, nodded at Sam, and approached the counter. He and Nicki spoke for a moment then the older man came over.

"Mind if I join you?"

Sam pointed to the empty chair.

"Getting back to normal?" the older man asked.

"This summer lost its chance to be normal."

Ernie harrumphed. "I don't like it when things aren't normal. Gives me indigestion."

Sam politely chuckled.

"Ain't funny. Wait until you're my age. Things give you an upset stomach for all sorts of reasons."

Behind the counter, food sizzled on the grill.

"Has a detective been by yet?" Sam asked.

"He came by yesterday. A fella by the name of Macklephee or some such."

"McAfee."

The older man tapped the table. "That's him. He was asking about the girl and her friends. I gave him Tom's phone number. The detective seemed a smart man."

Sam agreed.

"Didn't seem to like you much, though."

"Did he come out and say that?"

"Of course not." Ernie's smile was sly. "As I said, he's a smart man."

"Then why do you think he didn't like me?"

"Because when I mentioned your name, you should have seen his expression. It was as if I used the Lord's name in vain while in church. So, of course, I had to do it again just to make sure. I thought the man was gonna cover himself." Ernie made the sign of the cross over his chest. "That's what the ladies do whenever I slip up and say one of the words they're always correcting me about."

Nicki placed a Styrofoam cup filled with coffee in front of each man. "Are you guys talking about that detective?"

Both men looked up toward her. "He stopped in yesterday to ask about Izzy."

"Izzy," Ernie said. "Ain't no name for a lady."

The teenager smirked at the older man, and he mimicked the look back at her.

"You're crazy," she said, and Ernie shrugged in mild amusement. "Anyway," Nicki continued. "He came by to ask some questions."

"What kind of questions?" Sam asked.

"The usual kind. I mean, I guess they're the usual kind. I don't know. How often did she come here? Did she meet anyone? The same kinds of questions you asked."

"Looks like you still got it, kid," Ernie said to Sam.

"Did he ask about anything else?" Sam asked.

Nicki nodded. "He asked about Dom. He seemed really interested in him."

"How interested?"

The teenager glanced between the two men. "Pretty interested."

"Did you say something about him?"

Nicki's shoulders slumped, and she looked toward the ceiling.

"What is it? What did you say?"

"It wasn't that bad. I promise."

"*Nicki.*"

"I told him that Izzy went with Dom to deliver your boat. I figured that's how she learned about your place."

"If you knew that, why didn't you say that when we first talked?"

"I didn't want her to get into more trouble."

"But she was already dead."

Nicki looked to the ceiling again. "I know!"

"So, the detective—"

"Macklephee," Ernie interjected.

Sam continued, "—asked about Dom?"

The teenager said, "He wanted to know how much they talked. If they ever went to other places together. That kind of thing."

Sam stared at her.

"What?"

"Well? Did they? How much did they talk? Did you ever see them go to other places?"

"I don't know. Not much, I guess. He said hi to her when she was here. After they delivered your boat, I don't think I saw them speak to each other after that." Sadness etched onto her face. "Oh, yeah. She couldn't talk with him after that, could she?"

Ernie sniffed and said, "Is something burning?"

"Eggs!" Nicki shouted and ran behind the grill. "No, no, no," she muttered. "Gimme a minute," she hollered to the men. "I gotta start over."

The older man lifted his cup in mock salute. "I'm in no hurry."

Sam pulled his cell phone from his pocket and dialed Dominic's number. He'd just spoken to the man, so he expected his friend would answer, but the call went immediately to voice mail.

He didn't need to add to his friend's concerns, but Sam wanted to advise Dom to get a lawyer—just in case. There was no way McAfee would have results back from any DNA tests yet.

He silenced his phone and leaned back. Sam would run by Dom's place after he got his breakfast sandwich and continue their discussion.

"Happy to be back on the lake?" Ernie asked.

Sam briefly closed his eyes and thought about Hawaii. If he would've been willing to violate his rule, he could have stayed and spent another week with the woman he'd met there. Had he done that, he would have avoided all this mess.

But he hadn't, and now he had a real reason to investigate the murder of Isabella Taylor. He was concerned Detective McAfee might develop tunnel vision on Dom. Therefore, he needed to stick his nose into this situation further.

Sam opened his eyes and met Ernie's questioning gaze. "Yeah," he said. "I'm glad to be back."

# Chapter 19

After he secured the MasterCraft to his dock, Sam remained in his boat to eat his breakfast. His cabin was on the east side of the lake and faced the rising sun. Mornings and early afternoons were the best times for residents who lived on Honeymoon Bay.

By midday, this side of the lake would be covered in shade. It made the bay less desirable than the rest of Newman Lake—which was fine by the inhabitants who lived there. They tended to be the type who wanted a quieter life on the water. The residents who chased the sun—the types like Dominic—lived where the sun shined on them all day long.

Sam lifted his face to the morning sun while he chewed. The sandwich was completely cold now, but he didn't mind. He'd eaten plenty of cold egg sandwiches in his life.

He had stopped by Dominic's cabin after leaving Wagman's. His friend's boat was there, but Dom's truck was gone. To make sure, he walked through Dom's place—no one was home.

When he finished his sandwich, Sam balled the aluminum foil and climbed out of his boat. He walked up to his cabin with thoughts of Dominic Russo and Isabella Taylor playing out in his head.

The sun reflected off the sliding glass door as he stepped to it. He squinted from the glare and reached for the door handle. It sometimes stuck due to age and some possible settling of the house. Therefore, he used a little more force on it than was needed.

As soon as the door opened, his world flipped upside down.

***

Sam found himself staring at the ceiling of his cabin. He knew it was his ceiling because he'd been on this floor many times over the years for various reasons.

He remembered opening the sliding glass door and the sun reflecting upon it. Then there was a flash of movement from inside. His eyes hadn't fully adjusted to the change in light levels before his world spun wildly, and now he was here—on the floor.

Sam sensed the pain in his back before moving any part of it. He wiggled his jaw, then scrunched his nose. Sam lifted his fingers to his upper lip. No blood.

"Hello, sunshine," a woman said.

His head lolled toward the voice.

Seated on the couch was the dark-haired, tattooed woman from the coffee stand. He tried to recall her name. Sam blinked as he tried to remember.

What was her name?

"You must have hit the floor pretty hard."

"When he yanked open the door," another woman said, "I thought he was going to charge me. What was I supposed to do?"

This other woman's voice came from behind him. Sam tried to roll up onto the top of his head, but he only succeeded in seeing more of the ceiling. He dropped flat onto his back and winced.

"Sit up," the barista said.

Sam lolled his head to look at her again.

"Maybe I knocked him retarded," the other woman said.

The dark-haired woman leaned forward to study Sam. "At worst, he's got a concussion."

"That's what I meant."

The barista smirked. "Sure."

"Why do you have to be that way, Dee? You know what I meant."

Dee, Sam thought. *Deidre*. That was her name.

With considerable effort, Sam rolled over to his belly. As he pushed himself up to his hands and knees, he fought back a desire to barf. When he rocked back onto his heels, he saw the other woman. It was the same woman who'd punched him at Deidre's apartment—the one who looked like she could bench press a horse. Now, she'd struck him twice.

Sam attempted a joke. "There's more where that came from."

"Want me to hit him again?" the bodybuilder asked.

"Leave him alone, Andy."

Andy crossed her thick arms and twisted her lips. Sam reconsidered his appraisal of her. He no longer thought she could bench press a horse. Instead, he now thought this woman could bench press a horse trailer with the horse in it.

"Where's the stuff?" Deidre asked.

Sam turned his head slowly toward her. "The stuff?"

"I told you I knocked him slow," Andy said.

Deidre waved her off. To Sam, she said, "We know you have it."

He shook his head once and grimaced. A wave of nausea rolled over him. "It's gone," he muttered.

The dark-haired woman scowled. "If you know what's good for you, you'll tell me where it's at."

"I thought your friends had it."

"My friends?" Deidre glanced at Andy then back to him. "Listen, retard—"

"*See!*" Andy said. "I told you."

"If we had it, would I be here asking for it?"

"That's not polite."

The dark-haired woman tilted her head. "The hell?"

"You're supposed to say challenged." Sam touched his head. It was hard to think. Maybe he had a concussion. "Or special or something like that. Whatever it is, you're not supposed to say the R-word."

"The R-word?" Deidre asked.

"Retard," Andy said.

Deidre jumped to her feet and pointed at Sam. "You're giving me language lessons?" She turned to Andy. "Hit him again."

As Andy stepped forward, Sam covered his head with his arms and hollered, "Wait!"

When no blows immediately rained down, Sam poked his head up from the protection of his arms. He looked like a gopher peering out from the safety of its hole.

Andy's roundhouse punch caught him on the temple, and Sam fell to the floor.

When a second punch didn't follow, Sam was immediately thankful that there wouldn't be a fight. He'd been in several donnybrooks while as a deputy, but that had been some time ago. Still, his recent lack of pugilistic skills was embarrassing. He'd been assaulted by the football players in the grocery store parking lot. Andy had knocked him out at Deidre's apartment. Moments ago, she surprised him and flipped him onto his back. To top it all off, she just clocked him one on the temple.

Sam lay on his back with his hands and feet up and ready—an upended turtle prepared to do battle. That didn't sound tough enough, so Sam quickly modified his thinking. He was a combat turtle.

He and Andy stared at each other for a moment, then the bodybuilder frowned.

"You know I can kick your ass."

"I'm sure." He wasn't, but why provoke a fight and prove her right? Better to be agreeable and find out what they were doing in his house.

"I take classes."

"No doubt."

Andy cocked her head. "Not going to smart off about it?"

"Not this time." He lowered his feet to the floor but kept his hands up. He wasn't a complete fool.

When the bodybuilder sat on the edge of the couch, Sam realized the other woman was gone.

"Where's Deidre?"

Andy frowned. "How do you know her name?"

"You said it."

The bodybuilder scowled. "That means you know my name, too."

This wasn't starting well, especially since he was trying to be agreeable. Sam rolled slowly to his belly. "Listen," he moaned into the carpeted floor. "I don't know either of you. I just want you to leave me alone."

From the back of the cabin, the toilet flushed.

"It ain't happening until we get the stuff."

"Stuff? Why can't any of you call it what it is?"

"Any of us?" Deidre asked as she returned to the room. She wiped her hands on the back of her shorts.

Sam pushed himself up to his hands and knees.

"And who is us?" the dark-haired woman asked.

"The four of you who think smacking me around is a proper way to communicate."

Deidre stopped and glanced at Andy. She then squatted until she was at eye level with Sam. "Four of us?"

"You guys and the two football players."

Deidre straightened and slapped her hands. "Damn!"

"What?" Andy asked.

"*Izzy*," Deidre said. The word was full of venom.

"What's about Izzy?" Sam asked.

"She thought she was so smart," Andy said.

The dark-haired woman glared at her friend.

"*What?*" the bodybuilder asked.

"She wasn't smart," Deidre snapped.

"I didn't say she was," Andy whined. "I said she *thought* she was." To Sam, the bodybuilder continued, "The girl thought she should be running the coffee stand."

"Enough," Deidre snapped. She eyeballed Sam. "Where's the stuff?"

"The other guys took it. That's why my door was kicked in. I figure that's how you got into my house."

"Huh," Andy said. "So, that's why the front door—"

"Shut it," Deidre said, cutting her off.

Andy pouted at the dismissal.

Deidre lowered her head and began walking in small circles.

"So, what are you?" Sam asked the bodybuilder.

Her face darkened. "What's that supposed to mean?"

"Girlfriend or her muscle?"

It seemed to Sam that she wanted to be the former, but Andy reluctantly said, "Her trainer." She mimed pressing weights from a bench.

Deidre ran her fingers through her hair as she moved toward the sliding glass doors. She put her hands on her hips and stared out the large windows.

"That's where she died," Sam said.

Deidre sighed. "I know."

"You do?"

"The newspaper said she was found in a boat." She looked over her shoulder. "You see a boat in here?"

The bodybuilder glanced around. "No."

Deidre rolled her eyes and turned back toward the large windows.

The three of them remained quiet for a moment. Outside, a boat motored loudly across the lake.

Sam shifted his position and sat on his buttocks. His head pounded, but the immediate danger of the moment seemed to have passed. He decided to broach the subject he'd wanted an answer to since the beginning of this whole debacle. "You're into fitness," he started.

"Duh," Andy said.

"But you're selling drugs."

Andy faced Deidre as the other woman slowly spun toward Sam. "Excuse me?"

"You're into health and fitness, right? But you're selling drugs." He looked up at the ceiling while he thought. "It doesn't make sense."

For a moment, Deidre's frown deepened. As she watched Sam, she inhaled deeply, twisted her lips, and exhaled slowly. "What kind of question is that? Are you a cop?"

Sam's gaze bounced between Deidre and Andy. He didn't know how to answer her question now. Saying he wanted to solve Izzy's murder made him a private investigator, which made him a quasi-law enforcement officer. If they were dealing drugs, they wouldn't want him poking around.

And if he said he wanted to know what the drugs were for the sake of knowing, perhaps they would think he was a rival. That could be a threat.

His gaze continued to bounce as he tried to figure out an appropriate response. Perhaps he should say—

Deidre glared at Sam. "Stay out of it."

"Fine."

The barista's lip curled. Without looking at Andy, she said, "Let's go."

Sam brought his feet back up to reassume his combat turtle position. The barista and the bodybuilder walked out and left him on the floor.

"There's more where that came from," he muttered—but not too loud, in case the door was left open.

# Chapter 20

"Sam?" Sonja called.

"Out here," he muttered. He sat in the shade covering his deck and held an icepack on the back of his neck.

"Sam?" she called again.

"Out here," he repeated. It wasn't loud enough for her to hear, but she would find him soon enough. The cabin was small, and he wasn't hiding.

He watched a boat motor by. It was still too cold on the water to ski, so they were either visiting a friend, out for a tour, or headed to Wagman's.

Sam rechecked his phone. Still no call or text from Dom.

"There you are," she said.

He carefully placed his phone on the glass table next to him. "Here I am."

She wore a faded Green Bay Packers shirt, light blue jeans, and slip-on tennis shoes. The clothes tightly fit her curves, and she looked like she might have just come from a commercial shoot. Sonja wasn't a fan of the football team. Instead, she liked the colors and logo. She had multiple team shirts to go with different outfits. Sam had been out with her previously when she was dressed similarly, and it led to interesting discussions with die-hard fans. Sonja never minded, though. She loved the attention.

"What happened to you?" Sonja asked as she gently touched his shoulder. "Did you fall?"

"Several times," Sam said and lowered the ice pack. "And landed right on some woman's fist."

"You got into a fight? With a woman?"

"Fighting implies two people were involved."

Sonja studied Sam's face. "Why didn't you fight back?"

"I did," Sam said. "Her fist didn't know what hit it."

"Quit being a jackass," Sonja said.

He leaned back into his chair and moved the ice pack to the top of his head. "I'm sorry. I guess I'm a little embarrassed at how poorly I defended myself."

"Even the best fighters can't win them all."

Sam didn't bother to tell her that Andy had already bested him once and that he'd lost a confrontation against the football players. His fighting record this season was now a dismal 0-3.

Sonja asked, "What did they want?"

"Drugs."

"Are you running drugs now?"

Sam shook his head. "I found some drugs left behind from the party."

"What kind of drugs?"

He shrugged.

"You don't know?"

"Someone removed the brand labels from the baggies."

"Don't be a jerk. You said baggies, so they were clear then. You couldn't tell the drugs by the color?"

"Not just by sight. No."

She put her pinky against her tongue. "What about the taste?"

"You don't bake a cake with the drugs."

Sonja smirked.

"It doesn't work like that."

"So, with all that police training, you couldn't tell what kind of drugs they were."

"Sorry to disappoint."

Sonja shrugged. "What do I care? They aren't my drugs."

"They aren't mine, either. But it seems I'm stuck in the middle of a couple groups that want them. I'm not sure how the dead girl fits in, but I get the feeling she either stole them or was supposed to deliver them."

"Oh, my God," Sonja said. "The dead girl."

"What about her?"

"You didn't hear." It wasn't a question.

"I guess I didn't."

"It was all over the news. That's why I rushed over."

"What did I miss?"

She crossed her arms. "I thought you were friends."

"Sonja, you're not making sense."

"Dominic. They just arrested him for murder. It's breaking news."

Sam lowered the ice pack.

Sonja nodded. "No joke."

He tossed the cold pack on the table and grabbed his phone.

"I was sure you would have heard about it."

Dom still had not called or texted, but if what Sonja said was true, his silence suddenly made sense. He was supposed to meet with McAfee. Perhaps that's what the detective had planned all along. Sam stood and wobbled slightly.

"Where are you going?"

"To find out what's going on."

First, he wanted the Incident Report Card that McAfee had given him. Sam had left it on the kitchen counter. He found it—or what was left of it—shredded into little pieces. Either Deidre or Andy had done it. The light-blue roster of Spokane Demons players was crumpled into a ball.

The shredded incident card wouldn't stop him, though. It would require him to jump through a couple of hoops to get to the detective now, but it wasn't the hardest thing in the world to do.

He called the front desk of the Public Safety Building. The woman who answered transferred him to a receptionist at Major Crimes. The man who picked up was polite and sounded young. He informed Sam that Detective McAfee was away from the office.

When the Major Crimes receptionist offered to transfer him to McAfee's desk phone, Sam asked, "Can I have his cell phone number?"

"I'm sorry, sir. We don't give that number out."

Sam rolled his eyes even though he was on the phone. Maybe that's why he did it—because he was on the phone and the receptionist couldn't see him. He said, "This is regarding a case."

"Oh," the receptionist said. "Did he give you an Incident Report Card?"

Sam glanced at the shredded paper on the kitchen counter. "He did."

"If he wanted you to have his cell number, he would have written it on there. Did he do that?"

"He did."

"Well?"

"Someone tore up the card."

The receptionist harrumphed. "Well, then, I'm sorry, sir. I can't give you the number. I can, however, transfer you to his desk phone."

"That'll be fine."

Shane McAfee's voice mail greeting was extremely professional, which meant boring and ladened with too much information. As Sam listened to the detective drone on about the caller leaving the date and time along with their report number, he considered adding homicide detectives to his list of occupations to avoid. Before he could give it too much thought, though, the voice mail ended, and the phone beeped.

"Detective," he said, "this is Sam—Samuel Strait. I just heard that you've picked up Dominic Russo for the murder of that dead girl. Okay, that sounded stupid. No one murders a dead girl, right?" Sam chuckled.

*Why did I chuckle?*

He cleared his throat and continued. "I'm sorry about that. Listen, Dom didn't murder Izzy Taylor. I mean Isabella Taylor. Right."

Sonja watched him with growing concern. He shrugged and shook his head. The throbbing in his head seemed worse. Maybe he did have a concussion.

"Anyway, you've got the wrong man. Dom didn't do it. Please call, and I can explain everything."

He was about to hang up but hurriedly lifted the phone back to his ear. "I'm sorry I don't have the report number, but you remember who I am, right?" He felt stupid for adding that second part, especially when he remembered Ernie Holstrom's comments about McAfee. Sam said, "Yeah, of course, you remember me." Then he announced the date and time and recited his phone number before ending the call.

Sam stared at his cell phone.

Sonja asked, "Are you okay?"

Sam put his phone on the table. "Yeah."

"How hard did that woman hit you?"

"Hard enough."

"Do you need to go to the doctor?"

"I'm fine."

She watched him for several moments. "What are you going to do now?"

"I'm going to lay down. Maybe take a nap."

"You shouldn't sleep," she said. "You might have a concussion."

"I don't have a concussion."

"You might."

"I'm fine. I'm just tired."

"That could be a concussion!"

"It's not a concussion."

"Well, if you're going to take a nap, I'll take one with you."

Sam smirked. "Sonja, we don't nap together."

"We will this time. I'll make an exception—for your safety." She held out her hand. "I'll stay awake and watch you sleep."

His face scrunched. "That sounds creepy."

"Yeah," she said with a demented smile. "I know."

\*\*\*

When he awoke a couple of hours later, he was naked. Sonja lay next to him and softly purred in her sleep.

"For my safety," he muttered.

He slipped out of bed and quietly dressed. The pounding in his head was less now.

Barefoot, he padded into the living room where he checked his phone. There was a missed call and a text from a number he didn't know.

THIS IS MCAFEE. CALL ME.

Sam walked onto the deck and called the detective.

It was answered after the second ring. "McAfee."

"Detective, you've got the wrong man."

"No hello?"

"Oh, right. Hello, Detective. You've got the wrong man."

"I'm assuming you mean your friend, Dominic Russo."

"He didn't kill Isabella Taylor."

"You might be wrong."

Sonja walked out onto the deck with only her Green Bay Packers shirt on. It barely covered her bottom. She held out her hand for him.

Sam absently took her hand as he said into the phone, "Dom couldn't do it."

McAfee asked, "Did you know he showed Isabella Taylor your house?"

Sonja pulled Sam from his seat.

"And," the detective continued, "he had intercourse with the victim inside your residence?"

Sam remained silent as he considered the detective's words. Sonja led him back into the house.

"Your friend has scratches on his back and arms," McAfee said. "Those on his back are consistent with sex. Those on his arms could be seen as defensive wounds."

Sam wanted to protest, but it seemed the detective had spoken with Dom, and his friend hadn't held anything back.

"Dominic Russo knew the victim. He had been with her at the place of her ultimate demise. They had sexual contact, either by coercion or agreement. He is physically much larger than she was. He had means and opportunity."

Sonja led Sam down the hallway.

"What about motive?" Sam asked the detective.

"We don't need a motive. That's for prosecutors and juries to worry about."

"Well, he didn't do it," Sam said as resolutely as he could.

"For your friend's sake, let's hope you're right."

In his bedroom, Sonja turned Sam around. She reached for him as he said to McAfee, "I got jumped for the drugs."

"I know that."

"By two new people. The two women from the apartment we met at."

"The one from the coffee shop?"

"And her bodybuilder friend."

"Well," McAfee said.

"Weird, right? That's something to look into."

"It doesn't absolve your friend."

Sam waved a hand while he spoke. "But he's innocent."

A couple of seconds passed before McAfee said, "I'll look into it. I've got to go."

When the call ended, Sam realized he was naked again. "Sonja, I can't. Dom's in trouble—"

She slid her T-shirt over her head and climbed onto the bed. "He can wait." She patted his pillow.

Staring at Sonja, Sam internally argued with himself.

Dom needs my help, he thought.

*But what can I do at this very minute?*

Dom was in jail.

*Then there's no reason to hurry.*

No one was fighting for Dom right now.

*But Dom did start all this trouble by showing Izzy my house.*

When Sonja reached for him, Sam made up his mind.

Dom could wait.

# Chapter 21

Sonja was gone when he awoke. There'd been no huffing or slamming of doors, so everything must be right between them—for now. That made Sam smile as he stared at the ceiling. He liked no drama.

His smile evaporated, though, as he considered Dominic. Had his friend kept his desire to impress under control, none of this would have happened. But it did, and now he was in jail.

Sam's thoughts drifted to Detective Shane McAfee. He slowly sat upright and moved to the edge of the bed. Sam believed McAfee to be a good cop and a decent person. However, the detective probably figured he had solved Isabella Taylor's murder when he arrested Dominic. Which meant the cop was done looking for other suspects unless another fell into his lap.

Sam would have to make sure one did just that.

He grabbed his cell phone and saw the detective's text message from the day before. He didn't want to lose the number, so he added it to his directory. He was about to save it when he recalled Ernie Holstrom's name for the man—Macklephee—and he chuckled. It took only a few seconds, and he changed the entry.

Sam showered and dressed then. It was almost five now. The day had passed quickly by. A morning assault and an afternoon of lovemaking tended to do that.

He assessed his options. Right now, he figured there were two ways he could go.

First, there were the two football players. They had assaulted him and taken the drugs. He knew where the football players trained, but he imagined the training facility would be closed by now. Hanging out there, hoping to spot them, would be a waste of time until tomorrow.

Next, there was Deidre and Andy. They'd also assaulted him and wanted the drugs. He knew where Deidre worked. It was late for the coffee shop, and he could always find her in the morning. He also knew where she lived. Well, he assumed it was her apartment. It might have been Andy's. Regardless, one of them lived there, and it was a decent place to start.

He'd go back there. Sam grabbed his car keys and headed for the door. He pulled it open and was surprised to see Jordan Withers standing on the small porch. Her hand was poised to knock. She wore a sweatshirt, tan shorts, and canvas shoes.

"Hey there," she said.

"Hey."

"I didn't want to walk in. I didn't think lake rules applied to a reporter."

"They don't."

Jordan's smile faded.

"I'm headed out." Sam stepped onto the porch with her. He pulled the door behind him.

They were on the small landing together. In the confined space, he smelled her perfume again. Sam didn't want to be tempted to flirt with her. Another woman in his life would only bring drama.

He stepped off the porch to the sidewalk. Maybe he should add reporters to his list of occupations to avoid. He couldn't understand why he hadn't done it previously. It seemed like such a natural idea. Or was he thinking of adding reporters to the list just to avoid the temptation of talking with her? That would be the wrong reason to add them to the list.

As she followed Sam to his car, Jordan interrupted his thoughts. "Did you hear about Dominic Russo?"

He continued walking.

"He lives on the lake," she said.

Sam glanced over his shoulder.

"Do you know him?"

He paused to ask, "What are you after?"

"A story. I'm here to do some follow-up on him. Ask-the-neighbors type of stuff. I figured I'd start with you since you're the one person I know out here."

"Dom didn't do it."

"But the Sheriff's Office—"

"Made a mistake."

Jordan's eyes brightened.

"And you can quote me on that, but that's all you're getting."

He climbed into his car, started the engine, and drove off. Jordan Withers remained in his yard as he drove away.

\*\*\*

Sam could see the apartment from where he parked. He also saw Deidre's red Toyota parked where it had been earlier.

He opened the glove box and pulled out the empty *Standing Hampton* cassette case along with Cinderella's

*Night Songs.* Sam quickly swapped the cassettes in the radio and closed the glove box. He turned on the radio and leaned back.

Sam jumped in his seat when "Shake Me" roared through the car's speakers. He quickly turned down the volume. He'd forgotten how loud that album was.

While he watched the apartment, Sam imagined his father listening to this music when he was young. Unfortunately, he couldn't remember anything about him that wasn't attached to a story told by his grandparents or that came from a photograph.

Regardless, he envisioned his father listening to this album and wondered what it would have been like to have enjoyed this music when it was new. It was classic rock now, and younger generations openly mocked the looks associated with the musicians. But Sam didn't care. His father loved it, so he embraced it.

He caught movement from the corner of his eye. Deidre bounded down the stairs and then walked to her car. The Toyota Camry zipped out of the parking lot.

Sam followed her in his classic Crown Victoria as Cinderella's lead singer belted out, "Nobody's Fool."

\*\*\*

"Are you interested in a membership?"

From behind the counter, the woman's broad smile exposed unnaturally white teeth. Deeply defined muscles bulged underneath tanned skin the color of a Bengal tiger.

Deidre had led him to a nondescript concrete building on the old Trent Highway near the base of the Argonne hill. The small parking lot was filled with cars, and the pylon sign read *The Iron Way*.

"I was hoping to look around," Sam said. "Maybe see what you have to offer."

The receptionist stood then and leaned over the counter to fully take Sam in. Her eyes swept over his faded T-shirt and jeans. They lingered a little too long on his flip-flops. "This might not be—" she settled back onto her heels and regained eye contact "—the right gym for you. Maybe you should try yoga or a spin class. Something more your speed."

"I can lift weights," Sam said defensively.

"Can you?"

He couldn't tell if the woman was flirting with him or openly mocking him. Her crooked smile threw off his radar.

Deidre exited the women's locker room then and proceeded deeper into the gym. She didn't notice Sam in the lobby.

"We're geared for the hardcore trainer," the receptionist said. "Don't get me wrong—we're happy to take your money. But we try to manage expectations from day one. The worst thing that can happen for you and for us is to get you in here and have you learn that this isn't a place to hang out and meet women."

"I don't want to hang out."

"What about meeting women?"

As seriously as he could, he said, "I want to train."

"Okay." The woman once again stood on her tiptoes to lean over the counter. As she reappraised him, she muttered, "What's your bench?"

In other words, Sam thought, how much could he bench press? "No idea."

"Right," she said and dropped back to her usual level. "You want to train." Her crooked smile turned into a smirk. Not flirting, Sam decided. The receptionist jerked her head toward the weight room. "Why don't you look around? When you're done, come back and see me. You can decide then if you really want to train here."

"I appreciate it."

"Sure." She settled back into her chair and turned to face her computer. "Don't touch anything, and don't bother our clients."

Sam wandered for a bit and pretended to consider various pieces of equipment. He wasn't a stranger to a gym. He'd lifted weights during high school while he played baseball, and he lifted them during his time as a deputy. However, he never had any interest in getting big. Weights were always for strength and never for beauty. Looking at many of the people grunting and groaning in this gym, they fell into the latter category.

A muscular man and an overly toned woman posed together in front of a mirror. They switched positions, held them for a couple of seconds, and then critiqued each other's poses.

Further down the way, a man posed by himself. Using his cell phone, the guy took pictures of his reflection. Sam waited patiently to pass by as the man struggled to get the 'right' photograph of himself flexing. When he did so, he exhaled loudly and immediately checked his phone for the picture he'd just taken.

The gym smelled of sweat and menthol. Sam decided it was something akin to Ben-Gay. He remembered rubbing some of the ointment all over his throwing arm during junior high school to loosen up before practice. He'd found a tube of it belonging to his grandfather. Several guys on the team teased him about it, then they came to practice the next day smelling the same way. The coach ordered all of them to knock it off before they caused him brain damage from the cloying aroma.

Various marketing banners hung around the gym. Names like Weider, MuscleTech, and Monster Milk were prominently displayed. One banner—*Proud Sponsor of The Spokane Demons*—gave him pause.

Sam eventually made his way around the gym to Deidre, who worked in a seated squat rack. To the uninitiated, it might look like a medieval torture device. To the initiated, it looked like a modern torture device. Several forty-five-pound plates were placed on each side, and she repeatedly pressed up and down using only her legs.

Deidre didn't notice Sam standing nearby. White buds were stuck into her ears, and she excitedly chewed gum as she exercised. As the set of presses wore on, her face reddened, and beads of perspiration covered her forehead. She grunted loudly on the last repetition.

When she finished the set, Deidre secured it to the rack and climbed out. That's when she saw Sam. She straightened and said louder than necessary, "You."

Sam waved at her.

Her eyes narrowed, and she loudly asked, "What are you doing here?"

It was Sam's turn to look around. Several people watched them. The receptionist stood to take an interest in them.

"I want to know what you're after."

"What?" Again, her voice was louder than necessary.

Sam tapped his ears.

Deidre rolled her eyes, then removed her earbuds. A thump-thump-thump of hip-hop music emanated from them. "What do you want?" she hissed.

"What are you after?"

"What?"

The receptionist headed in their direction now. Her arms swung away from her body in an intimidating manner. She looked much bigger from behind the front counter.

"The stuff," Sam said. He was convinced the drugs played into the murder of Isabella Taylor. If he could find out how they figured into the scenario, he could help exonerate Dominic.

Deidre's scowl faded. "Do you have it?"

"What exactly is it?"

She shook her head as if she didn't comprehend his question. "What?"

The receptionist made it to them. "Sir, you were not to bother our clients."

Sam thumbed toward Deidre. "But Dee and I are old friends."

"Dee?"

Deidre half-heartedly shrugged.

"Well," the receptionist said as she disapprovingly assessed Sam once more, "you're not a member. You either carry on this conversation outside, or you complete the paperwork. Your choice."

He eyed Deidre. "I'll wait for you outside."

The dark-haired barista said, "Whatever," and turned back to her weights.

To the receptionist, Sam said, "You're right. I think yoga is more my speed."

He headed straight toward the exit.

\*\*\*

If he had expected Deidre to run out of the gym to finish their talk, he would have been disappointed. He leaned back against the headrest and listened to the music. Cinderella was now singing about "Once Around the Ride."

Deidre probably decided to finish her workout. Afterward, he guessed, she would probably shower and change. Taking her time would be a power play, he convinced himself. He shouldn't get angry or worked up over it.

Let it go and stay focused, he thought.

A vehicle with a low-rumbling engine pulled into the parking lot. After its engine quieted, two car doors slammed. He heard this over the music in his car. Sam rolled his head to the side but didn't see anyone walking nearby. He returned his attention to the front of the building.

When the two men walked toward the entrance, Sam bolted upright. His hand instinctively reached for the key stuck in the ignition. It was the football players—Toma Papani and Hoyt Jefferson. The two laughed as they walked, and each carried a gym bag.

Sam's fingers gripped the car key, but he didn't turn it. If they didn't notice him, he shouldn't call attention to himself by starting his car. Just let them go inside, and he could quietly drive away.

Hoyt grabbed the front door to the gym and pulled it open for his friend. As Toma passed by, the pale man glanced back toward the parking lot. Hoyt's face suddenly twisted in anger, and he muttered something. He dropped his gym bag, let go of the door, and stepped toward the parking lot. The entrance to the gym opened again, and Toma emerged. He'd left his bag inside.

Sam twisted the key, and the Ford revved to life. He dropped the car into reverse but immediately hit the brakes as a small Nissan passed behind him. The little car stopped suddenly as Hoyt and Toma walked in front of it.

The Nissan blocked Sam from behind. He couldn't pull forward due to the car parked in front. Sam was pinned in.

As the two bulky men ignored the danger the Nissan presented, the woman behind its steering wheel yelled and waved frustratedly at them.

Hoyt made it to Sam's car first. He slapped the trunk, then the roof, and the driver's window. He repeatedly yanked on the handle of the Ford's door. "Get out of the car!"

Sam was still looking over his shoulder at the driver of the Nissan. The young woman was confused as to what was occurring around her.

"Move your car!" Sam yelled and honked his horn.

Toma went to the other side of the Ford and followed the actions of his friend. The Samoan banged on the trunk and roof before smacking the passenger side window. With his free hand, Toma yanked on the door handle. "Open up!"

The two men played a loud, percussive rhythm on Sam's car. Hoyt's was slap—yank—slap—yank while Toma's was smack—tug—smack—tug.

Sam honked and yelled, "Move it, lady!" He was sure the woman couldn't hear his yelling, but she must have seen the anger in his face. The little car jerked forward and cleared a path for Sam.

He jammed the accelerator, and the Crown Victoria quickly reversed from its parking spot. Hoyt and Toma's banging rhythm suddenly stopped as the Ford launched away.

Sam hastily checked oncoming traffic and found the old highway to be clear. The Crown Vic bounced recklessly backward into Trent Avenue. Its front end careened wildly behind as the car reversed into the far lane.

The two men did not follow Sam into the roadway. Instead, they stood at the edge of the parking lot and continued to holler.

Sam dropped the gear shift into Drive, mashed the accelerator to the floor, and the car leaped forward.

# Chapter 22

"This is a surprise," she said. Sonja pushed the door to her apartment open wider. "I can't remember the last time you came over here."

It had been a couple of years, at least.

He walked by her and entered the apartment. "I've got some trouble."

Sonja's condo was near the entrance to the older portion of the Liberty Lake community. There were newer, flashier developments in the area, but they were further back from the water. With its dated shake siding and 1970s architectural elements, Sonja's building was better situated for those who wanted immediate access to the water and its lifestyle.

As a sweeping generalization, Liberty Lake was where the rich and beautiful folks lived. Newman Lake was the unattractive sister—the place where people moved when they couldn't afford the pricier homes on lakes named Liberty or Coeur d'Alene.

Sonja closed the door behind him. "What happened?"

Sam stopped in the living room and put his hands on his hips. He was about to comment when he realized her home had been remodeled. It looked modern now, like something from one of those HGTV shows he occasionally watched when he couldn't sleep. He turned to her and noticed how she waited expectantly.

"I don't know what happened," he said. "I followed the woman from the coffee stand and—"

"The one who punched you?"

Sam smirked. "She didn't punch me. Her girlfriend did. Well, her trainer, but she wants to be her girlfriend. It's complicated."

Sonja rolled her eyes. "So, you followed a woman, is what you're saying."

"To her gym. Yeah."

"Which one?"

"The Iron Way."

"Ugh. That place is nothing but meatheads."

"Seemed like it attracts a certain type."

"It's not a place to tone and tan, that's for sure."

"How do you know about it?"

Sonja's hip jutted out, and she rested a manicured hand on it. "My life isn't spent waiting for you to blow back into town."

"I wouldn't expect it."

She frowned. "You wouldn't?"

"You have a life to live."

"For your information, I've met some guys who train there."

"I understand."

"On location." She meant for photoshoots or a commercial. "They wanted a certain look."

"Naturally."

"You can guess the type."

Parroting her earlier word, he said, "Meatheads."

"Handsome," she corrected. "They were *handsome*."

"But you said meatheads went there."

Sonja rolled her eyes again. "Why do you have to be so difficult?"

"I agreed with you. How is that being difficult?"

She stared at him until he decided to continue. "So, I went inside to talk with her."

Sonja raised a hand as she considered his words. "Wait. *Why* were you following her?"

"Dom's in trouble."

"I know. I told you—remember? But what were you hoping to get by following this woman?"

"I wanted to know about the drugs everyone's after. I figure that's why Isabella Taylor was killed at my house."

Sonja crossed her arms. "And you don't think the cops could do this?"

"Why are you busting my chops?"

She impatiently tapped her toe as she spoke. "I'm making sure you're not following her for another reason."

"And what other reason would I have for following her?" As soon as the words tumbled from his mouth, he regretted them. Before she could protest, Sam lifted a hand to cut her off. He continued. "I'm not following her for any reason but to help Dom. Got it? When I talked with her at the gym, the receptionist said we needed to finish our conversation outside. They're sort of strict in that gym."

"Intense," Sonja agreed.

"Anyway, I waited for her in the parking lot."

"Where does the trouble come in?"

"The guys from the football team showed up."

"The ones that beat you up at the grocery store?"

"They didn't beat me up."

"I thought they did."

Sam shook his head. "One guy punched me."

"That sounds like getting beat up."

"It's not."

Sonja put her hands on her hips and considered Sam. "You get beat up a lot."

"No, I don't."

"I thought you were a better fighter."

"What gave you that impression?"

"You were a deputy."

"I fought better while in uniform."

"Uh-huh. Did they see you?"

"Who?"

"The football players," Sonja said exasperatedly. "Are you telling this story or not?"

He nodded. "They did see me. And as soon as they did, they beelined for my car and smacked the hell out of it. Hollered at me to get out. Like I was going to do that."

Sonja's face whitened. "That must have been scary."

"It was."

"What did you do?"

"I got out of there as fast as I could."

"Did you call the cops?"

"For what?"

"For them smacking your car. For scaring you."

Sam smirked. "No."

"Don't look at me that way. You still could have called the cops."

"I'd rather not."

"Whatever. Do you think this woman—what's her name?"

"Deidre."

"Do you think Deidre called these other guys?"

"I don't know. Maybe, but I doubt it."

"Why's that?"

"Because she and her trainer showed up at my cabin looking for their stuff." He air-quoted stuff just like McAfee did.

"I know. I was there."

"Well, if they were working together with the big boys, there would have been no need to come to my place. And Deidre was upset when I mentioned they might have taken the drugs."

"You didn't tell me that."

"I'm telling you now."

"Maybe someone else took it."

Sam hadn't thought about that. "Who?"

Sonja lifted her hands in the air. "How would I know? I'm not the detective here."

"Neither am I."

"You're acting like one."

"Thank you."

"At least, trying to act like one."

"I take it back."

Sonja smiled. "So, what's your plan now?"

"I don't want to go home. At least, not tonight. Deidre and Andy might show up there. And the two football players know where I live, too. It seems anyone and everyone might go there."

"But if you don't have the drugs, why would they go there?"

"I don't know. Can you just let me be paranoid without asking rational questions?"

She studied him for a moment, then slowly uncrossed her arms. Her hands slipped into her pants pockets and her shoulders hunched slightly. Her lips parted slightly before she said, "So..."

"So."

"Are you spending the night here?"

"If it's not too much trouble. We can order in. I'll let you pick."

Sonja grabbed his hand and said, "Who has time to eat?" She then led him toward the bedroom.

Sam was hungry, but he didn't protest being led away.

\*\*\*

"Sam?"

She nudged his shoulder, and his eyes fluttered open to darkness. "Huh?"

"Are you awake?"

"What time is it?"

"I don't know, but I had a thought."

Sam grabbed his cell phone and touched it to reveal its screen. It was shortly after midnight. He grunted in dismay and closed his eyes.

"The drugs," she said.

"What about them?"

"Why would they be after them?"

"Huh?"

"I mean The Iron Way is for serious trainers only."

"That's the impression I got."

"So why would Deidre and the other guys be after drugs?"

"To sell them." Thinking about Detective McAfee's words, he added, "Everything is about love or money."

"But this is about drugs."

"Which is a form of money."

Sonja continued to protest. "Why would they be involved with drugs, though?"

"I get what you're after. I already asked this question."

"Let me ask a different question. Do they care about what they put into their bodies?"

Sam's eyes opened into the darkness. Maybe it was the time of night, but the way she asked the question sparked something in him. It didn't take much consideration to know Deidre and Andy cared about their bodies. Andy looked as if she could be on the cover of Bodybuilder Today—if that were such a magazine—and Deidre could be on the cover of Fitness Woman—he knew that was a magazine as he'd flipped through one before at a grocery store.

It was the football players he had to ponder—Toma Papani and Hoyt Jefferson. The two men would be a case of looks being deceiving. They appeared to be fat, but they would indeed care about their bodies. The weight they carried was part of the game they played. However, they would need their bodies to operate at peak efficiency to compete amongst the other players.

"Yeah," Sam finally agreed. "They would care about what they put into their bodies."

"So, what if it wasn't cocaine or heroin?"

He blinked into the darkness. "You mean meth?"

"No. Not meth. You said it was a powder?"

"That's right."

Sonja stirred, and the light on the nightstand turned on. Sam repeatedly blinked while she flopped over to prop herself up on an elbow.

"Steroids are illegal," Sonja said.

"Okay."

"Are they powdered?"

Sam pushed himself slowly upright.

"Why are you looking at me like that?"

"That's a good question," Sam said.

"Thank you. I know they're liquid sometimes because people inject them. Like in a butt cheek, right?"

"I think so."

"But before its liquid, is it a powder? I mean, can it be a powder? Or can they convert it to a powder? I guess that's my question."

"That's the question."

Sam slipped out of bed and grabbed his pants.

"Where are you going?"

"To answer that question."

He padded into the living room.

\*\*\*

Wearing only his jeans, Sam sat at the kitchen island and worked his cell phone. He had called up several websites for information on steroids.

Sonja walked out wearing his T-shirt. He glanced up, smiled, then returned to his search.

"Are you hungry?" she asked.

"Starving."

"I'll make us some eggs."

For several minutes, Sonja moved about the kitchen. She pulled out a small pan from a lower cupboard and put it on the stove. Quickly, she cracked four eggs into the pan and then lay a glass cover on top. Then she placed a couple of pieces of wheat bread into a toaster. She depressed the button to start the timer.

"What have you found?" she asked.

When she reached into a cupboard, the T-shirt rode slightly up her backside. Sam noticed the reveal of skin and smiled.

Sonja glanced back at that moment and caught his eye. "Perv."

He shrugged and returned his attention to his phone. "I think I'm as confused as I was when I started. There's definitely a steroid powder, but I can't determine its legality."

She muttered, "Okay," as she grabbed two plates from another cupboard.

"It seems like the powders are coming from some companies that look to be Chinese or Russian."

"Eastern European."

"What?"

Sonja glanced back. "If you don't know for a fact that they're Russian companies, then you should say Eastern European. That way, you're not racist."

Sam pointed at his phone. "It says Russia."

Her face relaxed. "Oh. I'm sorry. As for China—"

"I know. I should say the drugs are coming from an Oriental company."

Her lips pursed, and she shook her head. "Now, you sound like Ernie Holstrom."

"Anyway," Sam continued, "the powders are coming from overseas, and the websites all have a hinky feel to them."

"Hinky?"

"Like they were put together in a hurry, and they used some translator program to write their copy. And they give it enough of a legit feel to make you think buying the powder is okay. It's weird. The whole thing feels weird."

The toast popped up, and Sonja removed it. She quickly tossed it onto a plate. Then she put two new pieces of bread into the toaster and restarted the process. She pulled the lid from the pan and scooped a couple of eggs from it. She slid a plate in front of Sam. Then she put a couple of eggs on a plate for herself and turned off the stove.

"Thank you," he said as he continued to flip through various websites.

She set a container of margarine and a knife on the counter. "What are you thinking?" she asked.

"I'm wondering why these drugs are so important." Sam set his phone to the side and began to butter his toast. "I mean, if anyone can already buy this stuff via the Internet, why assault me?"

"Twice," Sonja said. "You were assaulted twice for it."

Sam laid the knife across the margarine container. "Thank you for reminding me."

"I'm helping."

"And—" The toaster popped. While Sonja buttered her toast, he continued. "And would someone kill Isabella Taylor for illegal steroids?"

"They aren't worth as much as regular drugs, right?"

Sam's brow furrowed. "No. They aren't. Nowhere near as much."

They ate silently for several minutes. When they finished, Sonja asked, "Are you going to tell that detective about it?"

"McAfee? Yeah. I'll call him in the morning. By the way, that was a good idea you had."

"I know. I'm full of good ideas. Ready to go back to bed?"

# Chapter 23

"Steroids?"

"That's what I'm thinking," Sam said.

Detective Shane McAfee leaned back against his unmarked car and sipped his coffee. They were in the parking lot of Starbucks. Sam had called the detective and requested a meeting. McAfee said he had some follow-up on a different case that morning and would be in Liberty Lake. He could make that his first stop of the morning. "What led you to this conclusion?"

Sam laid out his theory about the drugs. A lot of it had to do with the fact that Officer Posluszny's test kits had not identified the white powder that Sam vacuumed up with the Dustbuster. To further his argument, Sam stated that it went against the goals of bodybuilders, fitness fanatics, and football players to be involved with illegal narcotics.

When he finished, Sam crossed his arms and confidently smiled. He felt he'd laid out a convincing argument. McAfee chuckled and slowly shook his head.

"What?" Sam asked.

"Have you never read the *Sports* page? Ever watched *ESPN*?"

"I've read it. Watched it. Yeah. Why?"

"Then you should know people in the sports community get hooked into illegal drugs all the time. Some of them use narcotics like its candy. Others deal in it like we're still living in the eighties."

"What's that mean?"

"It means maybe they got involved with the drugs before they went to college. Maybe they got involved after they met someone on the team. Who knows? But people in the sports community do stupid things that go against their self-interests all the time. Don't be naive."

Sam sighed. He had expected the detective to be a little excited about the possibility that the drugs were steroids. Maybe not enthusiastic, but at least intrigued by the concept. Sam decided to try a different tack. "Can you ask the lab to test for steroids? That way, we'll know for sure?"

McAfee shrugged. "They can test for anything. We won't get the results for months, though."

"But you'll ask?"

"I'll ask." The detective rubbed the side of his face. "I appreciate you calling me about this instead of running around trying to investigate it on your own. Any more than you already have."

Sam had told him about the dust-up at the gym.

"Because let me remind you, you're not a detective."

"I know that."

"You're also not a licensed private investigator."

"I know that, too."

"I'm just saying."

"I hear you, but what I can't figure is—"

"What did I just say?"

"What?"

"You're not a detective."

Sam's brow furrowed. "I know."

"So, stop trying to figure things out. Let them be."

"Can't we make conversation? A couple guys shooting the breeze. A former deputy to a detective."

McAfee's eyes narrowed as he sipped his coffee.

Expecting an interruption, Sam slowly said, "As I was saying…" When the detective didn't stop him, he continued. "I'm confused as to why either party attacked me for steroids. If only one attacked me, then that should account for both. Right?"

"Really? That's what you're hung up on?"

"If they're working together, why did both groups come after me? Unless them both being at the same gym is a coincidence."

"Coincidence?"

"You don't believe in that?"

"No, I don't. If they were both at the gym, it means something."

"Which goes back to my point, why would two groups working together attack me for the same reason? Aren't they talking?"

"There are too many variations. Maybe they aren't working together. That's the simplest explanation."

"Occam's Razor."

"Shut up," McAfee said.

"What?"

"If I have to hear another person try to explain Occam's Razor, I'm gonna puke."

"I used to be a deputy."

"Barely."

"Still," Sam said, "the simplest explanation is usually the right one. That's Occam's Razor."

McAfee rolled his eyes. "*Usually*. Every moron who learns that principle thinks they're a detective because of it. Just because it exists doesn't mean you throw away other possibilities without examining them. Maybe the folks you've come across in this really are working together, and they just don't trust each other."

Sam hadn't thought of that.

"Right there," the detective said, snapping his fingers. "That's two possibilities. The groups aren't working together, or they *are* working together, but they don't trust each other."

"Okay."

"Or maybe some unknown group stole your drugs, and both parties have braced you for them. You think they're coming at you separately, but they're actually working together. Did you ask the second group—that was the women, right? Did you ask them about the footballers?"

"I mentioned them."

"But did you *ask* about them?"

"No."

McAfee snapped his fingers again. "There you go. You don't know if they're working together or not. You're making a supposition that they're not."

"The women didn't know the men had taken the drugs."

"Maybe the women were there to double-cross the men, but the footballers got there first. Or maybe someone else stole the drugs, and both parties are trying to double-cross each other."

Sam's head was starting to hurt.

"So, in less than a minute, I gave you how many possibilities on why everything looks the way it does."

"A lot."

"A lot," McAfee said. "Occam's Razor is great, but it's only a starting place. It doesn't mean anything until you consider all possibilities. Maybe there is still a simpler explanation out there that you haven't found."

"What's simpler than saying they weren't working together?"

McAfee rubbed both hands over his face. "God, you're irritating."

"I'm only trying to figure out why I keep getting beat up."

"Because you're a terrible fighter. That's the simplest explanation. Occam's Razor."

Sam's shoulders slumped.

"Listen. Solving a case, regardless of whether it is a homicide or a garage burglary, is like putting together a puzzle."

"I'm not stupid."

The detective cocked his head at the interruption and waited. Sam realized McAfee was trying to share some wisdom. He turned his palms upward and said, "I apologize."

"So, a puzzle."

"Right, a puzzle."

"The problem is this. You don't get all the pieces when you start. You have to go out and find them—one at a time."

Sam wanted to tell him he knew all this, but McAfee seemed earnest in what he was saying. The man was on a roll.

"Some pieces are easy fits. Corner pieces if you will. You know exactly where they go and how they fit together with their neighbors."

"I've put a puzzle together."

"But while you're searching for pieces, you might stumble across one that belongs to another puzzle. But by God, you like the look of that piece. You want it to fit into your puzzle. It should fit, but it just doesn't. If you spend too much time focused on that single piece, you might miss another one—an innocuous little sucker that could bring the whole puzzle together. Get it?"

Sam nodded.

The detective glanced around before saying, "I had a murder once where a guy killed a kid for crossing his lawn."

"Really?"

"And it wasn't a harassment thing. This wasn't a neighborhood kid who tormented an old man. It was simply a guy having a bad day who took it out on a kid who was in the wrong place at the wrong time."

"You can't be suggesting I was in the wrong place for two assaults."

McAfee shook his head. "I'm not saying that. Stay focused. Sometimes the reasons people do things won't make sense. Stop trying to apply reason to the unreasonable."

"That I understand."

"I had another case where a woman tortured her roommate with a curling iron. Burned her repeatedly." McAfee touched the bottom of his coffee cup to his arm and made a sizzling sound. "Ssss."

"What'd she do that for?"

"Because the roommate ate her bag of M&Ms."

"Stop it."

"People are selfish and childish."

"Not everyone."

"If you expect others to act and think like you, you're going to be sorely disappointed. Think of the world as a giant middle school."

"You're kidding."

"I'm not. If you think of the world as a middle school, you won't be disappointed when people act out in unexpected or maniacal ways. What you must decide for yourself is, who are you going to be in that scenario? Are you going to be one of the selfish kids? Or are you going to one of the teachers?"

"Or a hall monitor like you?"

McAfee smirked. "I'm making a point."

"Not a very nice one."

"The point is this—they wanted the drugs, and they thought you had them. Sometimes, it's as simple as that."

"That's Occam's Razor."

McAfee shrugged. "Sometimes."

Sam closed his eyes and pinched the bridge of his nose. "Where was this conversation going?"

"I don't know. We're shooting the breeze like a couple guys. That's what you wanted, wasn't it?"

When he opened his eyes, Sam asked, "Can I ask you a personal question?"

"No."

"It's about your girlfriend."

The detective's face hardened. McAfee stepped back and opened his car door. "We're done."

"Wait," Sam said. "I'm sorry. I heard you were getting some pressure inside the department, and I wanted to tell you I understand what that's like."

"You want to be my friend? Is that what you're trying to say?"

Sam shook his head. "No."

"Good," the detective dropped into the driver's seat. "I don't need any new friends."

"Hey, have you charged Dom?"

"Russo? No, we let him go."

"That wasn't in the news."

McAfee settled his coffee cup into a center console holder. "It's not my job to alert the media when we decide not to charge someone."

"But you arrested him."

"No, we did not arrest him. We *detained* him. For once, the news got it right. Where did you see he was arrested?"

Sam hadn't read it or heard it anywhere official. The news had come second-hand from Sonja. He tried to replay the conversation with Jordan Withers. He couldn't remember if she said the word 'arrest' or not. "So, he's home now?"

"How would I know where he went?"

McAfee slammed his door closed and started his car. He drove away and left Sam standing in the parking lot.

* * *

Sam didn't return to his cabin to get his boat and cross the lake to Dom's house. That would have been the fun route, and he usually would have done just that, even if it added more time. Lake life usually dictated doing things the enjoyable way rather than the expedient way.

Instead, he drove around the lake to get to his friend's home. The winding road was lined with trees. Sam thought about pushing the Cinderella cassette back into the player, but decided he wanted silence instead.

He considered the problem of Isabella's murder, the drugs—which he now believed to be steroids—and his pursuers. He pushed the various thoughts back and forth, trying to make sense of them all.

When he couldn't, he came back to Detective McAfee's admonition. 'Stop trying to apply reason to the unreasonable.'

Maybe he should just let all the pieces he'd collected sit on the table of his mind. When he had enough of them, they would gel together naturally to form a picture.

While he was a deputy, most of the crimes he investigated were immediate. His thoughts drifted through a series of scenarios.

In a domestic violence call, the parties were easily identified, and he could quickly assess a situation.

Collisions were much the same way. Unless it was a hit and run, automobiles and witnesses remained on scene. The evidence and observer statements would quickly identify what happened. There often wasn't much mystery in the collisions he investigated.

Bar fights were similar. Combatants were separated, and deputies responded. More often than not, no one wanted to press charges. Mutual combat was agreed upon, and the parties went their ways. Easy peasy.

The more challenging cases, the ones without quick resolutions, received initial reports which were then kicked up to a detective. Sam didn't do any further work on those cases, and he never worried about them. Those ended up being someone else's responsibility—someone like Detective Shane McAfee.

The puzzles he had to solve as a deputy were substantially smaller than anything McAfee worked on, like a kid's puzzle in comparison. As a deputy, Sam applied a band-aid. Did that make Detective McAfee a surgeon?

He didn't like that analogy. Maybe as a deputy, he was a—

Sam was lost in thought when he focused on a Toyota Tundra coming his way. He glanced over at the driver.

Andy, he thought. *Andy!* Deidre's trainer?

Sam slammed his brakes and checked his rearview mirror. The truck disappeared around a bend. He considered making a U-turn, but the small road didn't offer an opportunity to do so. As another car appeared on Newman Lake Road behind him, Sam's chance to follow her vanished.

He pressed the accelerator and continued his journey to Dom's, which was only a couple of turns away. As he came to North Peninsula Drive, his thoughts flooded with questions about Andy.

What was she doing out here?

Did she know Dom?

Was she there to hurt him?

Sam dropped off the roadway and entered a long private driveway that serviced a multitude of addresses. Dom lived in the furthest cabin, and the driveway elevated up behind the place.

It belonged to Dom's parents, who only occasionally visited now due to their age. Dom didn't have any siblings, so it was his home year-round. When he was a kid, Dom's family only spent the summers there. It was a perfectly good place for year-round living, though.

Sam parked his car in the graveled driveway. He walked down the old wooden staircase to the cabin. He opened the door and said, "Dom?"

No answer.

He walked through the small home and called out again, "Dom?"

It only took a moment to pass through the cabin before he stepped out onto the elevated deck. He looked down onto the beach. Dom stood at the edge of his dock with his arms crossed.

"Dom?"

His friend looked up and stared for a moment. Then he nodded and began a slow walk toward the cabin.

# Chapter 24

The screen door slammed behind Dominic as he entered.

"Did you just have a visitor?" Sam asked.

"Why? You know her?"

"She's the one who punched me."

"At the grocery store?"

"No, at my—"

Dom stepped forward to study Sam's face. "Looks like she got you good. Just how many times did she hit you?"

"More than once."

"She's got a temper, that one." Dom continued into the small kitchen.

"Dude, this is serious. How do you know her?"

"The gym." Dom pulled a beer from the refrigerator. "How do you think?" He twisted the cap off the bottle and tossed it into the sink. Then he took a long pull from it. After he swallowed, he faced Sam and said, "What?"

"Are you serious? What's going on?"

"Nothing."

"Andy was here."

"Yeah, I know. Thank you. Just how hard did she hit you?"

"Hard."

"Speaking of, why did she hit you?"

"She knew Izzy."

Dom briefly scrunched his face then relaxed it. "Probably," he said and took another pull from his beer. "The girl worked with Deidre, so yeah—Andy might know her."

Sam shoved his hands in his pockets, bowed his head, and clicked his tongue against the back of his teeth.

"What are you doing?"

He glanced up.

Dom repeated, "What are you doing?"

"Trying to figure this out."

"What's to figure?"

"Isabella Taylor was killed in my house."

"In your boat," Dom corrected.

"I thought she was their connection to the lake. Now, I think it was you."

"Me? I had nothing to do with her death."

"But you brought them here."

"Them?"

"Andy and Deidre."

"I never showed them your place. Only Izzy. I told you that."

Sam pointed at the floor. "Was she here before?"

Dom wrinkled his nose. "Izzy?"

"Yes, Izzy. Was Izzy ever here—at your place?"

"No. Izzy was never here. I never met her before meeting her at Wagman's. I swear."

"But you knew Deidre and Andy from the gym?"

"So?"

"Doesn't that seem like too much of a coincidence?"

"Spokane is a small town. The Valley is even smaller."

"Did Izzy ever see you at the coffee stand?"

"I don't go through that kind of stand. I don't need cheap jollies."

"Did you know Izzy knew Deidre?"

"She told me where she worked, and I said I knew Deidre. That's all that was said. Nothing more."

"That's probably why she hooked up with you."

"Wow. Thanks for the kick to my ego."

Sam waved a hand. "I think there was some weird competition between those two."

Dom smirked. "Whatever you think, that's not why we hooked up. I would have known. Besides, I've never been with Deidre, so why would it matter?"

"What about Andy?"

"I've never been with her either."

Sam rolled his eyes. "Has she been out here before?"

"Today was the first time."

He considered Dom's build. His friend might have an undisciplined workout regime, but he was muscular throughout the upper body. "Are you buying steroids from her?"

"Andy? She doesn't sell steroids. Besides, I would never put that stuff into my body. Makes your wiener go small." He waggled his pinkie.

"Maybe she's selling it to others."

"Sam, buddy, you're not making sense."

"There were drugs in my house."

"You said something about that, but I'm still missing the connection to Andy."

"At first, I thought it was cocaine or heroin, but now I'm pretty sure it's steroids."

"That's a pretty weird drug for someone to bring to a party."

"A cop tested the drugs, and it came back negative for the majors. That means it has to be something else."

Dom sipped his beer, swished the liquid around his mouth, then swallowed. "I thought you said someone broke into your house for the drugs. So, they didn't get them?"

Sam shook his head. "They got them."

"Then what did the cop test?"

"I dropped one of the baggies, and it broke. I vacuumed up the mess."

"You vacuumed dope?" Dom's grin was full of disbelief.

"So?"

"And the cop tested the dirtbag? Is that what it's called?"

"How would I know?"

"Couldn't all that junk—the dirt and grime and such—affect the test? Maybe it really was cocaine and not steroids."

"It's steroids." Sam tapped his chest. "I can feel it in here."

"Okay. If you feel it."

"What was she doing here?"

"Andy?"

In frustration, Sam lifted his hands into the air. "Who else?"

"She wanted to know if I knew you."

"Why?"

"Why do you think?"

Sam's shoulders slumped. Why was Dom so difficult? "Because she's trying to find the stuff."

Dom cocked his head. "That would make more sense. Her story sounded fishy."

"Which was?"

"She wanted to know about you. She said you were stalking her girlfriend."

"Deidre's not her girlfriend. She's her client."

Dom pointed his beer bottle at Sam. "You know a lot about a woman you're supposedly not stalking. Now, I'm not judging. I've pursued a couple women that probably could have bordered on stalking."

Sam ignored Dom's comment. "How well do you know Deidre?"

"Not well. Just from around the gym. She's definitely a girl I could go for, but she's all about the jocks—"

"And Andy never mentioned drugs?"

"Never."

"She just asked about me?"

"That's right. She said she wanted to know about the guy who was stalking her girlfriend."

"She's not her—"

"I know, I know, but that's what she told me. And girlfriend doesn't have to mean lover. It can just mean friend. You don't have to be so literal."

"What did you tell her?"

"I said you were my friend, and you wouldn't stalk Deidre. It wasn't your style."

"Did that carry any weight?"

"I assumed so. She said thanks and left."

Sam put his hands on his hips. "What's Andy's full name?"

"It's a mouthful. Andriani Dimitriou."

"And Deidre?"

"Deidre Hearn."

"You're not bothered by any of this?"

"What's there to be bothered about?"

"Andy and Deidre are connected to Izzy."

Dom tilted the bottle of beer back and drained the remaining portion. Then he opened the fridge. "Want a beer?"

"No."

"Suit yourself." Dom twisted the cap off a new beer. He glanced toward Sam. "I'm sorry. I don't mean to be a jerk. You were asking if I was okay. Andy's an acquaintance from the gym, and she punched you."

"Don't remind me."

"You're the one who brought it up. Far as I'm concerned, she can fall off the face of the earth, and I won't lose any sleep."

"Are you okay after getting interviewed by the cops?"

His friend shook his head. "I am most definitely not okay after that."

"Why?"

"Because if any DNA results come back to me, I'm screwed. That detective is going to pin Izzy's murder on me. I've made a lot of stupid decisions in my life, Sam, but killing that girl isn't one of them."

"Then we should take a long, hard look at Deidre and Andy."

Dom slowly shook his head. "They didn't have anything to do with it. Somebody else killed her."

"How do you know?" Sam asked.

"I feel it in here," he said and tapped his chest.

"Okay," Sam said, "if you feel it."

# Chapter 25

After arriving home, Sam walked out to the deck. His mind was clouded with thoughts of Dom. He noticed Mary Jo Brakke on the beach behind her house. She stood near a clump of bushes and seemed interested in something she held in her hands. Mary Jo repeatedly flipped the item over as she examined it. Finally, she shrugged and began walking toward her cabin. The thing she held in her hand slapped absently against her right leg.

"Mrs. Brakke!" Sam called and trotted toward her.

She didn't hear him and continued to walk along the winding pathway at the rear of her cabin.

"Mrs. Brakke!"

This time she stopped and turned. Her face brightened, and she said, "Samuel." She walked back down the path toward the beach.

As Sam approached, he pointed to the square piece of cardboard she held in her hand. "What do you have there?"

"This? I found it in my bushes. It seems someone has lost the record that goes with it, though."

"May I see it?"

She handed the square piece of cardboard to Sam. It was the album cover for Night Ranger's *Midnight Madness*. The front image featured the five bandmates. The musician in the middle wore light-blue surgical scrubs and mirrored sunglasses. Sam didn't know the guy's name or the instrument he played but, based upon his appearance, Sam guessed he was a keyboardist or a drummer. Guitarists and lead singers didn't dress that way—like a dork. Across the guy's chest, someone had written a phone number.

Sam couldn't remember the last time he'd seen the album, but he recalled it being in good condition. All his father's collection was. Peter Strait had taken pride in his music, and Sam took care of the albums the same way. This cover was badly bent on one corner and heavily scraped.

"It must have blown in from somewhere," Mary Jo said.

"It's mine, Mrs. Brakke."

"Mary Jo."

"Mary Jo," he absently agreed as he studied the phone number on the album.

"There you go," she purred and rubbed the side of his arm. "Would you like to come up to the house? I can make us mimosas."

Sam's gaze drifted to her hand. "Huh?"

"And a light lunch. We can spend some time getting to know each other better."

As politely as he could, Sam said, "I'm not hungry."

Mary Jo demurely dipped her chin and caressed his arm. "Just the drinks then."

Sam stepped back. "I've got to go."

Disappointment swept across Mary Jo's face. "It's the middle of the day. Where do you have to be?"

"This." He lifted the album cover. "I've been looking for this."

"That explains nothing, Samuel."

Sam stumbled back. "I've got to go, Mrs. Brakke."

"Mary Jo," she muttered. "And you're welcome. I'm sure."

"Right." He lifted the album cover again, this time shaking it for emphasis. "Thank you." Sam turned and sprinted to his cabin.

***

He could have immediately called the number, but he waited until he was inside his cabin and away from the prying eyes of Mary Jo Brakke. She lingered on the beach until he closed his sliding glass door.

Sam pulled his cell phone from his pocket and dialed. It was answered on the first ring. A male voice said, "Tucker."

*Tucker?*

"Hello?" the man asked.

Where had he recently seen that name?

"Hello?"

The call ended.

Sam noticed the balled-up players list for the Spokane Demons on his kitchen counter. He grabbed it and smoothed it out. Near the top of the roster was the name he remembered.

Tucker Jacobson. Hometown—Post Falls, Idaho. College—North Dakota State.

He redialed the number. This time the phone was answered after the second ring.

"Who is this?" the man gruffly asked.

"Tucker Jacobson?"

Silence. He could hear the man breathing.

"Tucker?"

"What do you want?"

"Tucker Jacobson?"

The phone went dead.

Sam put his phone into his pocket and reconsidered the album cover. Why would someone write Tucker's phone number here? Wasn't it more convenient to just type it into a cell phone? Perhaps, they couldn't do that. Maybe this was a message passed on the sly.

*Then why write it on an album cover?*

He glanced around his house. There weren't many things to write on. Perhaps this was the only thing handy. So, what happened then?

Sam stepped back onto the deck. Maybe it blew away from here. Perhaps someone put it on the railing, and the wind caught it and carried it away.

Or perhaps someone angrily threw it like a Frisbee toward Mary Jo's house. Then the album cover could have blown into the bushes.

It was unlikely Izzy took it with her down to his boat. If that happened and the album cover blew away, it would have likely gone into the water.

No, Sam decided, the cover was lost up here, on the deck, before Izzy ever made it to the boat.

What to do about it now?

*** 

Detective Shane McAfee leaned against the kitchen counter. In his left hand, he held the *Midnight Madness* album cover. In his right, he had the wrinkled Spokane Demon's roster. "Tucker Jacobson," he said.

"The quarterback."

"And what exactly do you think he did?"

Sam shrugged. "I don't know if he did anything, but this album cover was missing when I came home. And it has his number on it."

"You're sure it's his number?"

"Well, no. But how many Tucker's do you know?"

"I've got a nephew named Tucker."

"Okay, but—"

"And there's a guy in Fleet Services named Tucker."

"I meant—"

"Although it's his last name, but we still call him Tucker. That counts, right?"

Sam fell silent and watched McAfee.

"Two Tuckers," the detective said. "I know two of them."

"Good for you."

"You're not sure it's the quarterback's number."

"No, I'm not, but when I asked if it was Tucker Jacobson, he hung up on me."

"That's why you called me. You want me to find out."

"That's not why I did it. I'm playing nice. Following the rules."

"So, that means you're done sticking your nose in my case?"

"I've learned my lesson."

"You haven't answered my question."

Sam rolled his eyes. "Okay, I'm done." He didn't want to be done investigating, but he was getting in over his head. He should leave well enough alone and just enjoy his time at the lake.

Idle hands, he thought and shoved both of his into his pockets. He needed to stop worrying about that and let things be.

McAfee stuck both the album cover and the crumpled paper into his left hand. "I'll look into Tucker."

"Wait. You're taking that?"

"It might be evidence."

"Maybe not. If it's needed, you can always come back and get it."

McAfee glanced at the cardboard cover.

"It belonged to my father."

The detective considered it a moment further and did the same for the roster of football players. He tossed the crinkled paper onto the counter. He waggled the Night Ranger album cover. "This," he said, "is evidence. I'm taking it."

McAfee started toward the door.

"Don't lose it," Sam said. "I want it back."

* * *

"Two nights in a row," Sonja said.

"I could have stayed at my cabin."

"No, I like this. It feels like we're a real couple. Some time here. Some at your place. It's nice."

Sonja moved about the kitchen as she fixed dinner. On the stove a pot of spaghetti worked toward a boil while a pan of red sauce simmered. She wore a little yellow sundress underneath a brown apron with stitched flowers on its front. Sam remained silent as he watched her.

Before adding the tomato sauce, Sonja had sauteed spicy sausage, green peppers, sweet onions, and garlic. Now, as she slowly stirred the concoction, she tossed some salt and pepper into it.

"No comment?" she asked.

"It smells good," Sam said.

Sonja faced him with her hands on her hips. In her right was a spatula that dripped red sauce. "About us being a real couple. I said, it feels like we're a real couple, and you remained quiet. It was like you swallowed your tongue."

Sam scrunched his face. "Had I done that, I would have gagged. I wouldn't be quiet at all."

She pointed the spatula at him and waggled it. More sauce dripped to the tile floor. "You know what I mean."

He had to be careful now. Sonja was laying relationship land mines in hopes of guiding the conversation to where she wanted it. He had to carefully navigate through that minefield without blowing himself up. "It does sound nice."

Sonja clucked. "Sounds nice," she said disapprovingly. She turned back to the stove and stirred the sauce. "That's all you can say—it sounds nice."

"What am I supposed to say?"

She glanced back. "How about you say you feel the same way? I said it feels like we're a couple, but you must not feel it." She angrily stirred the sauce. "It sounds nice. Who says that?"

Without realizing it, Sam had stepped on the first land mine—the one about feelings. What could he say now to avoid worsening the situation? If he agreed with her that it felt like they were a couple, he would deepen the relationship in a false manner, and he didn't want to do that to her. Sam cared for Sonja, but not in an until-death-do-them-part way.

Agreeing with her feelings wouldn't work. Neither would minimizing them because that would lead to an argument. He couldn't explain his feelings as they were in direct opposition to hers. To Sonja, it would sound like rationalizing. She wanted a long-term commitment from Sam, but he repeatedly told her he wasn't looking for that type of relationship. He couldn't help it if she refused to listen. She had her agenda for their future, and it didn't align with his goals.

He'd already stepped on one mine, and it happened so quickly that he now second-guessed himself. Sam wondered if he should have stayed at his cabin and risked another run-in with the football players or Deidre and Andy. At least a punch in the head could be dealt with easier than an emotional discussion with Sonja.

She glanced back. "You're giving me the silent treatment? Nice."

"What? No. I was thinking."

"About how to avoid my question?"

"Not avoid it, but to answer it honestly."

She flicked off the stove. "It's fine. You don't feel the same way. After last summer, I should be used to it by now."

"Sonja—"

"No."

She lifted the pan of spaghetti and took it to the sink. She turned it over and let the contents plop loudly into the basin.

"Oops," she muttered, "I ruined dinner."

Sonja dropped the pan on top of the noodles, then walked by him. She paused long enough to say, "You should go."

He remained seated at the table until he heard her bedroom door close.

# Chapter 26

Sam didn't want to go home.

It bothered him that his door had been kicked in and his house burgled. He still hadn't gotten the lock fixed, so anyone could push their way inside if they wanted.

He also couldn't shake the memory of Andy assaulting him on his deck and then inside his living room. Did it upset him that a woman had beat him up? Sure, he admitted. He'd like to think it was because she got the drop on him—surprised him—but the doubt remained that maybe he wasn't that good of a fighter. Even as a deputy, he'd never been in many fights.

His cabin had always been a safe, happy place for him—until now.

Sam drove aimlessly about for a time. Where could he go? he wondered. The better question might be—where should he go?

If he was still sticking his nose into the murder of Isabella Taylor, perhaps he should go to Deidre's apartment to continue the follow-up on that conversation.

But he wasn't in any hurry to see Andy again since the concern about his fighting skills lingered in the back of his mind. As Dom had said, that one had a temper, and Sam wasn't in the mood to provoke her.

He thought about Tucker Jacobson and wondered if Izzy knew the quarterback. Could the phone number on the Night Ranger album have been for her? Maybe he should track Tucker down. Since Izzy knew the two linemen, she might have known Tucker.

Would it even matter if she knew him? At that point, all Sam had concerning Tucker Jacobson was a phone number scrawled on an album cover. And was he even sure it belonged to Tucker Jacobson? No, he wasn't.

In the end, none of this mattered. He told Detective McAfee he would stay out of this. The least he could do was stay true to his word.

Sam pulled into the parking lot of The Super Fan. His stomach rumbled with hunger as he turned off his car's engine.

*** 

He pushed a French fry around in some ketchup before shoving it into his mouth. As he chewed, he watched the pitcher on the television inspect a baseball the umpire had just tossed to him.

At the top of the seventh, the Mariners and the Athletics were locked in a one-one tie. The game had been a yawner, but Sam enjoyed baseball—even a slow-moving match like this.

Dominic Russo slid onto the stool next to him. "I can't wait for football season."

"It's only May," Sam said. "Besides, football means winter's coming."

"Fair enough." Dom waved to the bartender, pointed to Sam's beer then himself. The bartender nodded his understanding. Dom then studied Sam's face. "I know that look."

"What look?"

"You two are back at it, aren't you?"

Sam stared at the TV for a few moments before shrugging.

"I knew it. Where is she?"

"Cooling off."

"What was it this time?"

"I don't share my feelings."

Dom patted Sam's back. "You've had that argument before, my friend."

"And I'm sure we'll have it again before the summer's over."

"Wouldn't it be better never to get involved with her again? There are plenty of chicks in the sea. Why torture yourself with this one?"

Sam didn't need Dom reminding him that he was violating his second rule—*No attachments*. He turned his attention back to the game. "I like her."

"Enough to take her with you when you leave for the winter?"

His shoulders slumped. "Not you, too."

"I'm helping you see the reality."

"Of what?"

"That you're a pig like the rest of us."

On the television, a batter drove a hard drive to the shortstop, who caught it after a single hop. The baseman zinged the throw to first for the out. That ended the side, and the game went to commercial.

Sam turned toward Dom. "I'm honest with her."

"Honesty doesn't mend a broken heart."

The bartender placed Dom's beer on the counter and asked Sam if he wanted another. He said he was fine.

To Dom, Sam said, "Why do I have to conform to what society dictates?"

"The hell does that mean?"

"I'm judged for how I live my life."

Dom sipped his beer. "Who's judging you?"

"Everyone."

"Everyone?" Dom smirked. "That sounds like hyper bowl."

"Hyperbole."

"Huh?"

"It's pronounced hyperbole," Sam said, "and I'll concede saying everyone might be hyperbolic."

Dom's face pinched. "Hyper *what*?"

"But I do get judged for snowbirding—especially at my age. And that grates on a guy after a while."

"People are jealous. Hell, I'm jealous, and I live at the lake."

"It's the same with relationships. I don't want to be in one. At least for the near term."

"And everyone judges you for that?"

"Exactly."

"Everyone is hyperbole." Dom pronounced it correctly that time.

"Why am I considered a bad person because I'm honest with what I want out of life?"

"I'm going to tell you something, and it might hurt your delicate sensitivities."

"What?"

"Most people don't care about you."

Sam lifted his eyebrows.

"I'm serious," Dom continued. "Most people don't give two damns what you do—whether it's good or bad. They're just trying to live their lives."

"Thank you, Dr. Russo."

"But the person who cares—"

"Is Sonja," Sam said. "I know."

"No, dummy. The person who cares is you."

"Me?"

Dom tapped Sam's chest. "Uh-huh. It bothers you that you live your life without a meaningful connection with a woman."

"That makes no sense."

"You're a romantic, Sam."

"Don't be stupid."

"I know your type. It's why you came home and reconnected so quickly with Sonja. You want to pretend you're a dog, but—"

"A dog?"

"—you're a scoundrel."

"Oh."

"See? You don't even like the idea of being a dirty dog. Me? I've embraced it."

"You're definitely a scoundrel."

"It's my nature. Your nature is to be a good guy. Which is why this whole thing with Sonja is so painful for her."

"So, I should what? Apologize?"

"You should break it off. Make it clean and quick."

Sam sipped his beer.

"Whatever you do, don't keep her in suspense. She's a great girl who deserves better than you keeping her on the line."

"Said the scoundrel."

"You're not me, though. It's not in your nature to treat a girl like that, and it bothers you."

"Knock it off."

"You need to make a decision and get comfortable with it. One way or another." Dom glanced toward the entrance of the bar. A tall, voluptuous woman walked in. She wore tight denim shorts and a sweatshirt. "I'll be back. I know that dancer. She'll expect me to come over and flirt."

"Scoundrel."

Dom patted Sam's shoulder as he left to talk with the stripper.

Sam stared at his beer and considered what he should do about Sonja.

***

He knocked several times, but she didn't answer. Sam wandered into the parking lot to find her stall. Her car wasn't there, which meant Sonja had left.

No kidding, he thought. Way to state the obvious.

Sam called her cell phone then, but it went straight to voice mail. Either her phone was off, or she was screening his calls and rejecting them. He sent her a text message— PLEASE CALL ME.

With nowhere left to go, he decided to return home— safety be damned.

Dom had said Sam wasn't the type of guy who liked meaningless relationships with women. Yet, he met many women while he traveled. Some had turned into relationships that lasted the entire length of his stays. Others were shorter in term—like the programming director he'd met in Hawaii. He could have imagined a longer relationship with her if the circumstances had been different.

But did that mean he should give up his life—the one he wanted to experience—to meet society's demands? Or should he ask a woman to join him on his travels? Would he enjoy that?

What would happen if it didn't turn out as he hoped? Could he send the woman home, or would he be forced to travel with her forever?

When Sam pulled in front of his home, he expected to find Sonja's car there. Unfortunately, the driveway was empty. He considered driving back to Sonja's, but he decided that was foolish, partly because his desire to leave was from a lingering fear that continued to plague him. The drugs were gone from his house. Therefore, no one was likely to return for them now.

This internal debate ended quickly, and Sam pulled into his driveway. He turned off the Ford and sat for a while in the quiet of the lakeside neighborhood. When he tired of that, he headed for the house. He pushed on the front door, and the lock popped open.

Sam frowned. He would need to get that fixed soon. The lock was only secure if someone respected it as such.

He went straight for the kitchen and pulled a beer from the refrigerator. The nerves about someone breaking into his house, along with the fight with Sonja, had him agitated. A cold beer and a few minutes on the deck would calm him down.

After snapping the can of beer open, Sam took a long pull. He nearly spit it out when a male voice said, "We've been wondering when you'd come home."

# Chapter 27

Sam spun to see Hoyt Jefferson—Mr. Potato Head—sitting on the living room couch. He'd been distracted walking into the cabin, but what would he have done if he had noticed the man? Jefferson sat with one ankle crossed over a knee—a relaxed position for waiting. He wasn't ready to fight.

Or in a position to pursue.

Sam tossed his beer into the sink—there was no need to create a mess—and bolted toward the front door.

Toma Papani stepped out of Sam's grandmother's room to block the small hallway. Sam's eyes widened, and he grabbed helplessly at the wall as he stumbled to a stop. He then hunched over, lifted his arms to protect his face, and tucked his elbows into his sides—the upright combat turtle.

With irritation clearly in his voice, Papani ordered, "Sit down."

Sam's arms tightened around his head as he waited for the bulky man to rain blows down upon him.

"Unless you want me to hit you. That I can do."

Sam spread his arms slightly so he could peer up through them. He knew better than to poke his head up like a gopher. The last time he did that, which was only earlier in the day, he'd gotten punched in the head by an ill-tempered female bodybuilder.

Toma Papani held a fist the size of a Christmas ham in front of Sam's face. "Choice is yours."

"I'll sit."

"Wise decision."

Sam quickly straightened then backpedaled into the living room.

"We were starting to get worried," Jefferson said.

"About?"

"You. We thought we made a mistake coming here."

Had Sam only listened to the little voice inside his head, he wouldn't have returned home. He could have stayed at Sonja's until she came back, and then he could have apologized for being a jerk. But hadn't he been thinking earlier that a punch to the head was easier than dealing with his feelings?

Where did all that big talk go? Sam wondered. Steeling his resolve, he asked in a surprisingly warbled voice, "What do you want?"

From behind him, Papani muttered, "Answers."

"And if you don't give the right ones, tough guy," Jefferson said, "my friend is going to knock the taste out of your mouth."

"Is that even possible?" Sam immediately regretted the wise-ass comment.

Since it came from behind, he never saw the blow that hit him alongside the head. And Sam could only assume it was made with Papani's open hand as it felt moderately padded. However, that's like saying a collision with a freight train could be cushioned by a mattress tied around the nose of its engine.

Sam's head jerked sideways from the blow, and he collapsed to one knee. A chorus of bells clanged inside his head. He blinked multiple times and opened his mouth repeatedly to release the sudden pressure inside his skull. He must have resembled a fish out of water.

Jefferson leaned forward in his chair. His big ears stuck out from the side of his head like Dumbo readying to take flight. "Still there?"

Sam scrunched his eyes. "Huh?"

"The taste in your mouth. Is it still there?"

He nodded and set off another chorus of bells.

"That's good," Jefferson said. "Now, about those answers."

"Ask away," Sam whispered as he struggled back to his feet.

"Why were you following us?"

"What are you talking about? I wasn't following you."

His response to Jefferson wasn't flippant or argumentative as Sam genuinely was confused by the man's question. Thus, the second blow from behind completely surprised him.

It was definitely from a fist, and it landed on his kidney—the right one. Sam arched his back and tried to scream, but the pain was so intense that only silence came from his lungs. He dropped to both knees as he continued his quiet shriek. Then he flopped to his side and clutched at his side. When his voice finally returned, he howled in pain.

Jefferson leaned forward. "Toma stung you good, huh?"

Sam writhed on the floor. He wanted to cry big, gushing tears—the type only seen in movies—but the excruciating pain seemed to stop all minor systems in his body from working.

"Why were you following us?" the pale lineman asked loudly.

As he continued to squeal, Sam spasmed and kicked his legs for several moments. When he finally calmed to a dull moan, Hoyt Jefferson repeated his question.

"Why were you following us?"

Sam rolled over to his hands and knees and sucked deeply for air. Time took on a surreal quality then. It was like a rubber band stretched to its limits—just hanging there in some sort of suspended moment.

He realized one of his flip-flops had fallen off. He looked languidly around for it. They were a new pair of flip-flops that he'd purchased in a specialty shop near Duke's in Honolulu. He couldn't find his favorite brand—Teva's Mush—so he bought a set of Reef's Fannings. Regardless, they were still a decent pair, and he would hate to have to replace them since they were so new.

Sam's gaze went under the couch that Jefferson sat on. The missing flip-flop wasn't there.

*Where could one flip-flop have gone?*

He had bought the new set after blowing out one while walking on the beach with the cinnamon-skinned beauty who smelled of... geez, he could never place that scent. Would he spend the rest of his days searching for that essence? Always wondering what it was and questioning those aromas that came close. Sam inhaled deeply in hopes of reminding himself of the scent.

Hoyt Jefferson leaned forward in his seat so he and Sam were almost face-to-face. Sam could smell the lineman's breath—hot and oniony—and he almost smiled at the ridiculousness of the man's ears.

"Avoiding the question is the same as a wrong answer."

The rubber band of time snapped back into place, and Sam immediately realized what the offensive lineman meant. He flopped onto his back and held his legs and hands out in a defensive position, much like that of an upside-down cockroach.

Toma Papani pulled his leg back, readying for a kick.

"Wait!" Sam hollered.

Jefferson lifted his hand to pause his friend from striking Sam. "What?"

"I was following the woman from the coffee stand. Not you." For added emphasis, Sam repeated, "Not you!"

"The coffee stand?" Jefferson asked.

"She was at that gym."

Jefferson glanced at Papani. "Deidre?"

"Yeah," the Samoan said and relaxed his leg.

"So, you weren't following us?" Jefferson asked. "You were following Deidre. Interesting. What do you want with her?"

Sam glanced between the two linemen. "I'm trying to find who killed Izzy."

"Why?" the pale lineman asked. "Do think Deidre killed her?"

Still on his back, Sam shrugged.

"You don't know."

"No," he said, "but she's involved somehow."

"How?"

"I don't know yet. I'm working on it."

Jefferson glanced at Papani, then back to Sam. "Are you a private investigator or something?"

"No."

"Then why do you care?"

"This is my house."

"So?" Papani said.

Sam looked up at the Samoan. "She was found in my boat."

Papani said "So" again and re-cocked his leg as if readying for a strike.

"I was mad," Sam blurted. "Mad that she was killed here. I figured that gave me a right to ask around."

Jefferson rolled his lower lip down and nodded. "I get that."

"Yeah," Papani said. "Me, too." The Samoan moved toward the kitchen and leaned against the counter.

When the darker lineman crossed his arms, Sam figured the beatings had stopped. He quickly crab-walked across the floor to sit with his back against the stereo system. "I'm sorry," he said. It seemed like an odd comment to say to a couple of guys who had just beat him, so he added a shrug for extra measure.

"What are you sorry for?" Jefferson asked.

"For thinking you guys killed Izzy."

Papani dropped his arms and stepped toward Sam. "The hell?"

Jefferson quickly lifted his hand to stop his friend. "Hold on."

The Samoan paused, but his face twisted in anger.

"Why would we do that?" Jefferson asked. "She was with us."

"Part of your crew?"

Papani rolled his eyes. "Our crew."

"She was our girl," Jefferson said.

"Your girl?"

"*Our* girl." Papani waggled his finger between him and Jefferson. "She was with us."

Gross, thought Sam.

Taking a full step toward Sam, Papani asked, "Got a problem with that?"

"No."

"Your face says otherwise."

"No, it doesn't."

"Yeah," Jefferson said, "it kind of does."

Papani now hovered over Sam, who suddenly flopped to his back and assumed the combat turtle position. He wasn't even trying to pretend he had fighting skills. "Wait!"

The darker lineman leaned over Sam with a menacing glare.

Jefferson remained on the couch and asked, "What are we waiting for?"

"Tell me about the drugs."

"No," Jefferson said.

"You guys came back for them."

Both men remained silent. "We already got them."

"Before," Sam said. "I meant before. What was so important about some steroids that you would break into a crime scene?"

"Steroids?" Papani snorted and straightened.

Sam glanced at Jefferson, who was shaking his head. "It wasn't steroids?"

The pale lineman stood and looked at his friend. "Let's go."

The Samoan jerked a thumb toward Sam. "Should I leave him with a parting gift?"

Jefferson shrugged. "If you want to."

Sam's eyes widened as Papani leaned over him. Sam turtled up as fast as he could. He pulled his legs tight into him and crossed them at the ankles. Even at that moment, he knew locking his ankles together was a silly move, but it still felt oddly comforting. His forearms pressed tight against his cheeks, and he interlaced his fingers over the top of his head. He could see the big Samoan through the space between his forearms.

Disappointment crossed Papani's face. "Forget it. He fights like a little girl." He shook his head and stepped away.

When the two linemen moved into the hallway, Sam scrambled to his feet. He kicked off the single flip-flop he still had on, so he was barefoot. Outside, Sam said, "Why don't you care?"

Both men turned toward him. "About?" they said in unison.

"Her death. Izzy's dead, and you don't care. You said she was your girl."

Papani moved toward Sam, but Jefferson held out an arm to stop him.

"Of course, we care," the pale lineman said. "We're sad she's dead, but it's the law's problem."

"That's all you feel for her?"

Jefferson shrugged. "She was a groupie."

"I thought she was a cheerleader," Sam said.

"Our cheerleaders aren't paid. They're basically groupies."

"Or wives," Papani said.

Jefferson sneered. "Forever groupies."

"The worst," the Samoan agreed.

"And she wasn't involved with the drugs?"

"Why do you care so much about the drugs?" Jefferson asked.

Papani clenched his fists. "You a cop?"

Sam lifted his hands in surrender. "No."

"Didn't think so," the darker lineman said. "You don't fight like one."

"I won't ask any more about the drugs, okay?"

Jefferson and Papani glanced at one another and turned to leave.

"Why did she have a party here? What did she tell people?"

Jefferson paused and looked back. "Hell, I don't know. Why do people do anything? At first, Izzy said this was her boyfriend's place, but after a while, people figured out that she hijacked somebody's cabin. That freaked out some people, and they left."

"Answer me this," Sam said, "Who brought her? There was no car here when I got home, so somebody brought her."

"We brought her," Jefferson said, "but we left before the party was over."

"Did she say who she was leaving with?"

"Leaving? She said she was spending the night even though we started to believe she broke into the cabin."

"And why did she hang out at Wagman's convenience store while you worked?"

"You ask questions like a cop," Papani said.

Jefferson put his hand on the Samoan's shoulder. "She liked us. Besides, she didn't have much else going on besides the coffee stand."

"What about the drugs? Who brought them to the party?"

Jefferson shook his head. "You said no more questions about the drugs, but here you are—asking more questions about them. I'm starting to agree with Toma. I think you're a narc."

Papani's fists balled, and he moved toward Sam.

"I'm not a cop." Sam stepped backward. "I swear. I don't care about the drugs. The drugs don't matter. I'm interested in the boyfriend."

Papani muttered, "Pfft."

"Were you jealous?"

"About a boyfriend?" Jefferson chuckled. The Samoan snickered as well.

"Izzy had plenty of boyfriends," the pale lineman said. "She was good for a tumble, was all. Understand, Izzy wasn't girlfriend material. She and the truth didn't spend a lot of time together."

"Meaning what? She lied?"

Jefferson looked at Papani briefly, then shrugged. When his focus returned to Sam, he said, "Tell us you're not a cop."

"I'm not a cop."

"You swear?" the two men asked in unison.

"Yes!"

Jefferson inhaled deeply and said, "She said her boyfriend was a buyer."

"Did you meet him?"

Both linemen shook their heads.

"He was a no show," Papani offered.

Jefferson added, "Or he never existed."

"If you guys sell—" Sam raised his hands in surrender. "I don't care about the drugs, and I'm not a cop. But why were you out here doing yard work for Ernie Holstrom if you're dealing?"

Jefferson shook his head. "We're not dealing. At least, not yet."

"Not yet," Papani agreed.

"This is our first score," the pale lineman said. "If we did this right, we would be on to bigger and better things. We could finally stop doing backbreaking work."

"Is that why you left the drugs behind? In hopes the buyer would show up and buy your score?"

"You think we left them behind on purpose?" Jefferson said. "We thought they were in the truck when we left. She must have gotten them out at some point."

"Izzy double-crossed you."

Jefferson blew out a force of air. "Double-crossed implies she was with us. She wasn't. She was a groupie."

"No loyalty," Papani added.

"Groupies don't have loyalty," Jefferson said. "It's in their nature."

Sam thought about Izzy's rendezvous with Dom inside his cabin. The statement about loyalty rang true. Still, it didn't mean she deserved to die over it.

"Plain and simple," Jefferson said, "she stole from us. We wouldn't have hurt her for it, though. We don't hit women."

Papani smirked. "Although we hit guys who fight like women."

Sam pretended to laugh.

"When we found out what happened," Jefferson continued, "that the stuff was missing, we came back, but the cops were here. We thought it was forever lost. Imagine our happiness to get it back."

The two linemen turned to leave, but Sam still had one unanswered question. "Has Detective McAfee contacted you yet?"

Jefferson stopped and faced Sam. "You're the one who told him about us."

Sam swallowed. "No."

The Samoan pointed at him. "Yeah, you are."

"Not me," Sam protested.

"Then how did you know he's looking for us?" Jefferson asked.

"He told me."

The two linemen glanced at each other.

Jefferson's eyes narrowed. "That still doesn't answer how he found out about us."

Sam shrugged. "He's a detective."

While Jefferson and Papani pondered his simple statement, Sam slowly backed inside his house and closed the door. He leaned his shoulder into the door. For a minute, he waited for a blunt force to slam against the home, but nothing happened. From somewhere down the road, a loud engine came to life and revved several times. Then it faded from the neighborhood.

With his back against the door, Sam slid to the floor.

# Chapter 28

When he awoke, Sam checked his phone. Still no response from Sonja to his last call or texts. He shuffled out to the kitchen and started a pot of coffee. Then he headed toward the bathroom.

In the shower, he took his time. The hot water soothed his aching body. Not only did he still feel tired, but various parts hurt from the damage inflicted by the offensive lineman and the female bodybuilder.

Sam turned the water up to the highest temperature he could tolerate and let it pulsate down upon him. He stayed that way for some time until the water cooled. Then he clicked off the shower and got out.

After dressing, he poured himself a cup of coffee and rechecked his phone—still nothing from Sonja. He went out on the deck and positioned himself so the low morning sun could shine on his face.

Sam considered calling Detective McAfee to update him on the contact he had with the two linemen. It probably wouldn't mean much in McAfee's investigation now. Sam believed the two men didn't kill Izzy. Of course, he could be wrong. He seemed to be in error a lot lately. Calling the detective could wait.

Sam sipped his coffee.

He wished Sonja would call or text. It didn't even have to be a positive message. Even an "I hate you" was better than nothing. He just wanted to know that she still existed.

Sitting there, wishing she would call him, made him feel powerless. He hated that feeling, especially considering the past couple of days. It also felt like a violation of the *No drama* rule. Since that was the case, he should do something about it.

***

It only took ten minutes to get to Sonja's condo. He drove through the parking lot and didn't see her car in its usual stall. That didn't stop him from getting out and ringing the doorbell to her unit.

No answer.

Sam hung around for a few minutes until he decided to cruise her local haunts. Well, what had been her local haunts last year. He wasn't sure she still went to them.

He drove to Liberty Lake Coffee Company and walked in. The small cafe teemed with activity. Along with hissing from an espresso machine, a cacophony of voices filled the small building.

Several attractive women seated at a table were engaged in eager conversation. As they sipped their iced coffees, they resembled clones of one another. Baseball hats and ponytails. Tight-fitting tops. Since they were sitting, Sam couldn't see what all of them wore, but the closest to him had on yoga pants and bright running shoes without socks. He imagined them all sporting the same garb. It was as if they proudly walked out of a secret meeting for Liberty Lake Mothers and took over a table at the cafe.

Two older men sat together at a smaller table. Each had a magazine and coffee, and neither bothered talking. They didn't look up at Sam, and every time one of the women laughed loudly, one of the men winced with displeasure.

The barista smiled at Sam as he approached. She was in her late twenties with dirty blond dreadlocks. She wore a wrinkled and stretched-out V-neck T-shirt. Tattoos of empty stars ran along the exposed portion of her chest. "What can I get you?"

"I was looking for my—" He hesitated to say the word. Speaking it would put him into a weird relationship position, and he hadn't said the word in at least a decade. Sam glanced around but didn't see Sonja, so he mumbled it. "—girlfriend."

The barista watched him expectantly.

"Sonja Boyd."

"Oh," the woman said, and her face brightened. "Sonja's the best, but I haven't seen her yet this morning."

"Okay."

"Are you expecting her?"

Sam glanced around the small cafe. "I was hoping to surprise her."

"And your name?"

He turned back to the barista. "Sam."

The young woman's face darkened. "She's mentioned you."

"She has?"

The barista grabbed an empty cup and turned away. "I'll let her know you stopped by."

He took that as his cue to leave.

*** 

After seeing Deidre's car parked in its stall, Sam parked in a visitor spot at the Argonne Vista apartments. He knew he shouldn't be there. The case was McAfee's, and he was supposed to be out of it, but the visit from the two linemen last night bothered him. Also, Sonja's disappearance left him feeling oddly alone. What he wanted right now was to distract himself with something—*anything*.

Idle hands, he thought.

Sam walked the concrete path to the front of Deidre's building then ascended the three flights of stairs. After pressing the doorbell, there was a pleasant bing-bong from inside. Footsteps came to the door, then a pause, and the door opened.

"Yeah?"

Sam didn't know what to say. He had expected Deidre or perhaps Andy, but standing in the doorway was a handsome man who stood several inches taller than Sam. He wore only unbuttoned faded jeans. His shoulders were broad and thick, but he had a mid-section paunch. Since he had almost no hair on his torso, it almost looked like the belly of a chubby baby.

"Help you?" the man said in an irritated tone.

Sam leaned to look around the man, but the guy moved to block his view. "Is Deidre here?"

"She's in the can."

Classy, thought Sam.

The guy studied Sam before asking, "You with the management company or something?"

"Or something."

"Girl scouts then."

Sam smirked.

"Nah. You're too relaxed to be management. Maybe you're trying to get with her."

"I'll come back."

"Probably should think twice about that." The guy tucked his chin and lowered his voice. "Unless you're going to tell me what this is about."

There was nothing to gain in arguing with the guy, and if he'd learned anything recently, it was that his fighting skills were not as sharp as he believed. Sam kept his mouth shut and turned to leave.

The guy's face suddenly relaxed. "You look familiar."

Sam stopped and glanced back. Now that he was staring at the guy, he had the same feeling—he looked familiar, too.

"How do I know you?"

"No idea," Sam said.

The guy muttered, "Huh," then swung the door closed in Sam's face.

Sam stood on the landing for a moment longer, then headed down to his car.

\*\*\*

He returned home, grabbed a sweatshirt and a beer, and walked onto the deck. It was a little past one in the afternoon, so the sun was just beyond its zenith. His cabin was mostly in the shade now. That made it a little cool to be sitting outside, so he slipped into thicker outerwear.

He sat and sipped the beer.

For a time, his mind wandered through his drama with Sonja. This was precisely why he had his rules and why he avoided long-term relationships. It was an unnecessary expenditure of time and energy to worry about this. She knew he was leaving at the end of the summer, yet she wanted to get into a relationship with him.

Should he even call it a relationship? No, he decided. Doing so would invite him to make poor decisions where she was concerned. He re-framed his statement.

Sonja knew he was leaving at the end of the summer, yet she wanted to get involved with him. Therefore, Sonja should have adjusted her expectations accordingly. He had not led her on. He had been quite clear of his plans.

This had happened before, he recalled. Not last year. No, last year, she was involved with someone when he returned. Wait, Sam thought, that wasn't correct. Sonja was most definitely in a relationship with somebody else. She made that very clear.

Then, near the end of the summer, after that relationship ended, she came around to rekindle with Sam. They had had an on-again/off-again— What was a better word than relationship? he wondered.

*Courtship?* Eww. Too old-fashioned.

*Thing?* No. That's terrible.

*Situation?* Sam shrugged. Situation would work fine.

They had occasionally lost touch throughout their twenties, which was probably a metaphorical dodging of the bullet. Who knows what could have happened if they actually dated when he was younger? Might they have ended up married with kids? Would that have been a bad thing?

He'd known Sonja during high school, but she was an overbearing force. She'd wanted them to go out, but he avoided her because of her forwardness. In fact, it was during their junior year that she first pronounced her love for him and that they would end up married one day. It wasn't like Sam to evade interested girls, but teenaged Sonja was not the calm, even-headed girl she was today.

He smiled at his joke.

The two of them finally hooked up after Sam started his snowbirding lifestyle. Sonja balked at the status of their circumstance when he left for the first winter. When he returned, she had a new boyfriend. She and Sam didn't even talk that year.

The next time he came home, Sonja announced she didn't want him snowbirding anymore. He didn't get a say in the matter. Well, Sam was not going to be involved with a woman making those demands. When he left for the next winter, she threatened to never speak to him again.

Then the fourth summer came—last summer—and they dated for a bit. Even though it was only for about a month, she called their situation—yeah, he liked that word much better than relationship—she called their situation off repeatedly, only to restart it a day or two later.

Sonja would never fully accept the way things were. Duh.

Sam sipped his beer.

Well, her acceptance of his snowbirding wasn't his concern. He couldn't control how she thought or how she acted. He could only control himself. He had told her his plans years ago. She could accept them for what they were and be with him, or she could reject his rules for living and not be with him. Whether she believed it or not, she had power in this relationship—*situation*, he corrected—and he wasn't going to allow her to make him feel bad for living the life he wanted to live.

A boat motored by, and the family inside waved up to Sam. He lifted his beer in return.

Sam's gaze dropped to his boat, and his thoughts drifted to Isabella Taylor and the football linemen. So, she was their girlfriend. Could a groupie be called a girlfriend?

Why not? thought Sam.

It might be a strange relationship, but the world was full of odd relationships. He'd seen plenty of them while he was a deputy, and he'd seen many more through his travels.

Thinking of relationships led his thoughts to Deidre and the familiar-looking guy at her apartment. A handsome guy with a doughy gut. Sam paused with his beer near his lips. That was twice that he thought the guy was handsome. That wasn't weird for him to think that, was it?

He shrugged and sipped.

The guy *was* handsome. It was a fact. There was nothing weird about it.

Andy the Trainer couldn't be happy about that arrangement. Fortunately, Andy was Deidre's trainer and not her roommate, which might create a challenging living situation.

Sam bolted out of his chair.

*Where the hell did Izzy Taylor live?*

He'd spent days looking for her killer and hadn't once thought about looking for where she lived. Why had he missed thinking about it?

Could it have been the drama with Sonja? Maybe.

Or the drama with Dom getting arrested? Unlikely.

What about interference from the linemen? Oh yeah.

And Deidre and Andy? Them, too.

But he should have thought about it sooner. God, he was out of practice being a deputy. Except, he wasn't a deputy, was he? Sam corrected his thinking—his investigating skills needed exercising. That was a better spin on things.

Sam stepped toward his cabin but stopped. Then he started toward the edge of the deck and stopped again. McAfee would surely have been to her apartment or her house or whatever she lived in. It would have been Homicide Detective 101 to go to the deceased's place of residence and search it.

Sam dropped back into his chair.

So, there was probably nothing to gain by searching there. Besides, he told the detective he would stay out of the man's case. Although, he violated that promise by going to Deidre's earlier.

Sam rechecked his phone and sighed. Nothing from Sonja. He could sit around waiting for her to call him, or he could do something.

Idle hands, he thought.

He pushed out of his chair and hurried down the steps to his dock.

*** 

"What am I looking for?" Nicki asked.

"Where she might have lived, or if she had a roommate."

Nicki sat at the table and worked her cell phone. Sam stood behind the counter and made himself a sandwich. In all his years of living on the lake, it was the first time he'd ever been behind the counter in Wagman's. He carefully placed several slices of meat—salami, turkey, and ham—along with provolone cheese onto a couple of wheat bread slices. Sam added lettuce, onions, and alfalfa sprouts. The sprouts were something new to the store. They hadn't had them on the lake in previous years, and he felt very Californian for adding them.

"Why didn't you think about this earlier?" Nicki asked.

"I don't know. I just didn't."

"Weren't you a deputy?"

Sam looked up from his work of culinary art. "Are you talking smack?"

"Talking smack," she repeated and chuckled.

He grabbed his sandwich and walked around the counter. "Talking trash?"

"Whatever, Boomer."

Sam ate while he watched the teenager work her phone. Nicki remained quiet as her fingers danced, hopped, and jumped across the screen. He got up and grabbed a bag of potato chips and a soda.

He continued to eat while she flicked through whatever she was doing. Sam closed his eyes and listened to the oldies coming through the radio. The one playing now was from his grandfather's era and was one Sam had heard many times before—Dave Clark Five's "Catch Us If You Can."

Sam wondered if God, the universe, or some hand of fate was challenging him from the ethereal.

"Wake up," Nicki said.

He opened his eyes to see the teenager holding her phone so he could read it.

"She lived with her mom."

"Huh."

"Looks like she moved in with her about a year ago. I found a comment she made to a friend about it being a drag." Nicki tapped the screen with her finger.

"Any idea what her mom's name is?"

"I should charge you for this."

Sam held up his half-eaten sandwich. "I thought you were."

"I meant for doing your dirty work."

"Ten bucks," he said.

"Twenty."

"Deal." He bit into the sandwich.

"Her name is Luann Taylor. I don't know where she lives, but it says she works at Webster Sheet Metal."

Sam stood, dug some bills from his pocket, and tossed them on the table.

"You're welcome," Nicki said sarcastically.

He lifted his sandwich and hurried out toward his boat.

# Chapter 29

Webster Sheet Metal sat off Freya Street on East Front Avenue in a large warehouse darkened with the grit and grime of the surrounding industrial area.

Sam parked his Ford in the side lot and walked into the small lobby. The office felt dirty—no doubt a by-product of the industry. Dated furniture was arranged around the room while old posters and faded pictures hung on the walls.

A woman Sam guessed to be in her early sixties sat behind a gun-metal desk. He estimated her age based upon her short, silver hair and the thick-rimmed glasses she wore. The yellow shawl draped over her shoulders didn't imply youth, either. She didn't appear to be a receptionist, but no one else in the small office seemed tasked with that responsibility. On the corner of her desk was a folded copy of the local newspaper.

Nearby sat another desk without an occupant. Its top was clean, although slightly cluttered with the knickknacks an employee might collect over time.

The woman looked up from her paperwork then tilted her head down slightly to peer over her glasses. She asked Sam, "May I help you?"

"Is Luann Taylor in?"

He knew it was a long shot coming to the business, but he decided to take it. Sam had typed Luann's name into his phone's web browser but didn't get any positive returns.

Several websites promised him all sorts of information on Luann Taylor if he would only pay for their services. Using a service felt wrong to Sam for two reasons.

First, he wasn't a licensed investigator, and he wasn't supposed to be traipsing around in Detective McAfee's investigation. Paying for the aid of a service would verify that he was indeed poking around into the killing of Isabella Taylor. Of course, that is what he was doing, but Sam wanted to pretend, at least—wink, wink—that he was discreet about it.

Second, he hated that so much information just sat out there on the Internet for the taking. If that much data was available on Luann Taylor, how many details were available on him? It felt like he should make some effort to learn this information before taking the easy way out.

"She's not in today," the woman said and glanced toward the empty desk. "Death in the family."

"She's at home then?"

The older woman stiffened and pulled the shawl tight around her shoulders.

"Would you mind telling me where she lives?"

"I think you should go."

Sam held up his hands. "I'm not trying to cause any problems, but I'd like to talk to her about her daughter, Isabella."

The woman's eyes widened, and she quickly reached for her phone.

"Hold on," Sam said.

She lifted the receiver.

"Izzy was killed at my house, and I'm trying to find out why."

The woman's finger hovered over the phone's button pad. "So, you're looking to bother Luann? What for?"

Sam lowered his hands, then shoved them into his pockets. "I found her. Nobody deserves to die that way."

The woman considered his words then slowly placed the receiver back into place.

"The Sheriff's Office is running the investigation, and I'm sure they're doing a fine job. However—"

The woman smirked. "You give them more credit than we do."

"Excuse me?"

"We've had several break-ins around here. Three, to be exact. Wait. Make that four after last week. Addicts. Always taking tools or metal. The cops can't stop them. I don't have much faith they'll find Isabella's killer."

Sam tapped his chest. "I've been asking around, talking to the people she knew."

"And you just decided to come see Luann now?"

He shrugged. "I was being respectful."

The woman pursed her lips, then pushed them side to side. "You used to be a deputy. That's what the newspaper said, isn't it? She was killed at the home of a former deputy?"

Sam nodded.

"And you want to look into it because she was killed there—at your home."

"That's right. Listen, you don't need to give me Luann's number or her address. I'll go outside, and you call her. If she wants to see me, great. If she doesn't, I'll understand and go about my business. I won't bother her anymore, and I'll stop looking into what happened to her daughter. I'll let the sheriff handle it."

The woman's lips continued to move from side to side. Finally, they stopped, pinched tighter for a brief second, then relaxed. "What's your name again?"

 ***

Luann Taylor lived in a dilapidated mobile home park in Spokane Valley. Her trailer was near the back and stood out like a llama in a field of cows.

It appeared to be freshly painted—bright white with red and black accents. A foot-high picket fence ran around the perimeter of her small yard. The green lawn appeared lush and was free of any furniture or yard art.

The inside of the little trailer smelled of stale cigarettes and perfume. Red curtains darkened the windows so much that the interior had a hazy lounge feel. A large television stood against the far wall. An episode of *Judge Judy* ran without the sound.

Sam could tell that the mobile home would have been immaculately maintained in regular times but, in the shadow of death, cleaning had become a secondary consideration.

Luann Taylor was a thin, pale woman in her mid-thirties. She wore denim shorts rolled at their edges and a black tank-top that read *The Pretty Reckless*. She also wore red low-top Converse shoes without socks. Her stringy blond hair appeared unwashed and dark bags hung under her eyes.

She sat cross-legged on a ratty, threadbare couch. On the armrest, a crushed cigarette butt still smoldered in a glass ashtray. Several empty coffee cups littered the low table between them.

Sam sat on a swivel recliner that leaned slightly to the left. A lace doily covered the end table near his elbow.

They were roughly the same age, he decided. That meant Luann must have been a teenaged parent, much like his own. For whatever reason, that allowed him to feel an immediate connection to her.

After he introduced himself at the door and made some initial small talk, she'd invited him in. Now, they had remained quiet for a few uncomfortable moments while she decided on her next question.

Luann rubbed her bare knees before asking, "Why are you doing this?"

"I found her."

"You told me that. You used to be a deputy, right? Are you like a private investigator now or something?"

He shook his head.

She leaned forward to glance over the coffee table to his flip-flops. He was still in jeans and a T-shirt. "You look like *Magnum P.I.*"

"I'm just a guy trying to understand why your daughter was murdered at my house."

Luann grimaced when he said 'murder' and flopped back into the couch. "The cops and the newspaper said she was found in a boat."

"That's right."

"That means you got, what, a lake place?"

Sam nodded.

"What do you do?"

He cocked his head.

"For a living."

"I'm unemployed."

She turned and pulled the curtain back from the window behind the couch. He supposed she was looking at his car parked in front of the trailer. After a couple of seconds, Luann lowered the curtain and eyed him suspiciously. "How do you afford to live on the lake?"

"My grandparents left me the cabin."

The answer must have satisfied something for her. She reached for her cigarettes. "What do you want to know?"

"Why was she at my place?"

Luann shrugged. "How would I know?"

He glanced around her house. "Did you allow her to throw parties here?"

"Not a chance. I don't even drink. She could never get away with that kinda crap around here."

That answered one question, Sam thought. Isabella Taylor lived with her mother, who wouldn't allow a party in her home. She found a vacant home courtesy of Dominic Russo and decided to throw a party. It could be as simple as that.

Sam shifted in his chair. "Did Isabella have problems with anyone?"

"Not that I know of." With a couple of jerks of her hand, she shook a cigarette loose from the soft pack. "I think she got along with most people."

"Mind if I look at her room?"

Using just her lips, Luann pulled the cigarette free. "In the back." She kept her head down, and the cigarette bounced while she spoke.

"You sure it's okay?"

She shrugged but didn't bother to make eye contact. "The cops already searched it. You looking now doesn't make much difference, does it?"

The chair turned and squeaked when Sam slipped from it. As he headed toward the rear of the trailer, he glanced back, expecting Luann to follow. Instead, the volume returned to the television.

He passed a bathroom, then a closed-door, before proceeding to an open bedroom. He paused at the doorway as he considered the room.

On the walls were photographs of NASCAR drivers and shirtless cowboys. The bed was carefully made, and a large teddy bear with a stuffed heart in its hands sat in the middle of it. On the dresser was an opened box of earrings and bracelets. A variety of make-up essentials were carefully arranged. The closet doors were open, and he could see various blouses and slacks organized by type and color.

It was the room of a grown little girl—someone who might have had her childhood stolen away by becoming a mother too soon.

Sam glanced back down the hall. Luann stood there with a cigarette burning between her fingers.

"That's my room," she said.

"Sorry."

"You didn't know." Luann motioned toward the closed door then turned toward the living room. "Izzy's is the other."

When Sam pushed the door open, it caught against a pile of clothing lumped on the floor. He stepped into the small room and immediately stopped. He scanned the bedroom as it appeared Izzy's entire wardrobe was on the floor. Nothing hung in the empty closet.

He left the room and returned to the front of the mobile home. "Did the cops do that? Throw her clothes on the floor?"

Luann exhaled a stream of smoke. "That's how Izzy lived. I loved the girl, but she was a pig. She'd wash her clothes then dump them on the floor. I didn't care what she did as long as she kept it in that room. Out here," Luann pointed to the living room's floor, "she had to pick up after herself. In there, it was a pig's life."

Sam frowned but returned to the bedroom. He spent twenty minutes moving clothes about in hopes of finding something that might point him in the direction of her killer. Unfortunately, he didn't find a secret journal, a locket with a hidden note, or any love letters. A thought occurred to him, and he searched again in earnest. Satisfied he hadn't missed something, he left Izzy's bedroom.

"Did she have a computer?" he asked.

Luann muted *Judge Judy*. "She did while in school, but it broke. She didn't use it much back then anyway, and I wasn't going to buy her another one. She didn't respect what I did for her, so why should I go out of my way to replace something she broke out of carelessness? Besides, she used her phone for whatever she needed. Same as I do."

Sam wondered if McAfee found a phone with Izzy's body. He wanted to ask the detective but doing so wasn't a possibility—not without alerting him that Sam was overstepping his boundaries—again. "Did the detectives say if they found her phone?"

Luann's eyes drifted to the muted television. "They asked if I had seen it."

"And?

Her gaze returned to Sam. "If I had, I would have given it to them." She reached for a cup of coffee, then settled back into her chair. "I may not like the cops, but I want them to find who did this."

Sam sat on the edge of the leaning recliner. "You don't seem too—"

"What?" she challenged. "Broken up?"

"Yeah."

She inhaled deeply then considered the lid of her coffee cup. "You know. I don't think I am." Luann met his gaze.

"It's messed up to say this, I know, but I don't think I'm as broken up as I'm supposed to be. I think I'm more upset that I'm not upset than being upset that she died. Does that make sense?"

"Sure," Sam said. Her logic twisted his brain, but he got the gist of what she was trying to communicate.

"I wanted her to have a better life. Better than what I had, and what did she do? She made worse decisions than me."

"How's that?"

Luann sipped from her cup. "I got pregnant at sixteen—my first real boyfriend. Second time we ever did it, and I ended up being a mother. He refused to be involved, and his parents weren't going to have anything to do with it. I think they even encouraged him not to talk with me. My mom, on the other hand, said I had to have the baby—that it was what Jesus would have wanted. But Jesus wasn't going raise the kid, was he?"

She put the coffee cup in between her legs then grabbed her cigarettes. With a couple of shakes of her hand, she loosened one from the pack. "I tried to tell Izzy not to be free with it. Value herself. But she didn't listen. She started spreading it around as soon as she could. As early as junior high school."

Luann flicked her lighter and inhaled deeply. When she exhaled, she continued. "Two abortions by the time she was out of high school. Thought she would have learned after the first one, but Izzy just went on doing what she was doing."

Sam remained quiet. There was nothing for him to say. Besides, Luann was finally talking.

"Izzy graduated, thank God. It was by the skin of her teeth, but she graduated. I thought she was getting her head on straight when she got a job working at Starbucks. I was proud of her. She did that for a bit, and then she started working at that bikini joint." Luann angrily inhaled on her cigarette then pointed at Sam. "That's what put her over the edge."

"The edge of what?"

"Men. Guys approached her all the time. I mean, how could they not? She was like a piece of meat at a butcher's counter. Always in a bikini. They could see what she had to offer. All that attention went to her head." Luann tapped her temple. "It made her crazy. She once told me she had so many boyfriends she couldn't keep them straight. And by boyfriends, she wasn't talking the type she held hands with."

That sounded like more than two, Sam thought. "Did you tell the detective about the extra boyfriends?"

Luann flicked her ash into the tray. "Of course, I did. I didn't hold anything back from him."

"Do you think any of them—the boyfriends—could have hurt her?"

She squinted as she inhaled deeply. "Who knows?" She exhaled. "I didn't know any of those supposed guys. She never brought them around. She knew I would disapprove. I didn't like that lifestyle. I'm not a prude, Mr. Strait," she pointed the two fingers that held her cigarette at him, "but I'm no whore either. She never introduced me to any of her male friends."

Sam lowered his gaze. It was the first time he noticed the color of the carpet. It was a light-brown Berber that looked in surprisingly good shape.

"Except Tucker," Luann muttered.

He glanced up, and his pulse quickened. "Tucker?"

"Tucker Jacobson. He was after Izzy, but she didn't see him in that way. At least, that's what she said."

"He wanted to be with her?"

"Of course. I saw the way he looked at her."

"He came over here?"

"A couple times. Yeah."

"Why would she bring him over and not the others?"

"Because they weren't—you know—doing it."

"But he wanted to?"

Luann snuffed out her cigarette. "From what I saw, yes. And I know that look in a man's eyes."

"What was wrong with him?"

"He was too needy, according to her."

"Then why let him come over?"

"He dropped her off once. Another time he came over to talk. When I asked what it was about, Izzy said he was just a friend and that she'd never go out with him."

"Too needy?"

Luann pushed out a stream of blueish smoke. "That's what she said. It was too bad, really. I sort of liked the guy."

# Chapter 30

Sam found the slightly crinkled roster where it had been left on his kitchen counter. His hand quickly smoothed it once more before he searched the names and faces of the Spokane Demons.

It took less than a second for him to find Tucker Jacobson. He studied the picture next to the name. The doughy field general with the cannon for an arm was the needy guy who had been inside Isabella Taylor's home.

Sam leaned in and further studied the picture. Tucker was *also* the shirtless guy with the baby belly paunch who'd greeted him at the door of Deidre Hearn's apartment.

Luann Taylor hadn't told Detective Shane McAfee about Izzy's connection with Tucker. Since he wasn't a boyfriend, she hadn't considered him a threat. Therefore, why would she worry about him?

Sam straightened but continued to consider Tucker's picture. The guy wanted to be with Izzy. According to Luann, her daughter had relationships with multiple men at the same time. The bulky linemen openly discussed Izzy being their girl. That alone was a problematic relationship to think about.

What might it have been like for a guy who wanted to be with Izzy? If the lovelorn quarterback knew her sexual proclivities, would he have been jealous, maybe angry, possibly vengeful? To Sam, that all added up to a motive for murder.

That gave him the three legs of the crime stool—opportunity, means, and motive. The last was often the hardest to prove and a luxury for prosecutors. The two essential legs of the stool were opportunity and means. Maybe he should have thought of it as a crime ladder with opportunity, means, and motive being rungs. Sam shook the meandering thought from his mind and returned to the problem at hand.

He considered the Night Ranger album and the number written on it. McAfee had taken the cover, so he did his best to remember it. Why hadn't he taken a picture of it before he gave it to the detective? It was too late to worry about it now.

Sam closed his eyes and tried to recall the digits. They were scribbled in the manner a man might do. But that didn't, or wouldn't, prove anything. Just because the number wasn't written in clear, looping lines didn't mean a woman couldn't have jotted them on the album. The number itself did little to prove Tucker was at the party. Sam needed to show that the doughy quarterback was in his cabin at the same time as Izzy. Without doing so, he couldn't confirm the guy had the *opportunity* to commit murder.

But the *means* to commit her murder was a slam dunk. Tucker Jacobson was a six-foot-four, two hundred twenty-pound quarterback—his statistics were listed on the roster. He easily towered over and outweighed Isabella Taylor. Strangling her would not be hard to accomplish.

It was now time to call Detective McAfee. Even though Sam traipsed through the investigation yet again, he figured the investigator wouldn't hold it against him if he turned over this kind of information.

When Sam reached into his pocket for his phone, the front door opened, and his head whipped in that direction. Fear was an abnormal reaction for him, but too many strangers had lately availed themselves of the lake rules.

Sonja marched down the center of the hallway. She wore a faded Chicago Cubs T-shirt that hugged her in all the right places, blue jeans that did the same, and high heels. A pair of sunglasses were pushed back upon her head.

She stopped in the middle of the living room and put her hands on her hips. "I'm done," she said.

"With?"

"Us, you moron." She pointed to him then herself. "I can't keep doing this."

Sam was afraid it would eventually come to this. "Okay," was all he could muster.

She threw her hands in the air. "That's all you're going to say?"

"What do you want me to say?"

"I want you to say you love me."

Sam stared at her.

Her glare hardened further, and she pointed angrily at him. "Why did I think you could even feel that?"

She turned to leave.

"Sonja." His voice was soft.

"What?" She didn't turn around.

"I can't say it."

Her shoulders slumped.

"It's not that I don't feel it, but I can't say it."

She turned slowly around, and her brow furrowed. "What does that even mean?"

Sam ran his fingers through his hair. "Everyone has their dreams."

"So?"

"Yours is to be an actress."

"That's not a dream. I'm doing it."

"But it's something you've wanted since you were little. Are you willing to give it up? For me?"

Her face pinched. "Why would I give it up?"

"If I say it, if I say those words, then there are only two options for us. The first," Sam held up a finger, "is for you to give up your dreams and follow me."

"I can be a traveling actress."

"Really? That's a thing? I didn't think that was possible."

Sonja's face slackened as she stared at Sam.

"You see, I've thought about all the connections it took for you to get to this point. All the interviews. All the networking. Even now, you run to Seattle at a moment's notice for an audition. Are you going to jump a flight every time you have a day shoot?"

Sonja lowered her head.

"Probably wouldn't make sense, would it?"

She lifted her eyes. "I could make new connections. New networks."

"I never go to the same place twice. That's part of the promise I made to myself. Your new connections, your new networks, would only be good for a season. Then—poof—gone."

Sonja's eyes dropped toward her feet again.

Sam held up a second finger. "The other option is I stay here year-round."

She looked up now, expectant. Her eyes were bright with hope. "You would do that?"

"No."

Her eyes narrowed, and the brightness faded.

"Is that what love is supposed to be? Giving up our dreams to be with another?"

"That's not fair."

"It's honest. I'm doing what I want with my life. If you want to come along, you can. But it will be hard for you to be an actress. You won't be around your friends and family. This is the life I want. Is it the life you can live?"

Her gaze moved toward the lake.

"Saying those words means one of us has to kill our dreams. I'm not willing to do that."

"This means you love me?"

Sam rolled his eyes. He decided to change the subject. "Where have you been?"

"Huh?"

"I came looking for you, but you weren't home, and you weren't answering your phone."

"You came looking for me?" Her face brightened.

"I was worried about you."

"You were worried?"

He rolled his eyes again.

"I spent the night with my parents." Sonja stepped forward and slipped into his arms. "You were worried about me?"

"I was." He closed his eyes and smelled her perfume.

There was a knock at the door. "It's open," Sam hollered.

Sonja bit his ear and cooed softly. "Do you know what this means?"

"What's that?"

"Make-up sex."

He softly grunted.

"Bad time?" a woman asked.

Sam's eyes popped open.

Sonja spun in his arms. "Who is she?"

Jordan Withers stood with her head cocked. "I know you."

"Well," Sonja said, "I don't know you." She pushed herself free of Sam's arms.

The reporter extended her hand. "Jordan With—"

Sonja smacked her hand to the side. "He's mine."

"Huh?"

Sam reached for Sonja, but she jerked her arm away.

"I think you've got the wrong idea," the reporter said.

"You're the one with the wrong idea."

"I'm not after him."

Sonja's head bounced while she spoke. "With the way you're dressed?"

Jordan wore a tight black T-shirt and blue jeans. "What's wrong with the way I'm dressed?"

"You look like a hoochie."

"Said the housewife from Beverly Hills."

Sonja inhaled loudly, and the reporter's face reddened.

"Okay," Sam said. "Let's cool it."

Both women turned to him.

"Sonja, this is Jordan. She's a reporter."

Sonja's eyes widened, and she turned slowly back to Jordan.

"Jordan, this is Sonja."

"I'm sorry," Sonja said. "I get sort of—"

"Crazy?"

Sonja's eyes narrowed. "Jealous."

"What can I do for you?" Sam asked.

"The dead girl," Jordan said with her gaze still fixed on Sonja. "I'm following up on that story." For added emphasis, she said, "Which is my job."

Sonja smirked.

"What's that got to do with me?"

"I keep hearing your name."

Sam cocked his head.

"Seems whenever I talk with someone, they mention you. For a former deputy who is supposed to be unemployed, you sure get around. Just to be sure, I checked the state, and you're not a licensed investigator. So, why are you sticking your nose in this story?"

"Who've you talked with?"

Jordan crossed her arms. She gnawed her lip and tapped her toe while she thought. Unconsciously, Sonja mimicked the gesture. It took a moment, but soon both women had their arms crossed, were gnawing their lower lips, and tapping a toe. Jordan studied him, and Sonja watched the reporter.

When she spoke, Jordan dropped her arms. Sonja did the same.

"Luann Taylor," the reporter said. "She said I missed you by minutes. Imagine my surprise. She said you're a regular *Magnum P.I.* Since I didn't see a Ferrari out front, I figured it's the flip-flops that were giving her that impression."

At the mention of his footwear, Sonja grunted her displeasure.

"I was offering my condolences," Sam said.

"Are you on your way to talk with Tucker Jacobson?"

"How do—"

"Luann told me. And by your response, I assume that's what you're going to do. Want to go together?"

"No," Sonja interjected. "He does *not* want to go with you."

The reporter ignored her and continued, "Or are you going to call the cops?"

"I was planning to, yes, but she walked in."

"Convenient story," Jordan said. "Why haven't you done it yet?"

Sam glanced at Sonja. "She can be distracting."

Jordan appraised Sonja. For her part, Sonja put her hands on her waist, cocked a hip, and looked skyward.

"As I said," Sam continued, "this one can be distracting."

Sonja's hands slipped from her waist, and she glared at him.

"Well," the reporter said, "I'm going to chase that lead. Either you can come with me or not."

"He is *not* going with you." Sonja shook her head.

Jordan smiled. "Okay, Mom."

"*Mom?*" Sonja almost choked on the word.

"I'm calling Detective McAfee," Sam said. "I'll let him know you're looking into Tucker Jacobson for him."

"You do that." Jordan gave both a final glance— Sonja's a little longer than his—then headed out of the cabin.

When the front door closed, Sonja spun toward him. "This one?"

"I didn't mean anything by it."

"It's going to cost you. You've got a lot to make up for."

"I need to call a detective."

"After," Sonja said and reached for his shirt.

Sam didn't argue with that.

***

They lay in bed when there was another knock at the door.

"It better not be that reporter again."

Sam sat upright. "I doubt she's coming back."

He grabbed his clothes and hurriedly dressed. When he stepped into the hallway, there was a second knock, louder than the first.

Sam padded down the hallway to the door and peered through the peephole. He opened the door to Tucker Jacobson standing on the porch. He wore a T-shirt, khaki shorts, and yellow running shoes without socks. His sandy hair was shaggy, and he did his best to affect an air of casual disregard.

"Hey man," he said with a half-hearted laugh and a point toward Sam. "I knew I knew you."

# Chapter 31

Tucker Jacobson walked around the corner of the living room and disappeared.

"Who's that?" Sonja whispered. She'd opened the bedroom door slightly and stuck her head out to watch Tucker walk away.

"He's a guy I've wanted to talk with."

"About what?" She leaned further into the hallway and revealed more of her nakedness.

Sam put his hand on Sonja's head and pushed her back into the bedroom.

"Get dressed."

Sonja appeared as if she were about to protest, but she vanished when he pulled the door. Sam heard her stamp her foot once.

Tucker Jacobson stood at the sliding glass doors in the living room and looked down at the dock. He glanced back when Sam entered the room. "Someone else here?"

"My cat." He didn't know what Tucker's intentions were for being there, so he didn't feel the necessity to be totally truthful with him.

"You talk to your cat?"

"Doesn't everyone?"

Tucker turned back to the sliding glass doors and motioned toward Sam's boat. His voice took on a hint of sadness when he asked, "That's where they found her?"

"You should know."

The quarterback looked over his shoulder. "How's that?"

"I figured you killed her."

Tucker fully faced him. "Me?"

"Uh-huh."

"*Me*." The quarterback tapped his chest.

"That's right."

"I killed her and returned to where it happened. For what reason?"

"It's called the scene of the crime."

Tucker lifted his eyebrows. "The scene of the crime." He said it as if trying the words on for size. "Okay, then. I returned to the scene of the crime. For what reason?"

"I don't know. You tell me."

"I already did. I remembered where I saw you."

Sam shook his head. "We've never met."

"Sure, we have."

"No, we haven't. I'm sure of it."

Tucker walked over to the wall of photographs. He pointed to one and said, "That's you. Right there. You're younger, but that's you. I'm positive."

It was Sam's high school graduation picture. He wore a letterman's jacket and stood on the dock.

"I remember thinking," Tucker continued, "how cool it must have been to grow up in a house like this. You grew up here, right?" He tapped the photograph of baby Sam with his parents. "Is that like your brother and his wife? I tried to figure out your life by these pictures, but now that you're here—"

"You're here," Sam said.

The quarterback glanced over his shoulder. "Huh?"

"You're here. This is my house."

Tucker nodded. "Right."

"Which begs the question—why?"

The quarterback pointed at Sam and smiled. "I knew I knew you, man. It was like a totally weird coincidence for you to show up at Dee's."

Sam crossed his arms. He might as well be straight with the guy and see how it played out. "I'm trying to find who killed Izzy."

Tucker scratched his head. "Aren't the cops doing that?"

"Yeah, but I have—"

"A detective even left his card for me at the training facility and where I work. He's trying to get a hold of me. I called him back, but we haven't talked yet. It's weird to leave messages for a detective—you know? I mean, calling the cops to talk is weird."

"Where do you work?"

"The produce section at Albertson's."

For a moment, Sam considered that a lettuce handler might have killed Izzy. It was a snarky and inappropriate comment for him to think. "You were here—at Izzy's party."

"Well, yeah, man. That's how I saw your picture." Tucker pointed at Sam's graduation photo again.

Knowing Tucker and Izzy were together at the party meant the guy had the opportunity to kill her. That meant all the pieces were now in place—opportunity, means, and motive.

"So, you're the new boyfriend?" He meant for it to be a statement, but at the last moment, it trailed off like a question. Luann Taylor's comment that Tucker wasn't her daughter's boyfriend raced to the front of his mind.

"Izzy's boyfriend?" His eyes widened with hope. "Oh, man. I wanted to be. Why? Did she say something?"

Sam stared at him until the quarterback's eyes returned to normal.

"Right," Tucker said. "You probably didn't talk to her before..." His voice drifted away as he turned to look toward the dock.

"Did you get mad when you found out about the others?"

Tucker glanced back at him. "What others?"

"For starters, Jefferson and Papani."

A short laugh burst from Tucker. "Hoyt and Toma?"

"They were hooking up."

The smile vanished from his face. "Which one?"

"Both."

He swallowed once, then asked, "She hooked up with them?"

"That's what they said."

Tucker's face scrunched. "Regularly? Like more than once?"

"That was the impression."

"You mean... all together?"

"Again, that was the impression."

The quarterback's shoulders slumped. He walked over to the couch and flopped onto it. "Those guys are supposed to protect me." His voice was soft. "How could they do that?"

"What about her?"

Tucker looked up. "Huh?"

"She's triple-timing you with a couple linemen." Sam wanted to sense some anger from the man. The motive he had expected was slipping away.

"I know," he muttered. "So wrong."

"Their relationship—the three of them—it doesn't bother you?"

"We weren't together." He shook his head and leaned forward. "Not yet at least. I thought we would be." Tucker lowered his gaze. "She went for a couple tackles," he muttered. "Who would've thought?"

"You don't seem too bothered by her death."

He looked up. "Huh?"

"She's dead."

"I know."

"You seem more upset by the fact she hooked up with Jefferson and Papani."

"*My* linemen," he reminded.

"*My* point."

"Huh?"

"You were at Deidre's place."

"Dee." He sighed and fell backward into the couch.

"How does she fit into this?"

"She didn't want us to break up."

"You guys are an item?"

Tucker nodded.

"And you were breaking up? Why?"

Tucker shrugged and smirked at the same time. It was a confusing message.

"Izzy," Sam said.

"I thought I was trading up."

"You broke it off with Deidre because of Izzy?"

"Not yet, but I think Dee knew I was going to. Izzy wanted to see me alone."

"Alone?"

"We had a three-way." Tucker's look of disappointment transformed into a smile of smugness. "It was my birthday present."

Sam shook his head in disbelief. "You just thought it was gross that she did that with your linemen."

His face scrunched. "That was with two dudes." He held up as many fingers. "That's one dude too many."

"That's a double standard."

He shrugged and said, "I'm a quarterback," as if that should explain away everything.

"She—"

"And they were linemen. That's, like, extra gross."

"She was—"

"If they were receivers, I'd get it, but linemen? Yuck."

"She was young."

Tucker pulled back and studied Sam for a moment. "She was twenty-one," he announced. He had a way of saying things that Sam suspected were supposed to end an argument. It was probably a perk of being a quarterback that allowed him to think that way.

"Twenty-one is young." Sam suddenly felt like an old man for saying such a thing.

The quarterback made a dismissive sound. "That's way more than legal. And I'm only twenty-eight. So, whatever. Besides, Dee was cool with it. Well, at the time, she was cool with it."

"I thought she didn't like Izzy."

Tucker rolled his eyes. "That was my fault. I paid too much attention to her, and Dee didn't like that. There's a lot of politics involved in a three-way, in case you didn't know."

He didn't.

"A piece of advice for the next time you find yourself in one. Always spend more effort on the one who brought you than the one who interests you." Disappointment crossed his face. "You're not going to get another opportunity if you don't."

Sam wanted to get away from Tucker Jacobson's advice on managing a menage a trois successfully. "I called you yesterday."

"That was you?"

"Your number was on an album cover."

Tucker seemed to think for a moment before saying, "Oh, yeah."

"Why did you write it?"

"For Izzy."

"Why didn't she just put it into her phone?"

"Because Dee threw it into the lake."

Sam glanced toward the body of water. "Deidre was at the party?"

"Sure. Izzy invited her. I thought the three of us might hook up here."

The idea of the three of them having sex in his bed, or worse, his grandmother's bed, bothered Sam. He fought back his anger. "Why did Deidre throw Izzy's phone in the lake?"

"Because she found out we'd been texting. She took me outside on the deck and yelled at me. Then the two of them went down to the dock and argued. Dee snatched Izzy's phone and hucked it into the water. That sort of calmed the argument down. Izzy couldn't believe she did that. Dee can be sort of crazy."

Deidre's yelling at Tucker and Izzy could explain the arguments that Mary Jo Brakke said she heard the night of the party.

Sam asked, "What happened after?"

"They came back up to the cabin—not together, of course."

"The party didn't end?"

"Seriously? It's not a party until something gets broken. No, man, it continued for a while."

Sam thought about the mess he was forced to clean up and had to fight the urge to punch Tucker as a little payback. Unfortunately, if he'd learned anything recently, it was that his fighting skills had atrophied.

"You wrote your number on the album because Izzy didn't have her phone. It's that simple."

Tucker shrugged. "Izzy said she wanted to make Deidre pay for doing that."

"Pay?"

A lascivious smile crossed the quarterback's lips. Sam wanted to pull back and say, "Eww," but he kept quiet.

"Revenge sex," Tucker said. "Ever get yourself some?"

He hadn't.

The quarterback looked toward the ceiling and sighed. "I didn't think I was ever going to get to hook-up with Izzy again until Dee threw her phone in the lake. Man, that closed the deal for me. And I gotta say I was looking forward to it. One on one with Izzy would have been insane. Know what I mean? We'd only been together that one time with Dee, but I could tell—"

Sam didn't want to listen to a play-by-play of Tucker's sex life, so he interrupted the man's ramblings. "Why did you guys pick that album? The Night Ranger one."

Tucker stared at him for a moment as his thoughts shifted gears. "It had that song on there. The one that our coach pumps us up with during practice. Something about rocking in America. It's not bad for being boomer music."

Sam crossed his arms and thought about what he'd just learned.

His house was chosen for the party because Izzy couldn't throw one at her home—her mother wouldn't permit it. The Night Ranger record was selected, and Tucker Jacobson's number was written upon it because Izzy's phone was at the bottom of the lake somewhere. It was unlikely McAfee would find it unless they brought a dive team out. Would the sheriff's department do such a thing? Probably not. Especially when they could subpoena the call logs and text records.

Besides the drugs, Sam now had another motivation for the murder of Isabella Taylor—jealousy.

But there was still the matter of the drugs. He didn't know what the drugs were or how they fit into the whole scheme of things.

"Drugs," Sam said.

"No, thanks. I'll pass, but if you got a beer, I'd take one of them."

Sam shook his head. "There were drugs here that night."

"Oh, it probably stunk when you got home, huh? A couple guys wanted to smoke weed in the house. We made them go outside since I hate that skunky smell, and Andy is worried about it showing up on tests."

"Andy was at the party, too?"

"How could she not be? She follows Dee around like a puppy. She was the one who made everyone go outside. Nobody is going to say no to that lady. Man, when she broke up the party, no one even questioned her. We all went home."

"Andy broke up the party? Why?"

Tucker's brow furrowed. "I don't think she ever said. She just told everybody to get the hell out. Even though she plays for the other team, I like that girl. I would if I could if you know what I mean."

He did but didn't have an interest in furthering that conversation.

"Back to the drugs," Sam said. "Was there other stuff? In baggies? Something that looked like cocaine?"

Tucker scrunched his nose. "Nobody was using that kind of junk. It wasn't that type of party."

"Somebody stored the drugs in my refrigerator."

"Seriously? I didn't know they spoiled."

"The drugs belonged to Jefferson and Hoyt."

"My linemen?"

"We've established that."

"But why?"

"That's what I want to know."

"Why wouldn't they tell me? I'm their quarterback."

"They brought the drugs because Izzy said her boyfriend was a buyer."

Tucker touched his chest. "I'm not a buyer."

"You weren't her boyfriend."

"Yeah," he said, disappointed.

"Maybe she had a boyfriend that she was helping with the drugs."

His face flattened. "Another guy?"

Sam didn't want to remind him of the revelation of her relationship with the two linemen. That would feel like rubbing it in the man's face. Instead, he said, "Deidre and Andy wanted the drugs, too."

"Dee doesn't do drugs."

"Does Andy?"

Tucker's nose crinkled. "I doubt it."

"Then what's with the drugs?"

"You sure it was drugs?"

If there was one thing Sam was sure about, it was that the powder was some sort of dope. The fact he'd been assaulted repeatedly meant for damn sure it wasn't flour or sugar. "I'm sure."

"Well, man, I don't know." The quarterback stood. "All I know is I got some things to talk about with my team. Loyalty, respect… loyalty."

"What about Deidre?"

"What about her?"

"Are you going to talk with her about anything?"

Tucker shook his head. "Dee and I don't talk, man. Our relationship is purely sexual—if you know what I mean."

He patted Sam's arm on the way past him to the door.

# Chapter 32

"If you know what I mean," Sonja said.

"That's what he said."

"I know. I heard it from the other room. What a moron."

"He's a quarterback."

"That doesn't explain anything."

"Sure, it does. It explains everything."

Sonja carefully placed her glass of iced tea on the table and stared at Sam. They were seated on the deck overlooking the lake. After Tucker Jacobson left, Sonja slipped from the bedroom—fully dressed—and pronounced she was hungry. She set about making a late lunch for them.

While she prepared sandwiches, Sam called Detective McAfee's cell phone. It went directly to voice mail. He left a message and then called the Major Crimes office. The overly polite receptionist informed Sam that the detective was on the scene of a homicide and might be unavailable for some time. Sam left a message there for McAfee to call him about information related to Isabella Taylor's murder before hanging up.

A few minutes later, he received a text message: THIS IS MCAFEE. TIED UP NOW. WILL CALL U IN A FEW. Sam responded with a double thumbs-up emoji.

While they ate salami sandwiches, Sonja and Sam discussed Tucker Jacobson's visit. Only a few potato chips littered his plate, but half of her sandwich remained. All of Sonja's chips were gone.

"How does his football role explain everything?" Sonja asked.

"His position," Sam began, "is like being the lead singer in a rock band. He's the guy who touches the ball on every play. He's naturally going to be the most popular player on the team."

Sonja flipped open the remaining portion of her sandwich and removed a slice of salami. "Lead singers don't touch the ball on every play."

"What?"

She pointed a floppy piece of salami at him. "Your analogy—or is it a metaphor? I can never keep those straight."

"Get on with it."

"It didn't make sense. You said quarterbacks are lead singers—that they touch the ball on every play. There is no ball in a band."

"You're overthinking it. I was drawing a parallel."

"A parallel. That's what you were making."

"All I'm saying is rock stars and quarterbacks are alike."

"In what way?"

"Women want them."

"I didn't want him."

"You didn't see him."

She rolled her eyes. "I heard him. That was enough."

"And the guys on his team would secretly resent him."

Sonja's face scrunched. "But he's their leader."

"So? The guy grabs all the glory just the same as a lead singer, which is why they would resent him."

"I clearly don't understand team dynamics." She selected another piece of salami. "Or band dynamics, for that matter."

Sam shifted in his chair. "It's simple. Quarterbacks, starting pitchers, goalies—" He had lifted fingers to correspond with each of those sports positions but frowned at the third one. "No, not goalies. They're behind a mask."

"But quarterbacks are behind a helmet."

"You can still see their faces. Besides, goalies mean hockey, and hockey players don't get girls."

"They don't?" She held a piece of salami in front of her open mouth.

"Have you ever dated a hockey player?"

"Ugh. They don't have all their teeth."

Sam spread his arms as if he'd just scored a point.

Sonja placed the spiced meat into her mouth. "So, this murdered girl wanted to be with the quarterback?"

"No. *Deidre* wanted to be with the quarterback."

"And Izzy?"

"Wanted to get even with Deidre."

"For what reason?"

He shrugged. "They worked together, and they had some weird competition going. Izzy thought she was smarter than Deidre, that she could run the coffee stand."

"Is that a reason for murder?"

"I don't think so, but remember Izzy hooked up with her boyfriend in a three-way. She was going to hook up with him again as payback."

Sonja's eyes narrowed. "We are never doing a three-way."

"I never asked."

"I'm just saying."

"Okay."

"Just so you know." She flipped a piece of lettuce away from the opened sandwich on her plate.

"I hear you."

"Still, killing a woman because she planned to steal your man after you invited her into a three-way seems like an extreme reaction."

"Deidre's an extreme woman."

Sonja twisted her lips. "What's that mean?"

"Nothing. And relax. I'm not interested in her."

"I don't know about that."

"Well," a female voice said as the person it belonged to moved heavily up the deck steps. "I can tell you she's not interested in him."

Both Sam and Sonja turned to see Andriani Dimitriou appear with a gun in her hand.

***

Sonja and Sam sat on the edge of the couch.

Andy paced back and forth. The gun—a revolver—waved as she spoke. "Dee didn't hurt anybody."

"Okay," Sam said as Sonja tightly gripped his left hand.

"She didn't do what you're saying around town."

"I haven't said anything to anyone."

Andy spun and pointed the gun at Sam. "Not true."

Sonja flinched, but Sam held steady. "Who said I did?"

The bodybuilder's lip curled. "Tucker."

"He told her about our conversation."

"That's right."

"And you overheard?"

Andy pushed the gun towards Sam. "Why else would I be here?"

"That's what I'm trying to understand."

The bodybuilder briefly sneered. "I was at her apartment when he showed up. God, I hate him—the whiny little bitch. It's always got to be about him. He told her what you said, and she got mad at him for coming over there. When they started yelling, I left."

"That's when you got a gun?"

"I've had it." Andy then considered the revolver in her hand. "It's my mom's."

"Why are you carrying it around?"

She pointed the gun at him again. "Because you're going to pin the murder on Dee."

Sam lifted his free hand in surrender. His other was still firmly in the grasp of Sonja's. She'd added her second hand to the vise grip he'd found himself in. His free hand ineffectually waved as he spoke. "I'm not trying to pin anything on anyone."

"Then what are you doing?"

Sam shrugged his right shoulder. His left was now occupied with Sonja's head being buried into his neck. "I'm asking around. That's all."

"About what?"

A nervous smile spread on Sam's lips.

"About what?" Andy pushed the gun forward, emphasizing each word.

"Izzy's murder."

Anger washed over Andy's face. "So you can pin it on Dee!"

Sonja squealed into Sam's neck, and he thrust his arm out in protection. He immediately realized it was a foolish response as an extended hand is no defense against a bullet. However, it still felt like a natural and rational thing to do. His hand continued to hover in the air between him and Andy's gun.

Sam said, "I just want to know what happened."

On the coffee table, Sam's phone buzzed. He'd brought it inside when Andy insisted they move off the deck and away from prying eyes. On the screen, he could easily see the two words identifying the caller—DETECTIVE MACKLEPHEE.

Sonja's head popped away from his neck to look at the screen. It was a natural reaction—almost primal—for her to look at who was calling Sam. When she saw the screen, her brow furrowed. Then she inhaled slightly and turned her face back into Sam's neck.

Andy lifted her chin toward the buzzing phone. "Who's that?"

"Wrong number."

The bodybuilder stepped forward to better see the illuminated screen. When she saw who was calling, Andy's eyes widened, and she grunted loudly. She angrily swept the gun past Sam's face. It was a frustrated outburst that served no purpose. He was out of her reach, so Andy wasn't about to pistol-whip him.

Sonja cried as she clung tighter to Sam.

"Why's a detective calling you?"

"We're friends." He didn't know why he lied, but it seemed better than stating he called the detective to discuss his conversation with Tucker Jacobson. That was the same reason Andy was now waving a gun in his face. Poking the proverbial bear didn't seem like the smartest choice in this matter.

"Friends?" Andy asked. "With a cop?"

"I used to be a deputy. I thought you would have known that."

Including the one with the gun, Andy brought her hands up to her head. "Oh, man." She turned slowly and repeated, "Oh, man."

Sam tried to slip his hand free from the grasp of Sonja's, but she held him tightly. He yanked repeatedly, but she failed to get his nonverbal signal to let go. Sam leaned away to get her to look at him, but her head remained pressed firmly into his neck. Whenever he wriggled and pulled, she moved and tugged. They were doing a seated version of the tango. All that was missing was the music.

"What are you doing?" Andy asked.

Sam stopped moving and looked up at the bodybuilder. If it was possible, and it certainly felt that way, Sonja clung to him tighter. He was afraid she was going to crawl into his lap. She made an odd mewing noise now.

"What were you doing?"

"Nothing." Sam tried unsuccessfully to push Sonja away.

Suspicion clouded Andy's eyes. "What'd he want?"

"Who?"

The bodybuilder nodded toward the now silent phone. "Your friend."

"How would I know?"

The phone buzzed again, indicating McAfee left a voice mail.

Andy's lip curled. "Play it."

"That wouldn't be polite. I mean, it's a message between friends and—"

"Play it!"

Sonja cried into his neck, threw a leg over his, and mewed. Sam leaned awkwardly forward to grab the phone.

The front door opened then, and a voice hollered, "Hey, Sam! You home?"

***

Stupid decisions are often made in a split second. That's how they must be made for them to be stupid. Otherwise, Sam knew, rationality enters with time, and stupidity is defeated. Yet, split-second decisions litter the course of our daily lives.

Sam believed most of life's choices were made in a fraction of a moment. On the freeway, driving seventy miles per hour, hundreds of decisions occur every minute.

*Is that car coming into my lane? Should I brake now? Should I speed up? Is that a cat?*

In police work, those split-second choices affect the lives of others. Sam had been forced to make many of these himself. Deputies see threats or opportunities, decide and act. Then the officers celebrate their successes, or they deal with the consequences of failure.

As his fingers wrapped around his cell phone, Sam didn't consider any consequences. When Andy turned toward the voice coming from the hallway, Sam lifted himself from the couch and reared his arm back for a throw.

He had played high school baseball. He'd been on recreational teams during college and his couple of years on the department. He may not have been the strongest hitter, but if there was one thing Samuel Roy Strait was good at during his baseball career, it was accurately throwing. Unfortunately, two things disrupted him at that very moment.

First, a cell phone is not a baseball. They're physically not even remotely close. One is a flat rectangle, while the other is a perfect sphere. The grip involved in throwing a cell phone is radically different than tossing a split-fingered fastball.

When Sam grabbed the phone, it lay flatly across the palm of his hand. One single finger—the index—hooked over the top of the phone. Even without stopping to consider his grip, he instinctively knew it was less than optimal. However, he didn't have time—or better yet, he couldn't give it time—to consider the consequences of throwing a cell phone with a less than optimal grip.

The second issue disrupting his throw, and this was what ultimately proved the most disruptive, was Sonja's fear that Sam was about to abandon her. At least, that's what he assumed she thought because as he stood, Sonja grabbed onto him fiercely—like a drowning woman clasping onto a life preserver—and yanked him back to the couch.

The combined effect of a poor grip and a full-grown woman tugging him downward was a less than graceful chuck of the cell phone. It arced through the air in an end-over-end fashion and slapped loudly onto the shoulder of the bodybuilder.

Andy arched her back in pain then spun around to Sam. "Hey!"

Suddenly, the gun barrel seemed more massive than before. Twice as large, perhaps. Maybe even three times. Sam grabbed Sonja and dove to the ground. They landed with an expelling of air—Sonja squeaked—and Sam waited for the impending gunshot to follow.

Instead, he heard Dominic say, "The hell are you doing?"

"What are you doing here?" Andy asked.

"Sam, you okay?"

"We're fine," he said into the back of Sonja's head. She mewed again.

Andy demanded, "Why are you here?"

"Why do you have a gun?"

Sam lifted his head. "She's protecting Deidre."

Andy pointed the gun at Sam. "Shut up!"

He dropped his head back onto Sonja, who squeaked once. Underneath him, she was trying to curl up into a ball.

Dom said, "Gimme the gun."

"No."

Sam started to lift his head, but there was a sound of a scuffle and a gunshot. He flinched and pulled Sonja tighter into him. She cried out and pulled her arms underneath her.

Something thudded on the floor nearby. In the following silence, Sam knew he should get up and move. Fight or flight should be his natural response. Instead, he remained where he was. Sonja was underneath him. Protecting her seemed to be his primary course of action now. Maybe he would get shot, perhaps he would die, but he if could save her—

"Get up," Dom said.

Sam popped his head up. The bodybuilder lay on the floor. "Is she—"

"No," his friend said as he picked up the revolver. "I hit her, and she shot your floor."

Sam quickly stood and pulled Sonja up with him. She tucked herself into his chest. She stared up at him with a strange look.

"You saved me," she said.

Dom clucked his tongue. "I saved you." He pointed to the unconscious form on the ground. "I was the one that did that."

"It means he loves me," Sonja said. "And he can't take it back."

"Are you serious?" Dom asked. "He laid on the floor. I fought the girl with a gun."

"Even if he can't say it," Sonja said, "he loves me."

Sam shrugged, and Dom moaned with displeasure.

# Chapter 33

Sam watched Detective Shane McAfee as the man considered the notes he'd written. "And that's when your friend, Dominic, entered the house and hit her—the Dimitriou woman?"

"Right," Sam said.

"While you huddled helplessly on the floor?"

They were back on the deck, and McAfee was interviewing Sam. Somewhere else, two deputies kept Dominic and Sonja separated while Andy was handcuffed and secured in the back of a patrol car.

An evidence technician was inside his cabin photographing where the bullet had been fired into the floor.

"I wasn't helpless," Sam said. "I was protecting Sonja."

"Do you think Dimitriou could have killed Isabella Taylor?"

Sam crossed his arms. "Maybe. The opportunity and means are there, right? She was at the party with Izzy."

McAfee rubbed his chin with the end of his pen. "What's the motive for it?"

"Deidre."

"Hearn? The apartment owner?"

"Andy is Deidre's trainer and friend. I think she has romantic feelings for Deidre, which aren't being returned."

"You think?"

"She hasn't admitted it, but I could read between the lines."

"And this connects how to the dead woman?"

"Deidre's involved with Tucker Jacobson—"

"The Demon's quarterback."

"—and she invited Izzy for a three-way for Tucker's birthday."

McAfee blinked repeatedly.

"I know," Sam said.

"So Dimitriou—Andy—was jealous of the three-way Izzy got to be in?"

Sam shook his head. "Andy wasn't jealous of Izzy."

"Where's Andy's motivation for killing Isabella Taylor?"

"To protect Deidre. Izzy was planning to hook-up with Tucker again—away from Deidre. Andy could have found out about it and killed her."

"Wouldn't Andy have wanted that to happen? To break up Tucker and Deidre? That'd clear the way for her to get with Deidre." McAfee frowned dubiously. "I think her motivation to kill Izzy is weak."

"I didn't say it was a good argument for her being the suspect. So, you think Deidre killed Izzy?"

McAfee closed his notebook and leaned against a railing. "Even after I told you to stop, you continued to muck around in my investigation. The linemen, quarterback, and the bodybuilder." McAfee's brow furrowed. "Sounds like a set-up to a joke."

"They came to me," Sam said. "I didn't chase them down."

"When you hit a hornet's nest, they buzz around you. That's how it works."

"I didn't mean for all this to happen."

"I'm sure you didn't."

"What about Deidre?"

"We've got units out looking for her. She's not at her apartment."

Sam glanced down to the beach where Sonja waited with a deputy. She waved up at him. He asked, "Anything else?"

"I need to interview your buddy and your girlfriend—"

He almost interrupted McAfee to challenge the use of the word, but Sonja was out of earshot, so what was the point?

"—but you're free to do what you want. Don't go into the house yet—not until forensics finishes up."

"I remember."

McAfee turned and headed down the deck stairs. Sam watched him approach Sonja and begin her interview.

***

"Samuel," Mary Jo Brakke said. "There sure have been a lot of police cars in the neighborhood lately. It hasn't been this way since…" Her voice trailed off.

"Since right before I was kicked off the department."

During that troubling time, his friends often stopped by while on duty to lend their support and give words of encouragement.

They stood on Mary Jo's front porch, observing the several deputy cars parked in front of his house. In his driveway, Dom's old Chevy pick-up sat.

Mary Jo forced a smile. "I'm sorry to bring that up."

"It's okay, Mrs. Brakke—"

"Mary Jo."

"—it's water under the bridge. I've moved on."

"What happened over there today?"

"A woman threatened me with a gun."

"Oh my."

Sam shrugged.

"Well," Mary Jo said with a wink. "It can't be the first time." She reached out to touch his arm but paused just before doing so. "So, we have nothing to fear?"

"No. Nothing to fear."

A white Mazda pulled in front of his house. From the passenger seat, Jordan Withers climbed out. A man in a T-shirt and khaki shorts that looked slightly familiar slipped from the driver's seat—the cameraman. Jordan glanced around the neighborhood and caught Sam's eye. She waved once.

"Who's that?" Mary Jo asked.

"The press."

"That's never a good sign, is it?"

He was about to turn back to Mary Jo when a little red car entered the neighborhood. His eyes narrowed and followed the Toyota as it passed slowly by his house. As it neared the patrol car that Andy sat in, it almost came to a complete stop. Suddenly, the Camry lurched forward.

"Damn," Sam muttered and sprinted away.

"Was it something I said?" Mary Jo called after him.

Jordan Withers stepped around the Mazda to intercept Sam. "Everything okay?"

Slightly out of breath, Sam asked, "Want to catch a murderer?"

"How?"

The little red car disappeared around the corner. Honeymoon Bay Road's narrowness did not provide an opportunity for it to turn around until it came to the small cul-de-sac after the bend. Soon, the Toyota Camry would come roaring back this way. He remembered how Deidre Hearn drove—like a crazy person.

"Put your car in the middle of the street."

"Just park it?" Jordan asked.

"Then get out and move to cover."

Jordan hurried to her cameraman, and Sam hollered for Detective McAfee. A deputy poked his head from around the back of his cabin and looked at him inquisitively.

"Get McAfee!" Sam yelled.

The deputy stepped fully into view now. "What?"

"McAfee!"

The Mazda moved into the middle of the road, blocking it completely. The driver's door popped opened, and the cameraman got out. He put his hands on his hips and cocked his head. "You sure this is a good idea?"

They heard the revving of the Toyota's engine before they saw it. The Camry zoomed around the corner of Honeymoon Bay Road. As Sam stood in the middle of the road, it sped toward him. He was on the wrong side of the Mazda—he was between it and the speeding Toyota.

Detective McAfee sprinted toward him with a deputy close behind. Sonja and Dom brought up the rear.

"Move," McAfee yelled as he waved his arms. "Move!"

The little red car sped toward Sam, its small engine whining in protest.

Sam took two steps, then dove from the roadway and into his yard. Sonja screamed, and Dom grabbed onto him. His friend dragged Sam further out of the way.

The brakes on the Toyota caught, and its tires squealed on the asphalt. It skidded and swerved but remained on the road. The collision with the white Mazda was small and anti-climactic—something that might have occurred in a grocery store parking lot by someone not paying attention while backing up.

The two deputies ran toward the Camry with their guns drawn. "Out of the car," one of them yelled. "Now!"

***

Deidre Hearn sat in the rear of the second patrol car with her head pressed against the back of the driver's seat.

Sam stood between Dom and Sonja and watched Detective McAfee approach.

"She's demanding a lawyer," the detective said.

"That's all she said?" Sam asked.

"The last refuge of the guilty."

Sonja pointed at Deidre. "She killed the girl in your boat?"

Sam nodded. "That's the way I figure it."

"Do you, Detective?" McAfee said.

Sam shrugged.

"And that one," Sonja continued by pointing to Andy, who sat in another patrol car, "was worried you were going to pin it on her. Do you think she knew?"

"Yeah. That's why she broke up the party."

"Who told you that?" the detective asked.

"Tucker Jacobson. He said Andy kicked everyone out and sent them home."

"So," McAfee said, "Deidre killed Izzy and Andy helped her get away. I can work with that."

Dom shook his head. "You think you know somebody."

"What about the drugs?" Sonja asked. "I thought Izzy was killed for drugs?"

Sam cocked his head. "What about the drugs, Detective?"

McAfee shrugged. "What about them?"

"We still don't know how they fit in."

"Does it matter?"

"There were drugs in my house. Deidre and Andy wanted them. Izzy said she had a buyer for them. There was a connection somewhere."

"And?" McAfee said.

Sam lifted his hands in frustration. "Doesn't it bother you not to know what was going on with the stuff?"

"Does it bother me? Not at all."

"Why not?"

"Because the drugs aren't the most important concern at this moment."

"They're not?" Sonja asked.

"Right now, we've got a suspected killer and her accomplice. And I emphasize *suspected* because the proof I have is weak. There's not much physical evidence, so witness statements are going to matter. Maybe I can get Andy to talk and admit how she felt about Deidre, but maybe I can't. Will the drugs come into play later? Who knows? Maybe not. But what's important is there's still a lot of work ahead before we can bring someone to justice for murder."

"But the drugs?" Sam protested. He wanted to know what they were.

McAfee shrugged. "Sometimes, not every question gets answered. Remember to focus on the important puzzle pieces—the ones that have been found and the picture they make."

"Puzzle pieces?" Sonja asked.

"It's a long story." Sam put his hand on his friend's shoulder. "This means Dom is in the clear?"

McAfee considered Dominic Russo, then shrugged. "Probably. We'll see."

"Probably?" Sam said.

"We'll see?" Dom added.

The detective walked off. "Stay out of trouble, fellas."

# Chapter 34

After Detective McAfee and the deputies left, Dominic invited Sam and Sonja out for a beer at The Super Fan. That was the reason he'd stopped by in the first place.

"We'll pass," Sonja quickly said.

Dom raised his eyebrows.

"I guess we're passing," Sam muttered.

"You're on a short leash, buddy."

"We have an agreement," Sonja said, "and he's on my time now."

Dom shook his head. "Well, if you ever want to come out and play—"

"Goodbye, Dom." Sonja escorted him to the door. "He'll call you tomorrow."

Sam dropped onto the couch. He heard the door close, but Sonja did not immediately return to the living room.

His mind wandered over the past few days. It had been a hectic start to his summer. It wasn't the way he wanted to live his life. He had a particular set of rules to make sure he avoided situations like this.

Sam pulled out the list from his wallet to review. As he went over them one by one, he came to the last—*Avoid people with repulsive careers.* He thought about adding homicide detectives to the list, but Shane McAfee ended up being a decent enough guy. No, he decided. He would not add homicide detectives to the list, even though he hoped he would never have to talk with one again.

Then he thought about Jordan Withers. Briefly, he thought about adding reporters to the list, but she turned out to be okay. Sonja stood next to him during her follow-up interview after the arrest of Deidre. When the reporter eventually left, Sonja muttered, "She might be all right." That was high praise from her about another woman.

Sam's thoughts then drifted to Izzy Taylor and Deidre Hearn. If he learned anything from this little adventure, it was omen in their profession attracted trouble. He grabbed a pen from the coffee table and added *Bikini Baristas* to his list of careers to avoid.

"What are you doing?"

Sam looked up. Sonja posed naked at the end of the hallway. One arm was extended over her head and pressed against the wall. It was an alluring position—almost everything she did was meant to have that effect.

"Reviewing my list."

Her come-hither look faltered. With venomous undertones, she said, "The list. What are you doing with that?"

"Adding to it."

"May I ask what?"

"To avoid bikini baristas in the future."

"Well, that's something."

"I thought so." He tossed the pen then carefully tucked the list back into his wallet.

She dropped her arm and strolled over. She climbed onto his lap, and he put his hands on her hips.

No more idle hands, he thought.

"Let's get something straight, Mr. Strait."

He smiled dreamily. "That's cute."

Her glare showed she wasn't messing around. "We don't have a moment to waste. June is around the corner, and that means summer is almost over."

"Technically, it hasn't even begun."

She grabbed his face with both of her hands. "Technically, you're an ass, but if you're leaving—"

"Which is my plan—"

"—then for the next three months, you're going to do what I say when I say it."

Sam looked away as he considered her words. He wasn't sure if he could abide by that rule. It seemed contrary to both his *No attachments* and *No drama* rules. Even though he made allowances when it came to Sonja, this was a significant deviation.

But it was only three months, he thought. One summer. How bad could it be? But it was for the entire length of his time home. Could he handle being with Sonja for that amount of time, doing what she wanted, when she wanted? It seemed like a high price to pay to—

Sonja shook his face until he refocused.

"Three months," she said. "You do what I say when I say? Got it?"

When Sonja tugged his shirt over his head, Sam finally got what she was saying.

# The Rules

1. Only be where flip-flops can be worn.
2. No attachments.
3. Leave when it's time.
4. No drama.
5. Avoid people with repulsive careers—lawyers, accountants, IRS agents, politicians, real estate brokers, preschool teachers, bikini baristas.

# Did You Enjoy the Book?

Thank you for reading *Strait Over Tackle*. This is a continuing series with Sam always on the move. I hope you'll check the other books out.

I'm always grateful when a reader takes time out of their day to comment on one of my novels. If you do write a review, please email me, and let me know.

I'd love to say thanks!

# About the Author

Colin Conway is the creator of the 509 Crime Stories, a series of novels set in Eastern Washington with revolving lead characters. They are standalone tales and can be read in any order.

He also created the Cozy Up series which pushes the envelope of the cozy genre. Libby Klein, author of the Poppy McAllister series, says *Cozy Up to Death* is "Not your grandma's cozy."

Colin co-authored the Charlie-316 series. The first novel in the series, *Charlie-316*, is a political/crime thriller that has been described as "riveting and compulsively readable," "the real deal," and "the ultimate ride-along."

He served in the U.S. Army and later was an officer of the Spokane Police Department. He's owned a laundromat, invested in a bar, and ran a karate school. Besides writing crime fiction, he is a commercial real estate broker.

Colin lives with his beautiful girlfriend, three wonderful children, and a codependent Vizsla that rules their world.

Find out more at colinconway.com.